SLEEP TIGHT

ALSO BY CAROLINE MITCHELL

DETECTIVE RUBY PRESTON SERIES
Love You to Death
Sleep Tight

DETECTIVE JENNIFER KNIGHT SERIES
Don't Turn Around
Time to Die
The Silent Twin

NON-FICTION
Paranormal Intruder

SLEEP TIGHT

CAROLINE MITCHELL

bookouture

Published by Bookouture
An imprint of StoryFire Ltd.
23 Sussex Road, Ickenham, UB10 8PN
United Kingdom
www.bookouture.com

ISBN: 978-1-78681-137-0
eBook ISBN: 978-1-78681-136-3

To my daughter Aoife. I know I gave you a name nobody can spell, but to me it reflects your undeniable uniqueness. You were always meant to shine bright in this world. Love you.

'Silently one by one, in the infinite meadows of heaven, blossomed the lovely stars, the forget-me-nots of the angels.'

– *Henry Wadsworth Longfellow*

PROLOGUE

The doctor gave a satisfied nod as he lifted the stethoscope from the woman's bare chest. 'Ah, the heart of a lion. We'll soon have you cleaned up. But now. . . a little music to ease the passage.' He did not expect a response because he was talking to himself. It had been that way ever since people could no longer bear to be in his presence. He turned, raising the needle of the old-fashioned record player as he set the music in place. Beethoven's *Moonlight Sonata* breathed life into the crumbling room. The haunting tune aided his movements, making them smooth and effortless. Classical music was something he'd fallen back on during the darkest of times when the pain of his disfigurement became too much. But now, in the privacy of his surgery, the turmoil of the last year floated away. The bones in his neck cracked as he craned his head towards the paint-flaked ceiling. He gazed in admiration as a union of colour and sound floated above. His ability to see colours in music was both a torment and a gift. But then he always saw the world differently to others.

Pushing a lever, he eased back the surgeon's chair. Earrings, necklace, bracelet... each piece of jewellery chimed as it hit the stainless steel bowl. Once used for harbouring freshly harvested organs, it made a suitable container for his exterior work. Jewellery removed, his eyes roamed over the woman's naked body. To him, it was a canvas, and there was so much work to be done. But then bringing beauty to a dark and unforgiving world was never going to be an effortless task. Unfolding the razor, he laid it on the side, admiring the glint of the freshly sharpened blade. It was called a cut throat for a reason. There was an art to using this implement, unlike the disposable razors used today. Too much pressure would initiate the onset of tiny beads of blood. Not enough, and you were merely scraping skin. It was why he had placed her in a comatose state, as still as the death which was yet to claim her.

The music played on, enveloping his senses in green, blue and purple as he prepared the soapy lather. The process was a meditative exercise, which acquainted him with every curve of the young woman's flesh. Goose pimples rose as an icy breeze snuck through the thin chipboard that boarded the window. He paused; he would have to purchase a heater. Such an appliance would make little demands on the generator, which purred in the corner of the room. Dipping the brush into the dish, he applied the frothy soap to the top of her thighs, working his way down in a slow, circular motion.

By the time she was lathered and shaved, her skin was mottled from the cold. He wiped his forehead with the back of his hand, stepping back to admire his handiwork. A warm throb of satisfaction pulsed inside him, and the left side of his mouth jerked upwards as he exposed his teeth in a ghoulish half-smile.

Up until now, he had kept his silence, but the time had come to make a statement to the world. Each work of art would be delivered publicly for all to admire and take pause. 'That's better,' he said, voicing his thoughts out loud. 'There's no better feeling than swiping your thumb over the grime of urban living to reveal something quite exquisite underneath.' Placing a blanket up to the girl's chest, he checked the leather straps were firmly in place. Her origins were no longer significant. Soon she would look like a fairy tale princess – but one without censor, fitting for the modern world. Art was reflected in life, and beauty could be found in dirty little things.

CHAPTER ONE

Her arms lay outstretched as if welcoming the cover of the night sky. Eyes open, mouth parted, her last breath was nothing but a ghost on her lips. Even without the trappings of jewellery and clothing, DS Ruby Preston could tell that this young woman was once loved. Somewhere there was a mother, a sister or a lover waiting for her to come home. Her platinum blonde hair lay splayed on the grass as if she were not human at all but an angel who had fallen from grace. Ruby fought the urge to cover her naked body. She was more than a girl whose life was abruptly snuffed out, she was a vessel carrying clues that could potentially lead them to the person responsible for the violence that had brought her life to an end. And there had been violence. The bruises dappling her ivory skin were a testament to that. But the vision of such a horrific act was not enough to dampen the stars shining brightly overhead.

The heat of summer was all but a memory now as the late November chill grew teeth and bit hard. Ruby buttoned up her coat, distancing herself from her all too human emotions of sorrow and anger – there would be time for that later. As she stood in Shoreditch Park, she knew that every second since the discovery of the body was precious. She lifted her airwaves radio to update control.

By the time DI Jack Downes arrived, the scene had been cordoned, a tent was being erected, and the streets were aglow with fluorescent jackets as uniformed officers assisted detectives knocking on doors.

'You look as if you've just got out of bed,' Ruby said, feeling as if the frost had permeated her bones.

Downes's finger combed his grey-flecked hair, looking over her shoulder to the crime scene. 'I have, as it happens. How did yous get here so quickly?'

'I was in the area dealing with a witness about an unrelated incident. Control called me up—'

'And you hotfooted it over here,' Downes said, finishing her sentence. 'Jesus, woman, don't you ever go home?'

'Married to the job, that's me,' Ruby said, stamping her boots on the frosted grass as she attempted to return some feeling to her toes. 'She's not been there very long.' Ruby did not need to be a coroner to work out that much. The girl's body was soft and limp, free of the rigor mortis that was yet to claim her. It was also a given that in such a public place she would not have lain undiscovered for long.

'Age?'

'I'd say early twenties, no puncture marks or tattoos; she doesn't fit the description of anyone in the missing persons database. I'm thinking a possible sexually motivated murder. Could be a boyfriend, but the bruising on her throat and thighs suggests a sudden, frenzied attack.'

Downes nodded. 'She'll have to stay here overnight. They won't want to be moving her until morning.' He sighed a frosted breath, pushing his hands deep into the pockets of his full-length tweed coat. 'I don't know, it's not that long since the door-knocker murders. Have you met the forensic pathologist yet?'

'Vera? Yeah, she's nice. Knows her stuff too.' Ruby stared at the ground for a few seconds, contemplating Christopher Douglas, the former pathologist. His loss had affected them all. The whump, whump of a police helicopter broke into her thoughts as it searched the park from the skies above her. She squinted as the powerful spotlight beamed from overhead, still seeing spots of light in her vision as it abruptly switched to heat-seeking mode. The park was filling up with onlookers. Unless the suspect was running around naked, it was unlikely they would pick him up now. Having taken what he wanted, he had most likely gone to ground.

'Away with ye to the station,' Downes said, drawing back her attention. 'I'll follow on. And grab us a bit of grub on your way. It's going to be a long night.' He clapped her heartily on the back before heading to the uniformed officer manning the crime scene.

But her time at Shoreditch police station was short-lived. Just hours later, Ruby was standing with Downes on the doorstep of Audrey Caldwell. She had reported her daughter missing and the description of the young woman matched the details of the body in the park. Lisa Caldwell, just twenty-one years old, had last been seen walking through it from Pitfield Street, after leaving the Britannia Leisure Centre prior to closing at 10 p.m. But that was over three hours ago. Ruby could have easily requested uniformed officers to speak to Lisa's mother but she had claimed ownership of the case the very moment she came upon the young woman's body, and would not shy away from her duties now. Taking strength in DI Downes's presence, she braced herself as a hall light flickered on. Her finger had barely pressed the door buzzer before urgent footsteps tip-tapped down the stairs.

The door swished open, and a pallid-looking Audrey Caldwell tightened the belt of her dressing gown, glancing from Ruby to Downes. She looked shockingly like her daughter, and a heavy sense of dread bloomed inside Ruby's chest. If there were any doubt that the woman lying in the park was not Lisa, it evaporated the moment she saw her mother's face.

'Mrs Caldwell?' Ruby said, opening her warrant card to introduce herself and her colleague. But Audrey was looking over their shoulders and into the darkened streets beyond.

'Is she with you? Have you brought her home?' she said, her voice strained.

'Can we come inside?' DI Downes said, his Northern Irish accent sounding as soft as butter in comparison.

Mrs Caldwell moved aside, and Downes ducked, stepping beneath the threshold. Ruby brushed against him as she followed Mrs Caldwell through to the living room on the left. His coat still carried the frost from the night air where they had found the young girl staring, dead-eyed, at the stars.

Ruby's eyes danced over the framed family photo on the dresser, which featured Mrs Caldwell with a young girl on each side. She felt her throat tighten as the face of the girl from the park stared back at her with a pink bloom to her cheeks and a carefree expression on her face. On the other side was a young woman in an army uniform, wearing a beret over her slicked-back blonde hair, and a wide grin on her face.

As Mrs Caldwell sat, Ruby delivered the news: 'The body of a young woman has been found in the park tonight.'

Mrs Caldwell drew in a sudden breath then clasped a hand to her mouth.

Grim-faced, Ruby pushed on. In her experience, it was best not to draw things out. Like ripping off a plaster, bad news should be delivered quickly and professionally. 'She's yet to be formally identified, but there's a strong possibility that it's your daughter.'

'Mum?' A young woman's voice spoke from the doorway. It was the other girl from the picture, her hair now hanging limply around her face. She took in the scene before taking her mother's side.

'Lisa's with a friend, that's all,' Mrs Caldwell said, taking small, quick breaths. 'She. . . she'll be home soon.'

'Have you seen her with your own eyes?' the girl asked, turning her gaze onto Ruby. 'This woman in the park?' She grabbed the framed photo from the dresser and waved it under Ruby's face. 'Is she the girl you saw?'

Ruby nodded. 'In all probability, yes, but she'll have to be formally identified in the morning. We'll assign a family liaison officer, who'll arrange to pick you up.'

Mrs Caldwell sprang from the sofa, wobbling slightly as her legs threatened to buckle. 'Now, I want you to take me now. This'll be a mistake. The sooner we get it sorted, the sooner you can look for my daughter.' Her voice was as brittle as shards of glass.

'I'm afraid we can't,' Downes said. 'We've got to leave the body in situ tonight. The most important thing we can do is preserve the scene and find out who's responsible. We've got a tent in place, and police will be standing guard until such time as we can take her to a mortuary. She won't be alone. I'm so sorry.'

'You needn't be sorry for me,' Mrs Caldwell said, 'because it's not my Lisa. She'll come in, any minute now, she'll. . .' Her words were overtaken by sudden violent sobs. Ruby watched as she fell into the arms of her daughter, wishing the woman could be spared the pain that lay ahead.

CHAPTER TWO

Nathan Crosby had eyes and ears all over London, and his network of homeless people provided him with intelligence that Ruby was keen to access. Her acquaintance with him held many advantages, but fraternising with a member of the criminal underworld would not meet with the approval of her superiors, particularly given the number of times she had ended up in his bed.

Ruby scanned the half empty café, the smell of cooked bacon and sausages making her stomach growl. She gave a nod of recognition to the unshaven man in the tattered coat. He sat hunched over his tea, his gloved hands drawing heat from the stained ceramic mug before he was forced to return to the chill of the streets. As always, he sat with his back against the wall. Ruby recognised the little mannerisms that went unnoticed to the untrained eye. He had served life in prison and old habits died hard. William Burke knew who Ruby was, and as always, she handed him a crisp ten-pound note before uttering a word.

A plump, middle-aged woman wearing a grease-stained apron brought Ruby a mug of tea. Two full English breakfasts were laid before them minutes later.

Hunched over his food, William wolfed it down, his elbows and arms wrapped around his plate in a stance to ward off imaginary inmates. Ruby tried to ignore the egg yolk dribbling down his chin. She had not eaten since yesterday, and it would take a lot more than bad table manners to turn her off breakfast.

'How's things?' she said, loading her fork with chunks of sausage and bacon.

'Rough,' William said. 'Me mate, Sam, died under the bridge last week. They say it's gonna be a brutal winter. This frost will kill off a few more before it's finished.'

Ruby nodded, knowing it was more than the frost that killed off his friend. Sam was a hopeless alcoholic, and it was more likely that his liver had packed up after years of abuse.

'You 'aven't brought me here to ask how I'm feeling, 'ave you?' William said, wiping his mouth with the back of his hand.

'No, I haven't.' Ruby waited until she had finished her meal before speaking again. 'We found a body in the park last night. Do you know anything about that?'

William shrugged. 'Lots of people walk through that park, I don't know 'em all.'

'So you've not heard anyone talking about it?'

William shook his head, mopping up his egg with a slice of fried bread.

Ruby delivered a hard stare, willing him to look her in the eye. The topic of conversation held more importance than his stomach and demanded their full attention. 'William,' she said as she leant forward, 'she was just a girl, barely twenty-one years old. Isn't there anything you can give me? Any new people on the radar? Anyone acting odd?'

'Acting odd?' William chuckled. 'I'm not being funny here, love, but I don't exactly mix with 'igh society. There're lots of weird fuckers out there, the best you can do is keep out of their way.'

'Her jewellery was stolen. They even took the earrings from her ears. I'm thinking maybe a smack head or someone new on the scene because behaviour like this doesn't just spring up out of nowhere. Do you know anyone down on their luck that's come back with a big score?'

'You know I don't touch that shit.'

'But you know someone who does?' Ruby said, detecting reluctance in his eyes. 'C'mon, mate, give me a dig out. I'll leave you out of it, I promise.'

'You're expecting an awful lot for a breakfast and a ten-pound note.' William downed the last of his second mug of tea. Any minute now he would rise to use the toilets and leave Ruby with nothing to show for their meeting, except a dent in her wallet.

She grasped his arm as he pushed back his chair. 'Please. I don't want to find another girl dead on the streets. Surely some things are about more than money?'

William snorted. 'That's the sort of thing rich folks say.'

The smile left his lips as Ruby slipped a photo across the table.

'This is her, pictured with her mother and sister. They're in bits. It might bring a little comfort if we could find—'

'Alright, alright,' William raised his hands in mock surrender. 'If I'd lifted some jewellery, and it was that hot, the first place I'd head to is Buster Turner on Bethnal Green Road.'

'Cheers,' Ruby said, grabbing her handbag from the seat beside her.

The café began to fill as an army of dust-clad builders piled in. Chairs and tables screeched as they took up the seats; the air filled with banter as they took the mickey out of the youngest member of the group.

Ruby handed William a battered card, along with some change for the telephone box. 'If you hear anything else, give me a ring.'

'Only for you,' William breathed a weary sigh.

Ruby paused, feeling a pang of guilt as she turned to leave. She dug a newly purchased pack of cigarettes and lighter from her pocket and placed them on the table. 'Here, it's about time I gave these up.'

There was no point in telling him to go down to the shelter for a night. After a lifetime of incarceration, she knew he preferred to sleep under the stars. Had he not been arrested for a breach of the peace the night before, he may well have been a person of interest himself.

After paying for their food, she slid her phone from her pocket and called up DC Owen Ludgrove's number. 'You busy?' It was a daft question. Every member of Shoreditch serious crime team was buried in work. But she knew the young detective constable would drop everything for her. 'Meet me outside Buster Turner's Jewellery Emporium on Bethnal Green Road. . . as soon as you can. Yeah, OK, see you in ten.'

She recognised the address, as it was one of the properties on Nathan Crosby's books. Not only was her ex-lover head of a criminal organisation, he fronted it with legitimate businesses, such as real estate, pubs and clubs. William Burke had never let her down with information before. The fact that Buster was fencing jewellery had dictated her route – she would not be going in through the front door.

CHAPTER THREE

'Wouldn't we be better off applying for a warrant?' Luddy said, following Ruby through the litter-strewn alleyway, which led to the rear of the pawnbroker's shop. 'And why are we going around the back?'

'Because the back is where all the fun happens,' Ruby said with a grin. 'I bet you were one of those kids who sat at the front of the bus on school trips, weren't you?' She knew she shouldn't enjoy being such a bad influence, but she could not help herself. Ruby had always been trouble. Being in the police could not change that.

She pushed open the wooden gate, lifting it slightly from the hinges to make her entrance. Luddy followed her through, his face taut. A burst of sound emitted from his police radio, and he swiftly turned the knob to silence the voice of the controller.

Ruby rapped hard on the blistered back door. A gust of wind howled around them, sending a tin can bumping along the alleyway. Somewhere in the distance a dog barked, but it was all lost on Ruby, who was focused on the task ahead.

'Best you leave the talking to me,' she said to Luddy as the sound of footsteps grew from the other side of the door.

Masked in a halo of cigarette smoke, Buster Turner peered through the door. 'The shop entrance is around the front.'

He was a greasy little man, his shoulder-length dark hair slicked back from his face. Two loose strands hung over his forehead, reminding Ruby of antennae. With his beady eyes and long pointed nose, everything about him was insectile.

Ruby raised her warrant card, her voice firm. 'We've come to speak to you.' She laid her hand on the door and pushed it open. 'Now, if you don't mind. We'll only be five minutes.'

With a grunt of annoyance Buster turned, allowing Ruby and Luddy to follow him inside as he treaded lightly on the linoleum. The smell of sour milk and cigarette smoke hung thick in the air. To the left was a poky kitchen. A variety of dead plants dotted the window ledge, and a pile of used teabags took up residence on the sink draining board. Ruby turned her attention to the door at the end of the hall, reading the words 'SHOP' scrawled in black marker pen over the blue paint. Buster entered the door on the right, following the sound of the tinny pop music playing from within. She should have asked DC Ash Baker along instead, she mused. He was old school and knew that sometimes you had to take a different approach. She felt a pang of guilt as the thought entered her mind. Luddy was studying for his sergeant's exams, and she would not drag him into a situation that could damage his chances of promotion. She was a copper first, and would play this by the book. She glanced around the poky room, a veritable Aladdin's cave: wall-to-wall with cabinets, their drawers stuffed with jewellery of every shape and size. One such drawer was laid on a wooden desk next to an eyepiece on its side, waiting for its owner to return.

On the radio, Kylie Minogue was singing about a locomotive, and Buster dragged his chair from behind his desk as he took a seat, leaving Ruby and Luddy to stand.

'What do you want?'

Luddy opened his mouth to speak, but Ruby beat him to it. This was her world, and she knew exactly how to deal with people like Buster Turner. 'We were making some local enquiries and saw your gate was open. You should be careful, there are some very dodgy people about.'

Buster narrowed his eyes in a mistrusting glare. 'Your concern is noted. Do you need me to see you out?' He leant forward to rise from his chair.

Ruby shook her head, satisfied she had come up with a suitable excuse for coming through the back entrance, in case he made anything of it later. 'Now that I'm here, I'd like to speak to you about some stolen jewellery. A silver designer bracelet was taken from a young woman who was found murdered in the park last night.' She produced her phone and drew up the picture of the missing piece. 'There's a pair of matching earrings too. They're quite distinctive, little silver keys with the numbers "21" on them. You wouldn't happen to know anything about those, would you?'

'I run a respectable establishment,' Buster said, impertinently. 'I do not take in stolen goods.'

'And the Pope doesn't pray,' Ruby said, poking some of the jewellery on the desk with her index finger.

Tiny beads of sweat glistened on Buster's forehead, and Ruby knew it was not from the two-bar heater weakly warming the room. 'My clients go through a strict signing in process, providing photographs and ID,' he added, his eyes darting from the jewellery and back to Ruby.

'What about the camera-shy customers who give you an extra cut?' Ruby said, arching an eyebrow.

Buster remained tight-lipped, and Ruby's frustration grew. Playing nicely was getting her nowhere. She exhaled sharply; she didn't have time for this.

'I think it's time you went,' Buster said, his hand drawn to the lip under his desk. He was probably trying to alert the gorilla working behind the front counter, and that was an encounter Ruby could do without.

She planted her hands firmly on his desk, her words like bullets. 'Do you want me to turn this place over?' She pointed at the jewellery to drive her message home. 'I don't care about your stolen gear, I'm only interested in the bracelet and earrings. I know you've got them.' Ruby was bluffing; well aware she was placing all her trust in a man who could be bought for a cooked breakfast and a ten-pound note. But it was too late to back out now. 'I can nick you for obstruction and close the place down for a search, or you can provide me with a statement, help us with our enquiries. What's it to be?' She glanced at Luddy, who was standing with his arms folded.

'This is police oppression,' Buster sneered. 'I'm going to report you for this.'

'Fine, if you want to play it that way,' Ruby said, knowing his arrest would give her the automatic right to conduct a premises search. But given her intelligence source, her justification was thin. 'You can make your complaint in custody while we're arranging for a solicitor to deal with your arrest.' Despite her cool veneer, Ruby's heart was hammering. Everything was riding on a bluff. It was the only way to deal with a snake like Buster, and William had never let her down before.

'I'll take my chances. In fact, I'll contact your superiors now rather than waste any more time,' Buster said, picking up the phone on his desk and dialling the first of three nines.

Ruby pressed the receiver to hang up the call. 'Go ahead, but first let me call your landlord, Nathan Crosby. He'd be very interested to hear one of his tenants is involved in a murder enquiry.' The irony was that, despite Nathan being a lawbreaker himself, he did not appreciate attention being drawn to his businesses. He would not be pleased, and of that Buster Turner was well aware.

'You wouldn't,' Buster said, recoiling from the desk phone as if it were a pit of snakes.

Ruby began searching through her list of contacts on her mobile phone. 'I've got his number on speed dial.' She waved it in his face, watching him visibly wilt. 'It's your choice. What's it to be?'

CHAPTER FOUR

Ruby wrapped her fingers around the steaming mug of tea. She was trying to ignore the fact Downes had omitted the sugar. It was such a rare event that he made a brew, it would not do to appear ungrateful. Their shift had ended hours ago, but given they had recovered the stolen jewellery from Buster Turner nobody would be going home tonight. Her methods of persuasion had improved the pawnbroker's memory, and by the time she left, she was equipped with an evidence bag containing the seized jewellery and a statement giving up Danny Smedley as the person who pawned it.

'I don't understand why we can't just go and arrest this guy,' she said, glancing around Downes's office. It was bigger than hers, but the extra space only served to house the clutter he had accumulated over the years. Old sporting trophies, group photos of police colleagues, and spare sets of clothes he had forgotten to take home and wash.

'DCI Worrow wants to get it right and, for once, I agree with her. They've got eyes on Smedley, he's not going anywhere tonight.'

Ruby threw up her hands in exasperation. 'We've got stolen jewellery and a positive fingerprint ID. If we bring him in now, he'll cough to it.'

'You know what he'll say in interview: that he found the jewellery in the park. We need time to build a case against him, and if he puts a foot wrong in the meantime, we'll catch him in the act.'

'I hope you're right,' Ruby grumbled. 'Nothing back from the post-mortem yet?'

Downes shook his head. 'Not yet.'

'In that case, I've got some enquiries to make.' Ruby shoved her arm through the sleeve of her blazer.

'Where are you off to?'

'Intel gathering. I want to know the motivation behind this murder.'

'Step lightly, don't go tipping anyone off,' Downes said.

Ruby arched her eyebrow in a knowing glance. 'I'll be on my radio if you need me.'

As she entered Nathan Crosby's club, she could not work out if she wanted to see her daughter or not. Building their relationship was taking longer than she had hoped. It seemed to suit Frances, Nathan's mother, who had taken to motherhood forty years too late. Ruby pushed past Nathan's staff as she made her way to the back office, giving the secure door three tentative knocks. It was further than most people were allowed to go, but her association with Nathan gave her the concession.

'It's me, Ruby,' she said, pressing down the leather-lined door handle. The little touches meant everything to Nathan, and despite his humble upbringing, every inch of his living space was designed and furnished to the highest quality.

Ruby cautiously opened the door to find him sitting behind his executive mahogany desk, feet up. It was a vast improvement on the cheap furniture that graced her office back in the nick. Her workspace smelt of print toner and takeaway food. Nathan's carried the scent of leather, freshly polished wood and the faintest hint of cigar smoke. It was something that his father would have approved of, but Ruby knew better than to mention Jimmy Crosby's name. She tilted her head to take in the view on all four shiny screens on his wall. One of the cameras was trained on his door, and only then did she realise that he'd seen her approach. 'They're new,' she said, knowing that a separate room downstairs was manned by his in-house security firm.

'Drink?' Nathan said, taking two cut-glass tumblers from a cabinet behind his desk.

'I'm on duty,' Ruby replied. 'Make it a small one.'

The corner of Nathan's mouth twitched into a smile. He pushed the glass beneath the ice machine before filling it with a generous helping of rum. Ruby took it without saying a word. They sat in amicable silence. Their gaze on the screens, they watched sweaty bodies mill about on the dance floor, merged in a kaleidoscope of colours.

'How's Cathy?' Ruby said, her eyes appraising him as he leant back in his chair. His maroon shirt and black trousers complemented his muscular form, and she sent herself a mental reminder that she was here on police business.

'Same as usual,' Nathan said. 'But you didn't come here for that, did you? I hear you've been terrorising my tenants.'

'I persuaded him to help me with my enquiries, that's all.' Ruby gave him a wicked grin. She knew he loved her rebellious streak, her inability to play by the rules. There would be no reprisals from Nathan tonight. 'What can you tell me about Danny Smedley? I take it you know about the murder?'

'For what it's worth, I don't believe it was a planned attack. He raped that girl because the opportunity presented itself. Then he was stupid enough to try and fence her jewellery on my patch.' The smile he was wearing dissolved from his face. 'That girl wasn't much older than Cathy. If he comes around here again, I'll slit his throat.'

'We've got eyeballs on him. We're bringing him in tomorrow,' Ruby said, taking a sip of rum.

Nathan nodded, then slid his mobile phone from his pocket and sent a text. Perhaps he had already given the order to kill and was calling his men off. Ruby licked her lips, enjoying the feel of the heavy crystal tumbler as she rested it on her palm. Would it have been such a bad thing, one less rapist and murderer on the streets? 'The thing is, I need evidence. If you happen to come up with any witnesses, let me know.'

'No need,' Nathan replied. 'If you're not able to get him under your own steam, we'll mop up after you when he's released. Just let me know the time and place, and we'll be happy to oblige.'

'You know I can't do that,' Ruby said.

'Ditto,' Nathan replied.

It always came down to a stalemate between them. 'I was thinking I might go back to the flat tonight. The tenants next door are having barneys every night. I've not had a proper night's sleep in ages.'

'It's your place, I don't know why you don't move in there.'

Ruby had been considering it. Nathan had gifted it to her months before under the guise of an inheritance from a long since dead aunt but she knew how it had been funded, and felt she was selling out. Either way, it seemed daft to have two flats, and she knew she would make up her mind soon.

Nathan stood, a signal that her time was up. 'Babe, it's not as if I'm gonna ask for it back. We've got Cathy. We're in it together, whether we like it or not.'

Ruby nodded, knowing the bond of having a daughter would always keep them in contact.

'And do you… like it?' Ruby said, stepping towards him until they were just inches apart.

'You know how I feel about you.' His voice was gentle now, comforting.

'I'll think about it,' Ruby said. 'The flat, I mean.' The proximity of his body was making her flustered.

A sharp knock at the door made Ruby jump, and she quickly pulled away.

'What?' Nathan said, his tone sharp as the door parted.

A gravelly voice responded from the other side. 'Sorry, boss, your three o'clock is here.'

Nathan's expression changed from someone she grew up with to a face made of stone. He swore under his breath. It was obviously someone he did not want Ruby to meet. 'Get Mike to stall him, take Ruby out the back.'

He turned to face her. 'Sorry, babe, next time you want to visit, call me first. I can't have you coming around here unannounced.'

'Don't worry, I'm going. I know when I'm not wanted,' Ruby said, her frustration growing at the barriers that rose in every direction she turned. She thought of Lisa's mother in the throes of grief. The fact Danny Smedley was still free after causing such devastation filled her with disgust.

As she left the club, she was hit by the sting of cold night air. She lifted the collar on her jacket, strengthening her resolve. She would speak to DCI Worrow, appeal to her better nature. Danny Smedley would not sleep another night a free man.

CHAPTER FIVE

'Skin white as snow, lips red as blood, hair dark as ebony wood,' the doctor recited the words as he slid the comb through the wig's short tresses. It shone beneath the surgical spotlight and was as black as the fairy tale suggested. He smiled in satisfaction. Gone were the nasty synthetic blonde strands. In their place was a bobbed wig made of real human hair. He had been pleased with his efforts. His skills with the scalpel had easily transferred to scissors, and he had worked diligently, trimming each strand of glossy black hair until it was just the right length. Her skin, once pockmarked and ashen, was now ivory white, free from unsightly hairs and blemishes. He had spent all night transforming it to the perfect tone, so engrossed in his work that he had forgotten to eat. If it weren't for the rats squeaking for food, he could have kept going until dawn. They gathered around his feet, whiskers twitching, as they rose on their hind legs. Their black beaded eyes shone with anticipation as they sniffed the air for food. In the last twelve months, they had become his closest allies. Sometimes they kept him warm as he slept – a pulsating blanket of fur. Like him, they appreciated the music that echoed around the derelict chamber. He moved towards the record player, setting it into life once more.

To the backdrop of colourful music, he transformed her lips to a fairy-tale red. Eyebrows, lashes, fingernails and toenails… every inch of her body received his full attention. He bent to inhale the scent of her skin and was rewarded with a pungent chemical smell. It equated to goodness, purity. It was his dream that his art would be picked up by the nationals and broadcast on TV. His fellow man could take comfort that even the dirtiest of street urchins might be transformed into something good and pure. Sacrifices would have to be made. But nobody said life was easy. He watched as her chest rose and fell from underneath the blue waffle blanket. Was she dreaming? Perhaps, in her world, she could sense the change. And he was almost ready to let her go.

The costume was quite extravagant, but he could afford the cost. He admired the cut of the long yellow dress as it hung from the wall, complete with a blue bolero top and a starched white collar. Red shoes matched the bow on the hairband yet to be placed on the crown of her head. But she was not ready to be dressed. Everything had to be timed to perfection in order to make his fairy-tale work of art complete. He had allocated three days for this particular creation and mapped his plans with precision. Day one was the stripping of the layers – a removal of the grime-infused outside world. Day two was when the detailed work took place: sizing her up for her outfit and bringing her back to life. It was one last parting moment for her to enjoy before death claimed her. Day three involved invasive surgery, those finishing touches which brought authenticity to his work. Just as in the fairy tale, his art would be both cruel and beautiful in its bidding. But this story did not come with a happy ending. Brothers Grimm folklore was more fitting for the modern world.

He snapped out of his thoughts as the woman stirred. It was almost time to draw her from the recesses of her coma. A full-length mirror stood at the end of the bed, ready to show her what she had become.

CHAPTER SIX

The musty smell wafting from the corner of the interview room suggested that Danny Smedley had not washed in several days. He ran a dirty finger around the neck of his custody tracksuit, emitting another blast of body odour into the box-sized interview room.

Danny's lack of personal hygiene was one of the reasons why Ruby had managed to persuade DCI Worrow to bring forward the arrest. There was still a possibility he carried Lisa's DNA and, given Danny's fingerprint, which they had obtained from the stolen jewellery, it was just cause. Upon entry into custody, Danny was requested to take part in a forensic examination, including penis swabs. Such a process was driven by consent, but if he disagreed to the examination, then an inference might be drawn, which meant people could wonder what he had to hide. Danny knew this because it was not the first time he'd been accused of rape. He had waved away the request, casting himself in a bad light by refusing to comply. Ruby was furious at how quickly he reoffended since his release from prison – so much for rehabilitation. She could only assume Nathan was right: there was no proper motive for it, other than Danny was stupid as hell and the opportunity had presented itself. Had it not been Lisa Caldwell it would have been another girl, maybe even Cathy. The thoughts made her flesh crawl. Ruby had always worked hard to bring offenders to justice but having a daughter of the same age made it personal.

She glared at Danny as he leaned back in the cheap plastic chair. She hated every fibre of his being, and every second of his sorry life that turned him into the person he was today. She had at least obtained some satisfaction that they had conducted gait analysis as he entered custody. Another one of her suggestions DCI Worrow seemed happy to take credit for. Given that Danny was bow-legged, it was too good an opportunity to miss, and Ruby was aware of other cases in which such analysis had helped convict. Sometimes it wasn't one huge surmounting piece of evidence but lots of little seeds of doubt during an investigation that meant justice could prevail.

DC Ash Baker also had a daughter around the same age as the victim but that was not why he sat beside Ruby as she ran through the introductions. It was his years of experience in dealing with such cases that earned him the right to be there. Ash Baker gained the most detections in her team, and Ruby wanted this wrapped up quickly. As they ran through the spiel that precluded every interview, Ruby kept her focus solely on the man in front of her. With dishevelled greasy hair and bloodshot eyes, personal hygiene appeared way down on his list of priorities. The duty solicitor sat next to him, a tall, stick-thin man, his suit a size too big for his bony frame. Glasses perched on the end of his nose, he shuffled the set of papers on his lap, having sped through a thirty-minute pre-interview consultation with his client. Ruby had dealt with him once before, and he had not given her too much grief then.

Her first question was open, designed to encourage the suspect to give a rundown of his day. Tell, explain, and describe were the words that precluded the open questions necessary to help her suspect confess – or lie, depending on what way you looked at it. Ruby laced her fingers together as she leant across the interview table. 'Tell me, what you were doing on the night of the 23rd November.'

'No comment,' Danny replied.

To the untrained person, an answer of 'no comment' may have seemed like a step backwards but to police, it was just another example of where an inference could be drawn. He had been given an opportunity but failed to explain his movements on the night of the murder. Danny may have thought he was smart, but, to Ruby, it was an indication of guilt or something very close to it.

The duty solicitor looked wholly disinterested. It pleased Ruby, although he was the last person she would want representing her if she got into trouble. Not that she would ever have to worry about that; Nathan Crosby had long since promised that he would look after her if she found herself on the wrong side of the law.

Such was not the case for the man before her. His solicitor had just travelled from a police station twenty miles away due to lack of cover and looked thoroughly exhausted. His advice to his client to respond with 'no comment' was something he seemed to recommend for those who were guilty or too thick to be trusted to provide a reasonable account. Ruby knew that if she prodded Danny enough, she would get a few words out of him before the interview was over. She took a deep breath, ready to burrow into the brain of the man before her.

CHAPTER SEVEN

'Do you understand why you've been arrested?' Ruby said, opening a Manila folder and placing it on the coffee-ringed table. It was more than just a sturdy piece of furniture, it was a barrier which provided time to react, should her suspect take exception to her line of questioning.

'No comment,' Danny replied, rocking back in his chair.

'I refer to exhibit AB01, which is a printout of a photo of the victim, Lisa Caldwell.'

She slid the picture across the table in the interview room. Danny's gaze fell on the image of the young girl, the face of someone who had everything to live for.

'Do you know this woman?'

'No comment.' His eyes still rested on the picture but he had withdrawn into himself, the upward curl of his lip suggesting he was reliving their last moments together.

Ruby snatched back the photo, unwilling to afford him the memory. All she could see in his face was arrogance and stupidity but it was something she was willing to take advantage of if she could prise some words from his sneering mouth.

'I refer to exhibit AB02. This is CCTV footage of the path before the cut through to Shoreditch Park at 10 p.m. that night.' Ruby turned the laptop to face him. 'I've provided a map with my disclosure, if you'd like to take another look at the area.'

His solicitor glanced up from his paperwork, pushing his glasses back up his face. He slipped his copy of the map Ruby had provided onto the desk.

Danny Smedley barely acknowledged it.

The CCTV footage displayed the black and white image of a young woman. Wearing a denim skirt and white T-shirt, she held onto a drawstring carrier bag. Her long blonde hair fell all the way down her back, and an image of the same girl flashed in Ruby's memory; the same blonde hair splayed around her on the frosted grass. She inhaled a soft breath, drawing strength from the intensity of her emotions.

She pointed to the screen. 'Here's footage of Lisa leaving the leisure centre. I'm just going to forward it a few minutes. . .' She clicked the image as a male figure came into view. It was as good an image as that camera could afford, given it was under cover of street lights, but not good enough to clearly identify him.

'This male was seen acting suspiciously, hanging around the park. It's my opinion that he was following Lisa. What can you tell me about that?'

Danny shrugged. He was so full of cockiness it warmed Ruby's heart but she would not allow him to know that. Her facial expression showed mild annoyance. It was a game she played only with those foolish enough to swallow it.

'For the benefit of the recording, Danny has shrugged.' Ruby needed to clarify every response in case the interview was played in court later. She dared not look at Ash, who was taking notes. The next few moments were crucial, and she could not break concentration.

'Do you know this person?' Ruby pointed at the still of the male. Head bowed, his hoodie was covering most of his features, although the shading on his jawbone suggested a thick growth of stubble akin to the facial hair Danny was sporting in the interview today.

'No comment,' Danny said, his tone flat.

'Is this you?' Ruby fired back.

'No comment.'

Ruby returned her attention to the screen. 'Now, why do you think someone would be following Lisa into the park like that? A young girl minding her own business.'

Danny sneered. 'She hardly minded her own business dressed like that.'

Ruby could have torn a strip off him, but, instead, she looked at him blankly. 'Like what? I don't understand.'

'These girls with their short skirts and flimsy tops. . .'

'It *was* pretty cold that night. . .' Ruby said, her voice trailing away.

'Too right. What do they expect, walking around with their tits on show? And then it's all over the newspapers, innocent this, and innocent that… Innocent, my arse!'

Ruby nodded, waiting for him to fill the silence. She could not reel him in anymore. The last thing she wanted was the court to think that she had any sympathy for this scumbag. 'So what happened? When you bumped into her, I mean.'

The words were nonchalant but the solicitor raised his gaze from his paperwork, his voice droll. 'My client has been advised to answer no comment.'

'I'd rather hear that from him,' Ruby said, annoyed at the break in momentum.

Danny folded his arms, confusion flashing across his face. It was as if he had just realised he was in a police interview room and not his local boozer. 'No comment.' He exhaled the words in sullen weariness.

But Ruby refused to allow his non-committal response to get in her way. 'What did you mean when you said Lisa had her breasts on display?' The fact the young girl had changed quickly from her swimsuit and not bothered to put her bra back on was not public knowledge. Ruby only knew it because a friend of Lisa's had mentioned her complaining about the underwire as she stuffed it into her bag in the changing room that night. Danny's comments gave scope for another inference to be drawn: a tiny one, but an inference just the same.

'I. . . I meant she probably dressed the same as most young women these days,' Danny said, forgetting his earlier advice of keeping shtum.

Ruby stared without blinking until he shifted under the weight of her gaze. 'So you're telling me this isn't you?' she clarified, waiting for his solicitor to complain that she was labouring the point.

He opened his hands wide in a gesture of innocence. 'It ain't me. I was at the hostel, in bed. I got in at around seven and stayed there until the next day. I left around twelve.'

'Yet nobody's seen you in all that time.'

Danny's shoulders jerked upwards in another shrug. 'I keep to meself. I watched some documentary on the telly from eight to nine, and then I fell asleep.'

It would not have been difficult for him to find out what was on TV, and he'd had time to get his story straight, although Ruby was grateful nobody had been stupid enough to provide him with an alibi. She allowed him to give a potted account of his movements before allowing Ash to follow up with extra questions, referring to his notes.

'You said you were in your room at the hostel from 7 p.m. until twelve the next morning. Is that correct?'

'That's what I told ya.' Danny nodded, tucking his hands under his sweat-stained armpits as he folded his arms across his chest.

'So how did your fingerprint get on what has been identified as Lisa Caldwell's jewellery?' Ash produced the exhibit, referencing it for the purpose of the recording.

'No idea,' Danny said with a shrug.

'Did you attend Buster Turner's Jewellery Emporium on the night of the murder?'

'No.'

'Did you try to pawn jewellery that night?'

'I told ya, I was in my room.'

Good, Ruby thought, paying close attention as Danny dug himself into a bigger hole. Ash finished up his questions before passing the baton back to Ruby. They had pre-arranged their interview questions and worked in harmony with one mutual goal. Ash had prepped their suspect and allowed him to lie. Now it was time for Ruby to move in for the kill. She cleared her throat as she inhaled the stench of fresh sweat rising from Danny's direction.

'You refused to allow police to take intimate samples when you entered custody. Can you tell me why?' They were an hour into the interview, and she itched to escape for a cigarette.

'I don't want no filthy copper touching my knob.'

Ruby almost laughed at the irony, but kept her amusement in check. 'It was the force medical examiner but you would have known that. It's not the first time you've found yourself in this situation, is it, Danny?'

He snorted in response, his face devoid of remorse.

Bad character was something Ruby would ask Ash to draw upon at the end of the interview; he'd read through Danny's past police history for the benefit of the recording. 'Thankfully, we don't need permission for other methods of analysis. You've got quite a distinctive walk, haven't you?'

Ruby was referring to his bow legs and the John Wayne type saunter that accompanied it.

'I've 'ad it since I was a kid, nothing I can do about it.'

'And it's relatively rare, isn't it? It usually stems from having rickets as a child.' She was all too aware of his deprived childhood. 'I requested a gait analysis when you came into custody. It's where experts analyse your walk against other footage and find a match. Much like this walk here,' she said, pressing 'play' on the laptop.

Danny paled as it displayed an image of his signature loping gait.

'As I said, being bow-legged is an unusual condition these days. I'm confident we'll come up with a match between your entrance into custody and the footage here. So, I'll ask you again. Is this you on the CCTV?'

Danny folded his arms, shrinking back from the screen. 'No comment.'

The duty solicitor peered over his glasses at the footage before sliding a sideways glance at him.

Ruby continued. 'I know we can't see your face here, but it's quite clear on CCTV when you ventured to Buster Turner's Jewellery Emporium on Bethnal Green Road to sell Lisa Caldwell's jewellery. The pawnbroker provided us with a statement, by the way. It contains an excellent description, by all accounts, matching the clothing seen on our CCTV.' Ruby pointed to the laptop with the tip of her pen. 'Black sweatshirt, baseball cap, torn jeans and boots. Oh, and the black rucksack on your back. The same black rucksack you had when you left prison. We've also obtained a further statement from an independent witness stating that a man fitting your description was hanging around that night.'

The witness had been the manager of the leisure centre. Ruby wished he had voiced his concerns at the time, in the form of a phone call to the police, instead of a statement the next day. But her colleagues were stretched thin, and it was doubtful they could have spared a chance to conduct a drive by in time anyway.

Ruby's heart lit like a furnace as she watched the arrogance drop from her suspect's face.

'I want to talk to my solicitor – in private,' Danny said, his hands dropping to the sides of his seat.

Ruby bit back her grin. She had him by the balls and was clenching them tighter by the second.

CHAPTER EIGHT

Danny nodded as Ruby checked his understanding of the murder charge she had just recited at the custody desk. His shoulders slumped, his head hung low, he was wearing the expression of a man who knew when he was banged to rights. The last twenty-four hours had been one result after another, and the small swell of pride she felt for her team was only marred by the pointless loss of a young life.

Thanks to her visit to Buster Turner, he had positively identified Danny Smedley as the person who sold him the stolen jewellery. As well as the positive fingerprint, Danny's bow-legged gait also proved to be his downfall. It was more than a coincidence that his clothing description along with his gait matched that of the person on CCTV, putting him at the scene moments after Lisa took a shortcut through the park. He could have used the excuse that he found the jewellery, just as DI Downes had warned, but the fact that Ruby had questioned Danny's whereabouts so early in the interview meant she had given him the perfect opportunity to lie. Had she provided full pre-interview disclosure about the evidence they had gathered it might have been a different story. Ruby had inhaled the stale smell of accelerant as his clothes were seized in custody and requested the helicopter go up a second time, confident they would discover the remains of a fire, where he disposed of Lisa's clothes. Because yes, Danny was that stupid, and stupid people usually got caught.

But Danny Smedley was not the only one to blame; the authorities deeming him at no risk to the public would be forced to take responsibility. Whatever happened now would only provide a droplet of comfort to Lisa Caldwell's mother as she fought for breath in a tide of grief.

Ruby's satisfaction with her team's efforts was short-lived as DI Downes approached her outside his office door. Bar of chocolate in hand, he was looking a lot better these days and seemed to have got over the worse of his grief since his wife's death the year before. For once, his steel grey suit was neatly pressed, the silver-flecked tie appeared new, and instead of whiskey lacing his breath, his skin carried the hint of Safari, a fragrance fitting for a man of his maturity.

'That helicopter we sent up, they've found something,' he said, as they both slid into his office.

But she knew by his expression that this was not good news. Biting off a chunk of chocolate, he clicked on his mouse and brought his computer screen to life. The image was streaming live, and Ruby inhaled a sharp intake of breath. For there, as they flew over a graveyard close to the original murder scene, was the body of a young woman laid out on what appeared to be a tomb. For a few seconds, the scene took on a surreal tone. Ghostly pale, the corpse had an ethereal quality as it lay over the cold unforgiving stone. Unlike Lisa Caldwell, she was fully dressed, wearing a full-length gown which flared in the violent wind.

'That's St Thomas's recreation ground,' Ruby said, rooting in her pocket for car keys. 'It's no distance from Lisa's dump site.'

Eyebrows raised, they shared a glance. She knew they were both thinking the same thing. Depending on the time of death, their suspect may have killed more than one girl.

CHAPTER NINE

Ruby was silent as she negotiated traffic, taking shortcuts only known to taxi drivers and those well versed with the maze. A former burial ground, St Thomas's recreation ground was overlooked by high terrace Victorian houses. As they reached it through the archway of Mare Street, Ruby's mind was working double time as she tried to second-guess what lay before her. Officers had conducted door-to-door checks in this area already. If Danny Smedley was responsible for this crime, how would he have dumped the body in such a public place without being seen?

Crime scene tape flapped around the borders of the park, attached to the trees, which had long since shed their leaves. Their bare branches shuddered left and right in the twilight breeze as if they were warding off the evil within. Ruby fingered her long dark hair from her face, tucking it behind her ear. Her earlier jubilance had disintegrated replaced by a dark sense of foreboding. The setting seemed to add to her unease. Moss-covered headstones, once plucked from their original resting place, lined the walls on one side. What was once a graveyard had now been converted to an open space, although some of the original headstones and resting places still remained, along with some tombs.

On one of the tombs lay the body of their latest victim. Stepping into a forensic suit and overshoes, Ruby felt heaviness descend on her shoulders as she walked towards the crime scene investigators.

They had got here in record time, and were already planning to erect a tent to assist them in their harvesting of forensics at the scene. A fourteen-year-old boy, pale-faced and shaking, was being led away.

She drew in a breath as she approached the body, tiptoeing through the dying nettles lining the single point of entry. The last thing she expected was another body turning up so soon. The job still managed to surprise her, even after all this time. The young woman, who looked in her early twenties, was carefully positioned but, unlike Lisa Caldwell, she was fully clothed.

Ruby listened as officers at the scene briefed DI Downes. At first, residents thought it was a shop window dummy, which someone had dressed up and left as a sick joke. The fourteen-year-old informant had got there the same time as the helicopter and, realising he had an audience in the sky, dialled 999 to report his findings. Most people in that area knew about Lisa Caldwell's murder, and most likely the boy did not want to be put in the frame.

It was as if Ruby had stepped into a scene of a fairy tale. The girl was positioned in a state of permanent sleep, eyes closed, the shock of her red ruby lips a contrast against her pale skin. Ruby took in the full-length yellow satin skirt, the blue and red velvet bodice and the dramatic white collar, which rested beneath her bobbed black hair.

The words left her voice in a whisper. 'Snow White.'

She touched the grey, weathered tombstone as if to remind herself that she was not caught in a dream. 'It's all so surreal,' she whispered, more to herself than anyone else. Unlike the girl who had been found staring up at the stars, this victim was not a natural beauty, but someone who had been tampered with to produce a shocking wax-like effect.

There was something about the lie of her chest that made Ruby look again. She itched to remove the outer clothing to see what lay beneath. This was nothing like the frenzied attack where the killer had fled the scene of the previous victim. This was a careful, deliberate killing, a crime scene, which had been carefully prepared. She frowned as her investigator's mind warned it was too early to discount a connection between this victim and the last one. She thought about the delay in arresting Danny Smedley due to Worrow's hesitation. Did this grant him enough time to find and kill another victim? They were no distance from the park where Lisa Caldwell's body was found.

She could feel the eyes of the nearby residents boring down upon her as she surveyed the area. The girl needed to be shielded but, with night closing in, time was not on their side. After photographing the scene from every angle, the tent was being erected to protect crime scene investigators as they worked inside. The light was fading, much to the hindrance of the fingertip search, which would also be organised with haste. Public parks were incredibly difficult scenes because of the amount of transient evidence. Chewing gum, cigarette butts and even condoms were often found. It would all need to be seized and bagged, but, given the amount of people trampling through the park, its value would be questionable.

Ruby stepped aside to allow CSI to get to work. One last glance at the victim's face made her blood freeze. 'I think I know this girl, our Snow White,' she said, the words cold on her breath, 'but I need to get closer.'

She felt Downes's firm grip on her arm. 'No rush, best we let Bones get on with it. That poor wee lass isn't going anywhere just yet.'

Bones was the head crime scene investigator, and Ruby knew him well enough to agree that he would not appreciate her interference. She drew back, impatient. Downes was right: she was always moving too fast, and the scene had to be treated with slow and steady deliberation. But she could not bear that somewhere out there was a family waiting for their girl to come home; a girl now lying on a cold slab of weathered stone.

CHAPTER TEN

Ellie Mason

Two Days Previously

Ellie nursed her cheekbone as she sat at her dressing table preparing to disguise her bruises for her evening shift. She wished she was back working for the Crosbys, with nice clients who granted them a little bit of respect. No one ever hit a Crosby girl. Lenny once said that hurting one of his girls was the same as keying his car. At first, she had not been impressed at being compared to a piece of property, but now she longed for the old days because at least it showed he cared in some way. Sleeping with Lenny had been something all the girls strived for because they got treated better than anyone else. He had a steely coldness about him, and wasn't as handsome as his brother Nathan, but he valued the girls in his own way. The only time she saw Nathan was when he gave her her marching orders, and that had been her own stupid fault – playing in the snow during working hours. It was hypocritical, she had told him, providing the clients with cocaine and not being able to take it herself. And now look where she was, about to stand on the streets and freeze her arse off for a few lousy quid. But her mum relied on the income, and there were no proper jobs for people like her anymore. She sighed at her reflection in the mirror, picking up her make-up brush to swirl concealer onto her cheekbone. She had been beaten up by pimps in the past, but Frankie enjoyed inflicting cruelty.

It was all because she had taken a liking to one of the clients. He had called himself John and made a change from the usual type: fat and sweaty with a paunch hanging over their nether regions. Finding their cock was like a game of hide-and-seek. At first, she thought John was a cop, but Frankie was always careful about things like that. Nobody pulled the wool over Frankie's eyes, and heaven help them if they tried. He ruled the underbelly of his portion of East London. Sure, he would bow down to people like the Crosbys, who were at the top of the chain. He looked up to them, and in his eyes they had achieved God-like status.

It was due to her spark of defiance that Frankie picked on her more than the other working girls. He had broken their spirit within weeks, but not hers. He could see she was trying to get off the gear, and she had confided to John that one day she would meet someone nice enough to encourage her to get out. Maybe Frankie had seen that hope in her eyes, or perhaps John had let it slip. A flicker of optimism was something Frankie would enjoy stamping out. That morning, he had set her up with Lorenzo, a man who wore his dinner in his beard, his breath carrying the remnants of his garlic lunch. She had seen him before but had always managed to wriggle out of having him as a client. His yellow-stained fingers were usually found burrowed halfway up his nose, and his body was covered in thick black hair that would give King Kong a run for his money. While personal hygiene meant nothing to him, he was a big player in the drugs industry and Frankie felt he had been holding out on him about a future deal.

The private session was a way of killing two birds with one stone. It would leave Lorenzo indebted to him because Ellie was so good, one meeting would never be enough. It would also serve to teach her a lesson for her continued defiance. She had masked her repulsion, telling herself that this method of punishment was preferable to the threat of physical violence. Or so she thought.

Wearing a broad grin, Lorenzo had left and, as Ellie gathered up her clothes, Frankie had entered the room. She expected him to say that she was off the hook but she had been wrong. Frankie had pinched her jaw tight between his fingers, telling her that he wasn't finished with her yet.

'Don't think you're above punishment just because you've done your job,' he said, his eyes fiendish as he reached for a bottle of nail varnish remover from his back pocket.

Today he had excelled himself by making her choose between having acetone in her eye or shaving off all her hair. He had shaken the bottle of remover while counting down the seconds as he awaited her response.

Ellie knew nothing of the effects, but she believed him when he claimed it could cause permanent damage to her sight. It was a no-brainer – she had to choose the loss of her hair over her eyesight because her hair would grow back, right? But her naturally highlighted blonde hair was the only thing about herself that she loved, which was why Frankie wanted to shave it all off. No amount of pleading or crying would sway him from his decision. As he pointed out, he owned her, and she should be grateful that he was giving her a choice.

'Now, what's it going to be? Because if you don't give me an answer in the next ten seconds, you're losing both eyes. Acetone eats into your cornea. Burns like hell, so I'm told.'

'Alright!' Ellie jerked back her jaw as she screamed. 'Take my hair, as long as I can wear a wig.'

Frankie's smile grew wider, his voice curling in mock sympathy. 'Of course you can, baby, I'm not cruel. Besides, who would want to fuck you bald?'

He laughed as he handed her the clippers, preferring to watch as she did it herself. Ellie sobbed as her hair fell to the ground, along with the last of her dignity. She retreated inside herself, masking the horror she felt as the final strands of hair fell to the floor.

But Frankie had taken it as another look of defiance, and slapped her hard across the cheek. Ellie recoiled, her heart plummeting as he reached for the nail varnish remover after all. Surely not after all he had put her through?

But as he threw the contents over her she realised he had been playing her all along.

'It's water, you stupid whore! Next time you think about leaving, it'll be the real thing.'

He left the room as she picked up her hair from the ground. Pulling a bobbin from her wrist, she tied the long blonde strands into a ponytail, sobbing for what she had lost. She would never be free. One day she was going to end up dead. If the punters didn't kill her then Frankie surely would.

Ellie realised she was sobbing. Puffy-eyed, she wiped away the trails of mascara running down her face. Her scalp itched underneath the blonde wig. Her hair would never grow the same again. She wanted to die. Anything was better than the life she led now.

She sat on the bed, the tears flowing freely along with her pent-up anger and frustration. Sliding her hand under the pillow, she curled her fingers around the ponytail she had fashioned, stroking the silky softness. She was not ready to touch her scalp and feel the nothingness. The power had gone to Frankie's head. He was fucked up. Snot bobbled from her nose and she wiped it away. Too scared to live and too afraid to die, she was in limbo. More tears fell, blurring her vision. All she could make out was the glint of blonde on her lap. But she had to clean herself up, she had an appointment with one of her regulars.

He was too embarrassed to attend because of his disfigurement, which was why she always went to him. He smelt of pee, but paid well, always making sure she kept some money aside for herself. It was easy money, and he took fifteen minutes of her time at the most. The extra cash would count towards her escape fund. Frankie may have won today, but she wasn't giving up.

She felt a pang of guilt as she thought of her mother, but she could not live this lifestyle to support her anymore. Pulling on her jeans she knew there was no need to dress up for the doctor, he had costumes of his own.

CHAPTER ELEVEN

Ellie Mason lived in humble accommodation. It reminded Ruby of the flat she used to squat in with Nathan before it was demolished, back in her teens. Situated over a newsagent's, it contained a small square living room-cum-diner, and two matchbox-sized bedrooms, which barely afforded room for their single beds. All the flats on that road were laid out much the same way, and the occupants were no strangers to the police.

Mary Mason was a diminutive woman. Years of worry were evident, having emerged as frown lines furrowing her face – a face that carried expressions of both fear and hope as she waited for answers. Ruby had come to see these expressions many times in her job. It was amazing how the human face could contort itself to simultaneously produce dual emotions. As Ruby introduced herself, Mary stepped back, almost tripping on her threadbare dressing gown as she silently allowed her inside.

'It's not good news, is it?' Mary's voice was thin and shaky as they entered the living room. 'I've had a bad feeling all day.' Picking strewn clothes off the tattered sofa, she indicated to Ruby to sit down.

'I'm sorry,' Ruby said. She hated platitudes, but today she meant the words.

She took a seat, trying not to imagine herself in Mary's place. It could so easily have been her, had her life not turned itself around. Mary had grown up on the street across from Ruby's home and had her fair share of problems, which she readily transferred to her daughter. Ellie was no stranger to trouble but always found her way back in one piece. But Mary seemed to realise that today her daughter's luck had run out. How sad it was, Ruby thought, that a bright young girl such as Ellie would end up on the streets. She was far from stupid, having done well in school. The certificates on the wall and numerous swimming trophies were a testament to that. But the boyfriend she had long since broken up with had introduced her to a dark pastime. With a father in prison and an alcoholic mother, it was easier to accept the promise of happiness gifted by narcotics than believe that she would ever get anywhere in life.

Ruby drew in a deep enough breath to accommodate the words she had not expected to repeat so soon. 'Today we found the body of a young woman. Fingerprint analysis has suggested it's your daughter, Ellie.' Ruby continued to echo the same words she had used in Lisa Caldwell's house: how Mrs Mason would be given the opportunity of a formal identification, and how a family liaison officer would be assigned to assist her with the process that lay ahead.

Mary Mason just nodded silently, her face stony grey. Numbed by a steady diet of alcohol, perhaps she was able to keep it together better than her counterpart, Mrs Caldwell.

'How long was she there?' Mary said. With a shaky hand, she lit a roll-up cigarette, leaving Ruby in a cloud of smoke as she exhaled.

'Not very long, we'll know more after the post-mortem.'

'Three days she's been gone. Three days.' Mary's eyes narrowed as she sent Ruby an accusing glare. 'This is your lot's fault. If you found her after I reported her missing, she'd be alive now.'

'Police took your report, which meant they looked into it,' Ruby said, knowing her words were of little comfort. It was no surprise that Mary was turning the blame onto her. After a lifetime of shrugging off her responsibilities, she was hardly going to accept her part in her daughter's death now. If she had been a better mother, taken care of them both instead of sending her out to work for some pimp. . . Ruby sighed. Who was she to judge? She had delivered the news, and now she was needed back at the station.

'But nobody cared,' Mary wailed, digging her fingers into Ruby's forearm as they both stood. 'It's because she was a prossie, isn't it? That's why you'd rather sit on your arse instead of going out to look for my girl. This is all your fault.'

Ruby thought of her colleagues who worked merciless hours, often completing full shifts without finding the time to eat. She thought of the endless paperwork, along with the pressure to gain detections, and the colleagues who risked their necks every time they walked the beat. She glanced around the flat littered with empty wine bottles and takeaway cartons; the air so stale you could cut it with a knife. She felt sympathy for Mary Mason just the same. Blaming the police was a knee-jerk reaction, and less painful than facing up to the fact she had let her daughter down.

Ruby wished she could have told her that they had pulled out all the stops, but she knew that the report of Ellie Mason would have been filed along with all the other missing person notifications they had received that day. Most of the time, such girls turned up of their own accord. There was nothing to indicate that Ellie Mason would be any different. But now, as her body lay on the cold slab of the mortuary, Ruby wished there was something more she could have done. It always came down to the same thing. They had to prioritise their work by a matter of urgency because they didn't have the manpower to deal with everything the same day.

Ruby had read the newspaper headlines for Lisa Caldwell, the young university student with a promising future ahead. She wondered what story would be created, if any, for Ellie Mason.

CHAPTER TWELVE

'It wasn't me,' Danny Smedley said, looking panicked at the prospect of being questioned about Ellie Mason's death. But Ruby knew better than to be lured in by his pleas of innocence. She breathed in the faint smell of cheap paint that hung in the inoffensive room: the result of some recent prison renovations.

Danny was currently being detained at Her Majesty's pleasure pending trial for the murder of Lisa Caldwell. He was a different picture to the outspoken man she and DC Ash Baker had encountered in Shoreditch police station. Now, as they sat across from him for the second time, Danny's arrogance melted away. So too had his long hair and shaggy beard. Clad in a grey prison issue tracksuit, a buzz cut exposed slivers of white lines on his scalp as old scars were revealed. Ruby wondered if he was wearing them as a badge of honour now he had returned to prison.

She, on the other hand, had worn her smartest designer suit, teaming it up with a pair of sharp black heels in the hope of being taken seriously. Her work wardrobe usually consisted of blazer jackets, tight-fitting black trousers and whatever blouse was clean on that day. Her Ted Baker tailored suit was reserved for special occasions only, and today she felt as if she meant business. She loosened the single button of her jacket.

DC Ash Baker was by her side, having both gone through the rigmarole of searches and scanners as they arrived. Police officers were checked the same as everybody else gaining entry, much to Ash's disconcertion. The short first account interview was designed to accomplish the facts quickly while they awaited the autopsy results of their latest murder victim. Timing was everything, although Ruby had been warned it was impossible to ascertain the exact time of death, checking out Danny's alibi would give them something to go on in the meantime.

Danny's lips parted in an anguished moan, his yellowed teeth exposed as he pleaded his innocence from across the table. 'You're not pinning that on me.'

Ruby had heard of his change of plea. The evidence had mounted up against him, and his solicitor would have advised pleading guilty in the hope of a shorter sentence. Given the crime, Ruby hoped that was unlikely to occur.

'So where were you on the night of Ellie's murder?' she said.

He took a deep breath, exhaling his words. 'I was in the hostel. This is the honest to God truth. I didn't kill that girl.'

'Killed *which* girl?' Ruby said, wondering if he could remember the name of the life he had snuffed out.

'Neither of them.' He rubbed the bristles of his shaven head. 'I coughed to that Lisa bird because I was on a promise, but I'm not owning up to this, no way. I'm no serial killer.'

Ruby's grimace was set by the disgust she felt inside. 'So let me get this straight. You denied murdering Lisa then pleaded guilty. Now you want to change your plea to not guilty?'

'Yes. I didn't kill either of those girls.' Danny's voice rose an octave. 'Speak to the hostel, I. . .' His voice trailed away and his eyebrows knit together in a frown. 'Ask the black woman on reception, the one with the dreads – she'll remember me.'

'If we find forensics on Ellie after you plead not guilty to her murder, the judge will come down hard.'

'You won't find nothin' belonging to me.' Danny shifted in his chair. In the distance, a bell shrilled – a reminder of the schedule that would rule his life for years to come.

'What did you mean when you said you were on a promise?'

'I came across Lisa in the park. Her body was still warm. At first I thought she was passed out, drunk. I was a bit bladdered meself, you see. . .' He cleared his throat. 'I took her jewellery. I figured she didn't need it anymore. I didn't kill her, I swear.'

'Are you taking the piss?' Ash said. His complexion had taken on a deep pink hue. Up until now, he had seemed happy to remain silent, scribbling Danny's responses onto his notepad.

Ruby glanced at her colleague, whose knuckles had curled over his pen. Repressed anger oozed from every pore. But Ash had dealt with murderers and abusers many times in his career. Why was he letting it get to him now?

Danny glanced from Ash to Ruby. 'It's true.'

'So why did you change your plea?' Ruby said, willing to humour him.

'Because I had a message from someone you don't say no to. He said he'd look after me if I coughed to Lisa's murder. I figured I was already in the frame, so I agreed.'

'Who?' Ruby said, her brows knitted in confusion. Just what was Danny Smedley playing at now?

'I can't tell you who it was. That'll get me killed.'

'So you're telling me you confessed to rape and murder because someone pressured you into it?'

Danny shrugged. 'I get hot meals, a bed for the night, and that lovely lady from the church comes and visits me.'

Ruby's face soured. She placed her clenched fists on the table, leaning forward as she stood. It took every ounce of her self-restraint not to smack him in the face. 'You don't feel the slightest bit of remorse, do you? How much pain is this going to cause the victim's family if they've got to watch this go to a full trial? The least you can do is plead guilty and put them out of their misery.'

He glanced around the bare walls. 'I was all ready to, until you tried to pin this other murder on me. I swear, I'm telling you the truth.'

Ruby sat back as she mulled things over. She glanced at Ash, who responded by rolling his eyes. But a small voice niggled at the back of her brain. There was something eerie about the way Lisa's body had been laid out. Arms outstretched, hair splayed. And then there was the unnatural curve of Ellie's chest. Latest updates stated she had received stitches, which suggested a recent operation. This was information not yet made public knowledge.

With both Lisa and Ellie's autopsies due soon, Ruby needed to get back. What if Danny Smedley really was telling the truth? What if the killer was still loose on the streets?

CHAPTER THIRTEEN

'Sorry I missed the autopsies.' Ruby closed her office door as the buzz of her team's activity filtered through. 'Traffic was a nightmare leaving prison. It seems like everyone wanted to visit their nearest and dearest today. Can you give me the lowdown?'

'Nae bother,' Vera said, a hint of a Scottish accent travelling down the phone. 'Your DI was able to make it after all. I'm putting together my report now, but I'm happy to give you the salient points in the meantime.'

Ruby smirked. DI Downes was a pure delegator. DCI Worrow had requested the presence of a member of the team, and Downes had volunteered Ruby to accompany her, citing he had an urgent appointment elsewhere. Appointment, my arse, Ruby thought. He was able to wriggle out of it quickly enough when push came to shove. She knew him well enough to recognise his little habits. Lately, he had been hinting that he would like her company, and not just in police time. She liked Jack, and it would have been easy to fall into a relationship with him, allow it to develop into something more. He rarely made demands on her, accepting her for who she was. But it wouldn't have been fair on either of them. Both their heads were filled with ghosts; his with his wife who had died the year before, and hers with Nathan Crosby, a man she was better off without.

Taking a gulp of tea, she listened as Vera ran through her observations. 'Given what your DI has said about him, I don't think Danny Smedley is your suspect.'

'For Ellie's murder?' Ruby said, recalling their Snow White girl.

'For either of them. Smedley's MO is rape, isn't it?'

'Yes, but such things have been known to progress to murder,' Ruby said, wondering where this was going.

'But Lisa wasn't raped,' Vera said, matter-of-factly.

'What makes you so sure?' Ruby said. 'I mean, I know there's usually bruising but what if he did it after she passed out?'

'Lisa was a virgin. Evidentially, she hadn't had sex with anyone, let alone our killer. She died from asphyxiation. The thumb marks on her windpipe demonstrated the killer knew exactly where to press for maximum results.'

Ruby rubbed her forehead. What started off as a straightforward case was now proving to be anything but. 'But I saw the bruises on her body.'

'There are signs of a struggle and, given the girl was naked, there's nothing to say the killer wasn't disturbed before he did the deed.'

'Yet he took the time to remove her earrings and the rest of her jewellery without making a mark.'

'Exactly,' Vera agreed. 'Such things are often ripped off. There's no sign of that.'

'But Danny Smedley's remanded in custody. He confessed to her rape and murder.'

'It's not up to me to tell you how to do your job, but I don't believe he murdered Ellie. Whoever killed this girl knew how to handle a scalpel.'

'Yes,' Ruby said, 'there was mention of a scar on her chest.'

'It's too fresh to be a scar, the stitches were still in place,' Vera said. 'They've gone to significant efforts to change her appearance too. Her hair has recently been clipped short, and her bodily hair – all of it – was removed.'

'When you say *all*. . .' Ruby said, her words trailing away as she tried to comprehend the news.

'I mean all. Eyebrows, eyelashes, arms, legs, pubic hair, the lot. The closeness of the shave would suggest a cut-throat razor was used or perhaps wax,' she mused, 'although I'd be more inclined to go for the blade.'

'That must have taken a fair bit of time,' Ruby said, scribbling the words *undisturbed location* on a piece of scrap paper.

'Not only that, but they've then glued on false eyelashes and drawn on a pair of eyebrows to boot.'

Ruby took another sip of tea. It tasted bitter as it hit her throat, but it was down to Vera's words rather than the quality of teabags. What sort of ghoulish makeover was this? She grasped for a semblance of normality. 'Couldn't she have done that herself? She was a working girl, and there's a bit of a trend for the fake look at the moment.'

'It's doubtful. Ellie was hair-free in places she could never have reached on her own. And then there's the skin bleaching. It would have stung like hell in her intimate areas. This was more than the disposal of forensic evidence, they've gone way beyond that.'

Ruby nodded into the phone. 'Any signs of a struggle?'

'The welts on her wrist suggest she was restrained.'

Echoes of the door-knocker killer found their way into Ruby's memory. Despite having solved the case, she could not rule out a copycat killer. 'Any rope burns? What about her ankles? Any lesions in her mouth?'

'No cuts. No rope burns – more like thick belt marks, and only on her wrists. She's got a few puncture marks and faded bruises, but that's not uncommon for a girl with her way of life. The trick is separating what happened before she met the killer. We can only surmise.'

'Any forensics on either of the girls?'

'It's early days. It's my estimation that Ellie may have been in captivity for a couple of days before she was murdered. Blood tests have been requested, but it wouldn't surprise me if she were drugged throughout.'

Ruby sighed, hoping that was the case if only to spare her the horrors of her ordeal. 'Time of death?' She knew how much Vera hated being pinned down on such things.

'Ach! I guessed you were going to ask me that. Lisa wasn't dead very long before being discovered. But Ellie. . .' She exhaled loudly. 'Sometime in the last twenty-four hours. Will that do you?'

'It definitely rules out Danny Smedley,' Ruby said. 'Although I won't be letting him off the hook just yet.'

'Looks like you need to cast your net wider,' Vera said. 'When your suspect finished cleaning up Ellie, and I mean deep cleaning, he conducted a little invasive surgery, hence the stitches on her chest.'

Outside a siren blared through the streets of London, and Ruby raised her voice to be heard. 'Surgery? I presumed she'd been injured and he'd stitched her up after she died.'

'More like he took a keepsake. He's removed some of her internal organs, her liver and lungs to be exact.'

Ruby frowned. She didn't like the sound of this. 'And done what with them?'

'Your guess is as good as mine. DI Downes is going to brief the team when he gets back.'

Ruby shuddered, thinking of a horror movie she had recently watched. 'I hope we don't have one of those cannibal killers on the loose.'

'I think you'd best be researching the origin of your story first.'

Ruby recalled the black wig, the ivory white skin. 'The Snow White theme?'

'Yes, we found the remnants of an apple in her stomach. We're analysing the remains for poison.'

Ruby sighed. If the apple was poisoned, it meant that Ellie would have been conscious for part of the attack. So much for being spared. 'No signs of sexual attack?'

'Not forced, although she was sexually active. But that's hardly a surprise given her profession. Oh, and there's one more thing.'

'What's that?' Ruby said, adding to her notes.

'She had rat droppings in her hair so perhaps you need to direct your search into areas that would be likely to carry vermin.'

Ruby thought it over. The killer's invasive deep clean could not have been solely born from the need to dispose of evidence. But why go to so much trouble to bleach skin and remove hair, then allow vermin to invade the body? Unless Ellie had been left alone for periods of time in a place where rats frequented. Questions flooded her mind, but Vera was still talking.

'Whoever the killer is they took great care in transforming her. She was almost unrecognisable from the photo that DI Downes supplied. Perhaps it was one of her clients who held a grudge, but then I'm not going to tell you how to do your job.'

'Let's hope it was a one-off,' Ruby said, a dragging feeling growing in her stomach. With briefing due in half an hour, it was going to be another late night.

CHAPTER FOURTEEN

Ruby stood at the head of the briefing room, hands on hips as she surveyed her team. It had taken her just minutes to bring them up to speed. They had been busy making enquiries of their own, evidenced by the countless updates being placed on the computer system at a rate of knots. It was a job to keep up with them, along with the endless amount of checking, approving and chasing up she had to do.

Eve sat to her left, the only other female in her room. Wearing a black linen dress, her pregnancy bump was barely visible.

With DCI Worrow and DI Downes being called away, it was up to Ruby to lead briefing. She wasted no time in getting stuck in. 'How's your workloads?'

The question invoked a low murmur of laughter and it rippled around the room. The Metropolitan Police Central Communications Command handled over twenty thousand calls each day. It was virtually impossible to keep up, due to the very nature of their role. Ruby knew that as well as they did, but she still insisted on asking the question.

'I'll rephrase that,' she said, conscious their time was precious. 'Everyone managing OK?'

DC Ash Baker tugged on his earlobe, the tips of his fingers yellowed from his nicotine habit. The most senior of detective constables, he was used to speaking on their behalf. 'No worries this end. Uniform have been giving us a dig out with some of the lesser enquiries, leaving us to progress the investigation.'

Ruby nodded. Of this she was aware. The Serious Crime Team had a decent overtime budget, unlike other departments in the force, but it was not a bottomless pit and the pressure for results was growing by the hour. She glanced at the board behind her. On one side was university student Lisa Caldwell, and on the other, young prostitute Ellie Mason. Even without the thick black line dividing the two cases, the gap between them could not have been any wider.

'DI Downes has reiterated that Ellie's case isn't linked to the murder of Lisa Caldwell.'

Despite Danny Smedley's change of heart, the court case was going ahead. But now Ruby was less convinced of his guilt. All she could do was comply with her superior's wishes and hope further evidence was unearthed. It was bizarre to say the least. Her eyes fell on the photograph of Ellie Mason in her vivid yellow, red and blue gown. The tombstone beneath her appeared drained of all colour, apart from the weeds creeping up at the base. 'Are we any closer to finding out the motive behind Ellie's body being staged?' she said, turning to her team for answers.

Eve shuffled her papers, her jacket draped across her shoulders. Whoever was in control of the heating seemed to be sparing it tonight. Ruby was used to the cold, but Eve was a creature of comfort, and huddled under her coat as she spoke. 'I've researched Snow White, and fairy stories in general. What you said about her lungs being removed seems to fit in with the original version of the Brothers Grimm.'

'Go on,' Ruby said, wondering why it always fell to Eve and not her male counterparts to research such things.

'In the Brothers Grimm version the huntsman was ordered to cut out Snow White's lungs and liver as proof that she had been killed, not her heart. He took pity on her and allowed her to live, palming the wicked stepmother, or mother in some versions, off with an animal's organs instead.' She glanced around the room before returning her attention to her notes. 'To cut a long story short, Snow White *was* poisoned with an apple but it became dislodged and she survived. Some of the details of the original story are disputed, but I imagine the removal of Ellie's organs and the clothing she was wearing when her body was found are a tribute to the original tale.'

Ruby's attention was drawn to DC Owen Ludgrove, who was rather annoyingly tapping his pen against the table. Luddy was a lovely young man but she had no doubt he had been read the sanitised version as a child.

'Why, though?' he piped up, frustration evident on his face. 'It's not even accurate.'

'That's what we've got to find out,' Ruby said. 'At this stage we don't know if the suspect is male or female, young or old, or if they're working with accomplices. Nothing can be ruled out until we know more.'

'I bet she had some dodgy clients though,' Luddy said. 'Things go wrong all the time, we know that.'

It was true; Ellie was not the first prostitute to be murdered on their patch. But there was more to this case than a one-off killing. It was the attention to detail that made the hairs stand up on the back of Ruby's neck. She kept her expression firm, a gaze of steady determination, as she interacted with her team.

But as they exchanged intelligence and delegated jobs, it appeared the answers were not forthcoming as of yet. An hour later, she masked a yawn, casting an eye over the clock on the wall.

'We're not going to get any further with this tonight. Go home, get some kip, and be back here bright and early in the morning. Except for you, Eve, you've got a pregnancy scan in the morning, haven't you?'

Eve smiled, a twinkle returning to her eyes. 'Yes, but I'll be here straight after.'

'Good, and make sure you bring that scan photo when you do. I'd like to get a glimpse of my namesake before the rest of the team.' Ruby winked. They were already taking bets on what the baby was going to be called.

As she saw the last of her colleagues out, Ruby flipped off the light switch, wearily hooking her jacket over her shoulder. She knew the faces of Lisa Caldwell and Ellie Mason would haunt her dreams tonight. She prayed for answers tomorrow before any more victims turned up on her patch.

CHAPTER FIFTEEN

'I need your help.' Those were four words Ruby never thought she would hear from Nathan's lips. It was five in the morning, and as she roused herself from sleep, she detected the sound of a car engine in the background of their call: he was on the road. Ruby rubbed her eyes with the heel of her palms as she sat up in bed. 'What do you mean? What's going on?'

As usual, Nathan's response was sharp and to the point. 'Have you still got the phone I gave you?'

'Yes,' Ruby said, a bolt of fear ripping through her as she flicked the plastic button of her bedside lamp. The tone of his voice told her something was very wrong. 'Are you OK? It's not Cathy, as it?'

'Cathy's fine. Ring me back on the other phone.'

'It's not charged,' Ruby said. But Nathan had already hung up.

A chill descended as she pushed back her duvet, the wintry night nipping at her skin. Nathan was no stranger to trouble, but he was a proud man. Hearing him call for help made her heart skip a beat. Tumbling out of bed, she wrapped her dressing gown around her. She cursed the electrics as the living room bulb blew for the second time that week. 'Shitty flipping flat,' she muttered, trying to distract herself from her concerns, each one spearing her heart like tiny needles of doom.

Kneeling in the corner, she rooted under the floorboards in her secret hiding place. It was hidden for a reason: the contents of that box could put her job in jeopardy. But, regardless of the risk, it was reassuring to know that the firearm Nathan had gifted her was still there. She patted the old tin biscuit box without opening it. Reaching into the old Tesco plastic bag, she took the phone, and slid the wooden board back, standing on it until she heard the satisfying click as it fell into place. Like her, Nathan had a spare phone, one that could not be traced.

Her heart was hammering by the time she plugged the Nokia into a charger. Dialling Nathan's number, she held her breath, releasing it only when he answered after two rings.

'What's going on?' she said. Sitting back on her bed, she was ready to jump into action at a second's notice.

But Nathan's voice had taken on a hard edge as if he'd had time to reconsider his call. 'You wouldn't happen to know anything about the drugs raid at my place, would you?'

Ruby frowned. One minute he was calling her for help, and the next he was accusing her of having it in for him. 'You know better than to ask me that. It must have been the drug squad.' But why was he calling her at this hour over a drugs raid? Nathan wasn't stupid enough to keep the product in his home. His quick wit and intelligence had kept him out of prison all these years, and he wouldn't begin taking stupid risks now. She strained to hear the sound of traffic in the background, knowing that he would not be making telephone calls from the back of the police car. His silence unnerved her. She had to keep him talking before he changed his mind and hung up. 'Just tell me – what's happened?'

'I came home to find the place was swarming with Old Bill. Mum texted to warn me so I didn't go in. The place was clean, but they found something else. . . something that puts me right in the shit.'

'What is it?' Ruby asked, wanting to get dressed, but unable to leave the phone while it was plugged into the charger.

'It's a set-up, that's what it is. Someone's trying to frame me for that girl's murder, the one you found dressed as Snow White.'

News of the killing had hit the media early. It was hard to avoid, given that both Lisa and Ellie's bodies were found in such public places.

'You're not making any sense,' Ruby said, 'Are you talking about Ellie Mason? Why would they frame you for that?'

'They found it under my bed in a gift box. They must have thought there were drugs inside. It's fucking disgusting! I don't know how they got in, but someone's going to pay.'

Ruby leant into the phone, her mind swimming in confusion as she tried but failed to work things out. 'This is doing my head in. One minute I'm fast asleep, and the next you're ringing me up, talking about drug raids and gift boxes. I'm sorry, Nathan, but can you get to the bit where you start making sense?'

'It belongs to that girl you found. I know it does.'

'What?' Ruby said, her tone insistent. 'What was in the box?'

'Her lungs and liver – the dirty bastards. Someone put them in a box under my bed.'

Ruby drew in a sudden breath as the seriousness of the situation sunk in. 'I see. Where are you now?'

But Nathan's inability to answer a direct question was painfully evident as she tried to access the truth.

'It's a set-up. They'll waste no time in getting a warrant for my arrest,' Nathan said. 'I need to lay low for a while. You need to sort this out, I'm not going to prison.'

'There'll be a trace on your car,' Ruby said. 'And don't use a cash machine. There's CCTV everywhere. It's only a matter of time until they find you.'

'I've got no problem laying low,' Nathan said, his voice clear as the steady hum of the car engine extinguished in the background. Wherever he was, he had arrived at his destination. His tone lowered, almost pleading. As if she was the only person in the world he could rely upon. 'Can I trust you?'

Ruby frowned. She sensed he was coming to the end of the call. 'What kind of question is that? Of course you can. How did they get into your house to plant the box? I thought that place was a fortress.'

'It is. The cops have seized the CCTV. I wouldn't put it past them to corrupt the evidence.'

'Now hang on. . .'

'You know how long they've been waiting to collar me. They're not gonna let a little thing like CCTV get in the way. But that's the least of my worries now. I'm staying at your new flat tonight, and then I'm moving on. I'm relying on you to clear my name; I'm not going to prison.'

'You won't,' Ruby said, heaving a sigh so deep it made her feel like she was drawing up air from inside her toes.

Her head was spinning. Soon dawn would be filtering through the flimsy bedroom curtains. She needed to get dressed and go to work, but what would she do then? DI Downes knew all about her on-off relationship with Nathan, and he wasn't one of his biggest fans. There was no way she could share Nathan's location but she was a member of the Establishment that was hunting him down. She had never felt so torn, wanting to see her lover but unwilling to draw attention to his location. Nobody knew about that flat apart from the two of them – he had always kept it a secret, even from his brother. It was well stocked. There was no reason that he could not stay there until this died down. But did he trust her? Was that what this was really all about?

Her investigator's mind taking over, Ruby returned her attention to their conversation. 'I'll help you, but it works both ways. I need a list of all the people who could be setting you up for this.'

'That's a fucking long list, babe,' Nathan said, the night breeze taking his whispers as a car door slammed behind him.

Ruby imagined him leaving the car and taking cautious steps as he entered the walkway to the flat. 'I know, but there's a lot easier ways for people to get revenge than planting a set of internal organs under your bed. This is someone who's inventive, and would go to any lengths.' She tapped her bottom lip as she thought it through. 'I'll keep my phone hidden, but, if you need to reach me in an emergency, you'll have to block your number before texting my work mobile. Just say something like "thanks for the flowers," so if my texts are interrogated, it won't show up on the history that we've spoken.'

The jingle of keys was followed by the sound of a door closing. At least he was inside, safe for now.

'OK. You go to work as normal,' Nathan replied. 'Don't act like you know anything until they tell you.' He inhaled a terse breath. 'I hope I can trust you, Ruby.'

A bloom of outrage rose from within, and Ruby pulled the phone from its charger as she paced the floor. 'That's three times you've brought my loyalty into question. After all we've been through, do you know how hurtful that is?'

'Hmm.' Nathan groaned, falling silent as he formed an appropriate response. He never was very good at conveying his emotions. 'I don't mean it that way. You'd only serve me up if you thought it was for my own good. You'd want me to turn myself in because I'm innocent. But it doesn't work like that. They'll put me away for this, they've been looking for an excuse for a long time now.'

Ruby wanted to tell him that that would never happen, but she could not find the words. Sometimes police relied on other means to catch known criminals, such as traffic offences or financial matters, instead of what was really going down. But they would never manufacture evidence. Then again, her colleagues would not need to search hard for forensics when it was so conveniently planted under Nathan's bed.

'I swear, I won't say a word. Just hang tight where you are. I'll do everything I can to sort this out, but I need to know what I'm dealing with. What about your car?'

'You don't need to worry about that,' Nathan said.

Of course. Nathan was well versed in covering his tracks and had most likely swapped it on the way over.

Ruby jumped as her mobile phone played out. She glanced at the screen before returning her attention to Nathan. 'It's Downes. I'll find out what we're dealing with, and I'll call you as soon as I can. In the meantime, I need you to compile a list of all the people you've pissed off over the last year, including any recent prison releases. You know what these people are capable of. We'll have this cleared up soon.'

Ruby tried to sound hopeful as she ended the call but she knew the truth: if she wanted to clear Nathan's name, she had a fight on her hands.

CHAPTER SIXTEEN

As DI Downes called Ruby inside, she threw her eyes over the empty takeaway cartons on his desk. His office stank of last night's curry. The tie loosely hanging around his neck harboured a matching stain, and she wondered if he had slept in his clothes. They had finished just before two, which meant she was motoring with only a couple of hours' sleep in the tank. Not that it was worth mentioning. By the look on Downes's face, he was in no mood to offer sympathy.

'What's going on?' she asked, doing her best to project a look of confusion.

'Don't pretend you don't know,' Downes said. After catching her disapproving glance, he turned to throw the takeaway wrappers in the bin, still grumbling as he opened the window, allowing the spicy smell an escape. Spikes of rain dappled the blinds as they swung from left to right. Wind and rain were gathering outside with the promise of a storm. It was going to be a rotten day. 'I'm no eejit,' Downes grumbled, taking a seat in his swivel chair. 'And I've known you too long to believe you're in the dark about this.'

Ruby leant against the side of his desk. It was too late to change tack now. 'Boss, I've no idea what you're talking about, but it better be good for you to drag me in here at this ungodly hour. Is it the murder case? You know I still think Danny Smedley could be telling the truth.'

Arms folded, Downes delivered a relentless stare, as if he was trying to see into her soul. But lengthy silences meant nothing to Ruby. She was the queen of long pauses and would be the last person to crack.

'It's Nathan Crosby,' he relented. 'The drugs squad carried out a raid on his home last night, and they found evidence connecting him with Ellie Mason's murder.'

Ruby's eyes widened. It was hard enough hearing it from Nathan, but it still felt like a hammer blow to the stomach to hear it from her superior officer. Deep down, she had hoped that Nathan had got it wrong. 'Evidence? What evidence? You're having me on, right?'

'Do I look like I'm joking?' Downes said, with a face as thunderous as the storm clouds outside. 'He's wanted for murder.'

'Wanted for murder? So he's not been arrested yet?' Ruby said, repeating Downes's words for effect.

She knew she could trust Jack enough to tell him that she had spoken to Nathan, but she could not trust herself. Downes had a way of getting around her. In no time at all he would be persuading her to make Nathan turn himself in. She could see it now: him clasping his hands over hers, his soft honeyed voice convincing her that if Nathan were innocent, he would have nothing to be concerned about. But she knew that was not true. Nathan had plenty to worry about, and so did she. She could not bear to think of him spending time in police custody, where officers would be tempted to administer some justice of their own. He was at the top of his empire, but there were always people willing to topple him down. She could not afford to tell Downes anything, and once again she found herself being put in an impossible situation as her loyalties were tested.

'It's got to be a mistake,' Ruby said. 'What did they find?'

'Well, I'm hardly likely to tell you that now, am I?' Downes said. 'Don't you see? I can't allow you to handle this case. It's a conflict of interest.' A gust of wind whooped in through the window, scattering a pile of paperwork onto the floor. 'Feck's sake,' Downes grumbled, slamming the windowpane shut.

Together they picked up the paperwork from the thinly carpeted floor. Ruby contemplated Downes's outburst: so that was why he was so annoyed, it wasn't just about her. If DCI Worrow found out about her connection with the Crosby family, Downes would get his arse kicked for allowing her to handle the case. Ruby stacked the pile of overtime sheets back onto his desk. She would not beg, but she had to find a way of keeping ownership. She stood firm, grateful they were the only ones in the darkened office. Soon her team would be filtering in, and she did not want them to witness their disagreement. She closed the blinds, blocking out the view into the office that housed her team. Downes's office was situated across the room from hers, and both were contained on the expansive floor that made up Shoreditch Serious Crime Unit. Satisfied her conversation was private, she turned to her DI.

'You can't take me off the case, people will ask questions.' No reply. She took it as a good sign and continued. 'It's not the first time I've been compromised, is it?' she said, referring to her previous case, the door-knocker killer. 'But that turned out OK.'

Downes grunted. 'If you call nearly getting killed "turning out OK". What if you find some potentially damning evidence against the Crosby family, what then?'

'I think that ship has sailed, don't you?' Ruby said. 'If you remove me from the case, the team will be asking why. Nobody will know about my connection with Nathan, not unless you tell them.' She softened her voice, touching Downes on the arm. His muscles tensed beneath her fingers, and she slowly drew her hand away. 'Boss, please,' she said, hoping her face would speak the truth, because she meant what she was about to say. 'I won't defend a murderer, especially after he's killed a girl young enough to be my daughter. Neither would I allow a man to blinker me from finding out the truth. You do believe me, don't you?'

Downes gnawed on his thumbnail as he mulled it over. 'If we find out that Nathan Crosby's responsible, you can't put the brakes on. You have to see it through to the end. But if you can't do that, you need to step away from this investigation now.'

Ruby was quick to respond. 'I'll find justice for Ellie. Think about it, I have an insight to the Crosby family, and yes, of course, I'd be investigating the possibilities of planted evidence. But I'll see it from both sides, and maybe bring in some new suspects. I heard about the post-mortem. Nathan's no surgeon.'

'Maybe, but . . .'

'I'll be privy to some good intel, and you can always overturn my findings if you don't agree.' Ruby could see he was softening. Her heart lit like a beacon; she was winning him over. 'I promise I won't impact on this case in a negative way. You know I'm the right person to oversee this. Please.' She stared at him, her dark eyes beseeching.

Downes nodded wearily, handing her the folder on his desk. 'It's the photographs of the evidence found under Crosby's bed. It's not pretty. They're undergoing testing but we're confident they belong to Ellie Mason.'

Slipping them from the folder, she flicked through the crime scene photos. The organs were contained in a zip-locked plastic bag within a macabre black-ribboned gift box. Zip-lock was good, it would explain why Nathan didn't smell the freshly harvested organs when he proclaimed his innocence.

'And anything else?' Ruby said. 'Any drugs?'

'No,' Downes said, 'nothing was found.'

'Of course it wasn't. Nathan may be a lot of things but he's not stupid. You know as well as I do that he wouldn't keep coke in his house. That warrant was a bit convenient, don't you think?'

Downes rubbed his chin, for once short of words.

'C'mon, why keep a set of organs under his bed? It's obvious what's going on here, Jack. You must see that.'

'Then why has he run away? If he's so innocent, why didn't he stand his ground? It's not as if he can't afford the best lawyers.'

'Well, would you blame him? I'd do the same thing in his shoes. Evidence is evidence, and a lot of people won't care who planted it there as long as he gets banged up.'

A door closed in the distance, and Ruby peeped through the blinds as lights were switched on. 'It's Ash,' she said. 'He's in early. I'll put the kettle on, make us a cuppa before they all roll in. Everything's gonna be OK, I can feel it in my bones.' But she was trying to convince herself more than anything, and Downes was not finished with her yet.

'Ruby...'

'Yes?' she said, as nonchalantly as she could.

'When you talk to him, and you *will* talk to him, you tell him to hand himself in. The longer he stays away, the worse it looks.' Another rub of the chin. 'Ask yourself: if what you're saying is true, and he's been set up, what the hell has he done to deserve this sort of revenge?'

'I've already asked the Crosbys to provide a list of people who hold grudges—' Her words jolted to a halt as she realised she had let the cat out of the bag. She cringed as he thumped a hand on her shoulder, but Downes was smiling, a bemused look on his face.

'I knew you were lying. Very well, we'll do it your way. But put a foot wrong and we're both for the high jump. Don't let me down.'

'I won't, I promise,' Ruby said, grateful that at least she had said 'The Crosbys' instead of Nathan's name.

'Update your enquiries under "Operation Lancelot". I'll grant permission to carry out internal checks on Crosby and his acquaintances. It'll do ya some good to find out what's going on with that lot.'

Ruby nodded. She may have let her knowledge of the case slip but she was pleased with the clearance to carry on background checks. It would have been tricky otherwise. Hinting she was on the side of the Crosbys was enough bait for Jack to insist that she check them out. She knew all along that was what he had wanted – for her to see the Crosbys for what they really were. She was under no illusions as to what they did for a living, but his reaction suited her just fine. Now she had carte blanche to do as she wished with the investigation. She turned to leave, trying not to look too smug.

Downes's voice echoed behind her. 'Just don't forget who you're dealing with. And if you do bump into Nathan Crosby, I expect you to nick him and bring him in. But call for backup. In a situation like this they're capable of anything.'

'Yes, boss.' Ruby rolled her eyes, glad the blinds were shut so he could not see her reflection. Nathan would never hurt her and, whatever she discovered about him or his family, she would never allow it to come between them. So why did she feel so nervous about digging into his past?

Her phone beeped with a Facebook message from her daughter, worrying about her dad. Ruby shoved it back in her pocket. She would speak to her later. Try to offer reassurance. Tell her that Nathan would soon be in the clear. Because he would, wouldn't he? A rumble of thunder from outside halted her thoughts, filling her with a sudden sense of dread.

CHAPTER SEVENTEEN

'Wakey, wakey,' Ruby said, gently shaking DC Ash Baker by the shoulder. 'Can I have a word in my office, please?'

Ash slowly lifted his head from the paperwork, peeling back the list of taskings from his cheek. 'What?' he said, pausing to dry wash his face with his hands. 'I. . . I must've fallen asleep.'

'Here,' Ruby said, minutes later, handing him a mug of tea as they took a seat in her office.

Sipping from their mugs, they listened to the relentless winds screeching through the cracks in her window. Rain hammered on the glass outside. Daylight had finally prevailed and a dull slate colour washed over the city sky, doing nothing for her morale.

'You look knackered. You shouldn't have come in so early,' she said. But as Ash's shoulders drooped, Ruby could tell that home was not a place where sleep came easily.

Tipping back his head, he ingested a mouthful of tea. 'Mmm...' He smacked his lips and smiled appreciatively. 'There's more than tea in this.'

Ruby leant forward conspiratorially. 'Just a drop of whisky, nothing to set you over the limit. Want to talk about it?'

'I'm sure you've got enough going on with this case and everything.'

But the haunted look in his eyes told her he was desperate to get it off his chest. With briefing due in ten minutes, soon neither of them would have a second to spare. Ruby's priority sat with the members of her team, and she couldn't help but worry that she was pushing them too hard.

'Mate, there'll always be cases,' she said, closing the door. 'It doesn't mean I don't have the time to listen to you.'

Ash took another gulp of tea. The deep frown lines embedded in his forehead told her this was a problem that had been worrying him for some time.

'C'mon, don't pull all that macho keep-everything-in stuff with me. God knows the job puts enough weight on our shoulders without added problems at home. I take it that's what it is, home?'

'It's the missus,' Ash said, still staring at the floor. 'Her depression's getting worse. Mum can't cope with her anymore, and I've had to make some tough decisions.'

'Really? I'm sorry to hear that. What are you going to do?'

'We don't have any choice, she's gonna have to be sectioned.' His hands were clasped around the mug as if it were a lifebuoy in a sea of despair. Rain battered the window from outside, adding to the bleakness of the situation. Ash sighed, his gaze finally meeting Ruby's. 'I just can't face going home. What sort of a husband does that make me? What kind of a dad?'

His voice cracked, and Ruby could feel the stress emanating from his body. She hated to hear him wracked with guilt when he was doing everything he could. It was a place she had been to herself with her mother's dementia, and it didn't seem all that long ago.

'Stop it, you silly sod. You're the bravest person I know, and not just in the job. How's the kids?'

'The girls have gone to live with my sister, but the missus can't be left alone now she's threatening suicide.'

Ruby nodded. She had to keep Ash buoyant if she wanted to help him get through it. 'But they're OK? I guess it's easier now they've started uni.'

'Oh yeah,' he paused as he threw her a wry grin. 'They love Canterbury. They seem to be a lot happier living with my sister than they ever were with me and Abigail.'

'I guess it makes sense, with your sister living so near the university,' Ruby said. 'And it's not as if they're little kids anymore.'

'Hmm… Thankfully, Fiona, my sister, loves to have them. If it wasn't for her, I don't know what I'd do.'

Ruby crossed her legs, deliberately ignoring the clock on the wall. The briefing would have to wait. 'So is it arranged for tomorrow?' Memories of putting her mother into care sprinkled her thoughts.

'Yeah. I'm not looking forward to it because I know she's going to kick off. She's outraged when I mention treatment, becomes violent. It's not her fault.' He placed his empty mug on the desk and glanced out the window.

Ruby's forehead creased. 'You've never reported any violence.'

'Why should she be criminalised because of an illness? Besides, if I were a better dad and husband, maybe none of this would have happened. Yet here I am, burying myself at work because I can't bear to be at home.'

If Ruby were to follow procedure, she should document their conversation and ensure any allegations of violence were reported. But Ash's wife was getting sectioned, and police involvement at this stage could only make things worse. Ruby had vowed to be a human being rather than a walking, talking police procedure handbook; it was why her team respected her as much as they did.

She took a deep breath. 'When I put Mum into care I was sinking in guilt. We couldn't cope living together anymore, and her senility had got so bad that she was a danger to herself. But it didn't stop me from feeling responsible somehow. Sometimes she would shout and scream, and I didn't know where to turn. But you know what? She's used to her care home now. There's nowhere else she'd rather be. I know it's not the same thing but there's a good chance Abigail will get better. It's not too late for things to go back to what they were when you first met.'

'But that's the thing,' Ash said, his expression pained as he voiced the words. 'The love I felt for her died years ago. It's such a mess.'

Ruby was lost for words. Who was she to give relationship advice? 'Have you spoken to occupational health? Maybe take some time off, go to Canterbury, see the girls? It sounds like you need a holiday.'

'To be honest, all I want to do is to work. When I'm investigating, I feel occupied, you know? Useful. I don't have to think about what's going on at home.'

It was a feeling Ruby knew all too well. Her personal life was a mess, work was all she had to cling to. It was the one place in the world where she felt valued. 'What about taking the rest of the day off then? Get some sleep so you're at full strength.'

'No offence, Sarge, but I'd rather be here. I've taken a half-day off tomorrow. I've arranged for a uniformed officer to come round to help me get her into the ambulance – Aoife Daly, remember her, that nice PC that helped me with the house-to-house enquiries in my last case? It turns out her mum has schizophrenia. She's very supportive.'

Ruby felt a pang of disappointment that Ash had not come to her first. 'I would have been glad to support you, mate, had you asked.'

'I'm always bending your ear. Besides, it's all taken care of. If Abigail's not sectioned soon, she'll do herself in. She keeps going on about this spaceship. . . says it's going to bring her to a better place, but the only way she can get there is by dying and coming back to life.' He rubbed his face, which seemed to have aged by ten years. 'Sometimes I get so tired, you know? I think my family would be better off without me. I don't know the girls anymore, not really. They don't know what to say to me. We're like strangers.'

'They're teenagers,' Ruby said. 'Comes with the territory from what I've heard.' She paused, her internal alarm bells still ringing from his earlier comments. 'When you said they're better off without you. . . You're not thinking of doing anything stupid, are you?'

Ash threw on his well-worn smile, waving away her concerns as he rose. 'Ah, don't mind me, I'm just maudlin. You're right, things will be a lot better when Abigail gets the help she needs.' His eyes rose to the clock on the wall. 'We'd better get moving before Worrow sends out a search party.'

Hitching up his trousers, he tucked in the shirt that was straining over his expansive belly. Eating junk food at random times had gained him enough weight to make him unrecognisable from his joining photo, taken almost thirty years before.

Gathering up her paperwork Ruby stifled a yawn, making a mental note to keep a close eye on Ash. It was a long day ahead, and she would have to draw upon her reserves of strength if she wanted to get through what lay ahead.

* * *

'Sergeant Preston, nice of you to join us,' DCI Worrow said, casting a cold eye over her shoulder as Ash Baker skulked behind her, squeezing in between Luddy and Eve. She stood at the head of the table, her black bob skimming her jawline. Her face was pinched and tight, making it clear that their tardiness was an unacceptable interruption.

Ruby narrowed her eyes. If her DCI wanted to show her up she could not have picked a worse time. But her superior seemed to sense Ruby's annoyance and drew her gaze back to the team. The room was full with as many officers connected to the case as they could squeeze in.

'As I was saying,' Worrow said, spreading the newspapers out on the table, 'our capital city is no stranger to murders, but this recent one appears to have caught the attention of the media. It features in all of these papers, albeit in a small section. It's up to us to ensure this progresses no further, particularly now a member of the Crosby family is suspected of being involved.'

Ruby pursed her lips, as if trying to contain her words. Yes, a splash in the newspapers could provoke an adverse reaction, setting the police in a bad light. But it wasn't the end of the world. Despite her and DCI Worrow having a mutual interest, they saw things in a completely different way: Worrow worried about headlines and its reflection on her as the DCI, Ruby thought only of Lisa and Ellie lying frozen in a mortuary drawer. Such young lives to be snuffed out so suddenly. The fact they were so publicly displayed hinted at arrogance, a willingness to want to play. It was *her* priority to ensure the bastard that so brutally killed them was swept off the streets, *her streets*, before he struck again. She folded her arms, feeling crestfallen as her superior planned Nathan's arrest with the team.

CHAPTER EIGHTEEN

The doctor shuffled on the rotting mattress, shifting his bones to get comfortable. Underneath the material of his long military coat, small warm bodies stirred. A set of whiskers brushed against his own, a long black tail slithering across his neck as the rodents sharing his space settled down. The storm had brought them inside seeking warmth and shelter. He had not turned them away. Their bellies full from the food that he had brought them, they had kept him company as he plotted his next move. Surrounded by newspapers he had scanned each word under torchlight, absorbing the titles that referred to his victim as a young prostitute who had been transformed before her death. It had filled him with warm glee to see his art spoken of in the nationals. Not that they saw it as art, not yet. But they would, he would make sure of that. He must have fallen asleep around three when his flashlight dimmed, and his eyelids turned leaden. Waking up with his faithful creatures wrapped around him, he no longer felt alone.

It was not as if he didn't have a home to go to – however his flat in Shoreditch no longer felt safe. The people who disfigured him had left him with nightmares, and it had taken some time to feel back in control. His art was a testament to his recovery, and his victims gave him strength. Not that he saw them as victims, empathy was not an emotion he was familiar with.

Even throughout his childhood, he had known he was different to the others. As his friends buried their pets in makeshift graveyards, he threw his bug-eyed goldfish down the toilet. He remembered wondering, as he urinated on him, how long it would be before he could persuade his mother to buy him another one. Pets, like people, were disposable objects. There were too many of them in the world, and the loss of a few would make it a better place.

Just because he didn't care about his fellow human beings did not mean they were not a subject of great fascination – and in what other occupation would he be able to place his hands on real-life subjects? He smiled at the thought. People were so trusting back then. Over the years things had changed. The respect faded, and he was forced to move his profession into the shadows of the darkness. Illegal abortions were highly paid, and it was something he developed a great fascination for. Word got around that he could be trusted. Soon he was employed by darker characters to treat gunshot wounds and life-threatening injuries. He had even dabbled in facial reconstruction. He had treated them all and been well paid for it.

Now he was an outcast. Money was no longer a necessity, and he was at least free to treat his betrayers with the contempt he felt.

He had already lined up his next work of art, and he could not wait to get his hands on her. He stroked the fur of the rat nestling underneath his coat. Like humans, they could turn on him without a moment's notice. That was what he liked about the creatures that visited him in the night: they never pretended to be any more than they were, and he trusted them more than they deserved. Like the rats, he had learned to walk in the shadows and immerse himself in a community that rejected him long ago. With his long grey hair and oversized coat, he prowled the night with his head low, his offensive features hidden away from view.

He had known April for some time now. Granted, she recoiled beneath his touch, but he worked hard to demonstrate a gentle and grateful side to his nature, much unlike the brutish behaviour of some of her younger clients. And when that failed the promise of more money always won them over in the end. He slid himself upwards, freeing the rats as they squeaked and swooped for cover. Shaking his leg as he stood, he loosened one from within the thin material of his trouser leg. Its long yellow teeth embedded in the stitching as it attempted to nip him on the way down. Like a footballer, the doctor kicked out, releasing it across the room. Skittering on its back, it hit the skirting board with a thud.

Shaking the stiffness from his limbs, the doctor walked across the room and ran his hand over the rusted surgeon's chair. It was time to prepare. Today was the day, and he had something very special lined up for April. His eyes crept over to his scalpel, which glinted in the dim light. It was good to be reacquainted with his old friend. Killing the girl in the park had been unplanned but he had enjoyed submerging himself in violence again. It had given him the confidence to move on to greater things. He had something even greater in store for his next masterpiece. His thin lips stretched into a smile. It would be the talk of the East End, and there wouldn't be a newspaper in the land that would not want to cover it.

CHAPTER NINETEEN

April

April popped a chewing gum bubble as she checked the website for bookings. Her inbox was empty apart from the usual lurid crap she had come to expect.

BigPenis52: I want 2 do U up the arse. U will beg 4 more.

Unlikely. She rolled her eyes as she pressed delete and moved on to the next one.

RogerUSensless: U so fine babes, msg me so U can suck my cock.

'I don't think so,' April said, pressing delete. She clicked on the third, a small groan escaping her lips.

ServantOfGod69: You have sinned, but I can help you see the light. Let me save your soul.

'Really?' she said, binning the email until there was nothing left. Three lousy emails: two from people who were illiterate, and one from a self-proclaimed servant of God who used a sexually suggestive username. She rested her chin on her hand, still chewing mechanically as she clicked through her website pictures. That photo of her sitting naked in the bucket chair was as hot as hell, so why had all her bookings dropped off? It would have been nice to raise some extra cash given it was her last day but it was slim pickings as the market was flooded with women offering themselves up for little or nothing. At least her profile pictures were real, unlike the fresh-faced nymphs on her competitors' sites. It was a far cry from the emaciated, grey-skinned reality. Back in the day, when she aspired to better things, hers were taken by a proper modelling agency in London.

There used to be a time when she could command £300 a client, but now she couldn't even keep a roof over her head. Sex trafficking was big business in the city, and the women brought in to service the punters were in no position to complain.

April shut down the laptop, vowing to count her blessings. At least she was free. Tomorrow she would start her new life. But she could not help but feel sad for what could have been. At just seventeen, she had travelled from Essex to London with a head full of dreams. Too short for modelling, she was told that being a high-class escort was the next best thing. She had a nice body and certainly wasn't shy when it came to showing it off. Sex was something she enjoyed, and she never had to get up for work in the morning and squeeze herself into the tube for a daily commute. Working for the Crosbys had been the perfect arrangement. She had met Lenny at a party in London, and he offered her a job, after requesting a 'test drive' that night. She had heard all about the Crosby family, and Lenny's lavish lifestyle was something she wanted for herself one day. Crosby girls had the opportunity of meeting footballers and politicians, he told her, and bagging herself a sugar daddy was something she had always dreamed of. He wooed her with the promise of upmarket clients and offered some much-needed protection.

And now, less than two years later, he refused to answer her calls. Losing her job was the beginning of her downfall. She had become too accustomed to the champagne lifestyle; when the bubbles flowed freely, so did the coke. And who could blame a girl if she wanted a little pre-sex booster? If the clients took it, it seemed only natural that she would too. She still missed it, still got the itch for the euphoria only a cocaine high could bring.

She had tried his number only this morning because she was too upset to face the facts. It was time to leave London, give up her dreams and go home. Besides, there was more than just her to take into consideration. When her friend, Lorna, called and offered a lifeline it seemed like it was meant to be. The hotel her friend was working in was taking on staff. She had a spare room, and April could begin paying rent as soon as she was earning. So she had said yes. Today was her last day in the big city. The train tickets were booked, and tomorrow she would begin her new life in Essex. Near home.

It went somewhere towards building back up a relationship with social services, who had placed her little girl in foster care. Not that she could blame them. She had committed a cardinal sin by choosing to party over her child. They knew what she did and said it was too dangerous for a small baby to be embroiled in such a hedonistic lifestyle. It wasn't as if she hadn't tried but it had been so hard. The incessant crying had drilled into her brain along with the torturous lack of sleep. It's why she wheeled little Charley into the same hospital where she was born and just left her there. It hadn't taken them long to catch up with her and get the social involved.

April shook away the thoughts. It was all in the past now. She was going to be a good mum; she would learn how. She clutched a packet of cigarettes as she left her flat. God! It was pissing down outside. That was all she needed. She certainly wasn't going to miss this. Another pang of regret. Gone were the cocktail dresses and yacht parties. Her standards had hit rock bottom in the last six months. She sighed as she pulled up the hood of her jacket, wishing she hadn't lost her umbrella. It had been a nice one too. Burberry.

Flecks of rain spiked her face, and she swore as she walked the rain-splashed path. Just one more job, she told herself. The doctor had surprised her this morning by requesting her company. She had hoped for something better, so she could cancel their appointment. He wasn't the most pleasant of clients but a good earner nonetheless. A man of little words, he requested just minutes of her time, promising to pay her double the hourly rate. She was about to say no when she thought of the money, and it would be OK, over in a flash. She had to work hard to suppress the feeling of her flesh crawling when she was with such an unattractive client. She would keep her eyes tightly shut and imagine she was screwing one of those Hollywood stars instead. It had taken a good stretch of the imagination in Doctor Tanner's case. It was more than his disfigurement that made her shudder, he smelt as if he had crawled from the belly of the sewers. A dab of Vicks under her nose helped block out the pong.

That was a trick taught to her by a copper when he told her stories of jobs he had been to and things he had done. A regular client, he was a good man. A little bit sad, in need of female company.

She crossed the road, her fingers gripping the hood of her jacket. Rain slashed against her bare legs, and she felt her internal alarm flash a warning. *What are you doing? There's a murderer on the loose.* She paused, biting her lip as she tried to recall the directions. Trying to ignore the slice of cold fear. Should she go there on her own? People had asked her to do it in the strangest of places but in a derelict building? Was it safe? She had known Ellie Mason, and now she was dead. Poor cow. Unable to get off the gear, her life had spiralled since she stopped working for the Crosbys. It was reading about Ellie's death that had helped convince April to throw in the towel. The police had advised all working girls to keep themselves safe yet she was going to a derelict building, without telling anyone that she was there. She pushed away the warnings; she was being paranoid. Doctor Tanner was a regular. All the girls knew him and, if she didn't hurry up, she'd be late. Besides, he must have been a respectable man once. She had seen the certificates on the wall of his flat. *Get a grip*, she told herself. Ten or fifteen minutes, max, and you'll have enough money to keep yourself going for a week. Her teeth chattered as the cold air brushed against her legs. Marching on, she lowered her head against the rain.

CHAPTER TWENTY

'Ruby, come in,' Frances Crosby said, giving her arm a squeeze. 'Isn't this a dreadful business? Still, I'm sure it's only a matter of time until you can sort it out.'

Ruby nodded, unwilling to commit to an answer. 'How's Cathy?' she asked, glancing up the stairs.

'Out with her friends. I don't expect her back until late. It's been good for her, having some stability in her life, someone who can give her what she needs.'

Ruby knew the barbed comment was aimed at her. Frances would never forgive her for giving Cathy up for adoption, but she was in no position to offer her a stable home.

'Oh, it's just that I was hoping to see her,' Ruby said, unable to let the subject go.

'Well then you need to be patient, my dear. She's a Crosby through and through. And Crosbys find it hard to forgive.'

Ruby set her jaw. She and Nathan had been loved-up teenagers, living rough on the streets. Life had been different then, and they had given Cathy up because they had no choice. Now she had returned, Frances would waste no time in pouring poison in her granddaughter's ear.

'I've just got to make a phone call.' Frances imparted another sharp smile. 'You head into the drawing room, and I'll be with you in a minute.'

To an outsider looking in, it would appear that the diminutive woman had offered Ruby the warmest of welcomes. She looked almost cute, with her blonde bobbed hair and pink designer trouser suit. But beneath the smile Ruby envisioned the sharpest of teeth, capable of ripping a person in two. The nicer Frances appeared, the more guarded Ruby became. Her footsteps echoed down the vast corridor, the hairs on the back of Ruby's neck prickling as she walked.

Fresh from briefing, she had journeyed to the luxurious Crosby residence in Chigwell in the guise of making some urgent enquiries. Not that she had to hide now that Downes had given her free rein. It felt strange for her visit to the family of gangsters to be above board for once. She should have come double crewed, but there were a few reasons why she had chosen to attend alone. For one thing, she did not want anyone else knowing about her relationship with Nathan Crosby. For another, Frances would not speak quite so candidly with another officer in the room, and it could compromise her position as sergeant when their close acquaintance became apparent. How she had managed to keep it under her hat this long, she did not know, but there was no way she was going to jeopardise her job now. As always, when she thought of how much she valued her role, the scales tipped the other way. Her emotions were a continuous see-saw. Since joining the police, she had never known it any other way. She'd think about her job, the driving force in her life, then she'd imagine Nathan, the type of man she would usually put behind bars. Growing up next to the Crosbys had given her an insight not afforded to many and brought with it added complications when it came to her job.

She wondered what he was doing and if he was OK. Unlike his brother, Nathan had done well to avoid prison all these years. The only time he came close to being discovered by the police was when his movements were orchestrated by his brother, Lenny. The brothers had both grown up the same way, both victims of their father's heavy hand, yet they couldn't be more unalike. The only thing that kept them together was the sense of family loyalty their mother had embedded since an early age.

Ruby slowly opened the heavy drawing-room door. It was just as she thought: Lenny was waiting for her, and Frances's phone call had been a ploy to give the two of them some time alone. Her stomach tightened at the sight of him. She gathered up her reserves of strength as she confidently pushed her way through. Lenny would be keen to impose some of his more persuasive tactics to get what he wanted, and Frances had no problem in turning a blind eye.

Dressed smartly in trousers and shirt, he sat next to the blazing open fire, his crossed leg bobbing as nervous energy overrode his senses. Lenny was jittery, Ruby thought. Probably on a comedown from the last lot of coke he had shoved up his nose. He stood as she entered, his hands shoved deep into his trouser pockets. His hair slicked back, he wore a tight expression, offering Ruby a glare which suggested she had been the bane of his life. That was the trouble with Lenny. He could never take responsibility for his actions.

'Well? Have you sorted it out yet?' he asked, wrinkling his nose at Ruby's presence as if she had just walked in dog shit and come swanning in.

Ruby held back from rolling her eyes as she walked towards him. Her childish reaction came from a lifetime of deflecting his annoying traits. It may have worked when she was eight, but they were adults now. Lenny was unpredictable, and the fact he both fancied and disliked her in equal measures left her uneasy.

'That's what I'm here for,' she said, 'in an official capacity. I don't think Nathan is responsible for this any more than you do, but we need to work together. Someone has had access to his home. I'll need a list of suspects, people you've angered over the years. Then I'll need. . .'

'No, no, no, that's not how this works,' Lenny said, his finger moving from left to right in a tick-tock fashion. 'I tell *you* what to do.' Seizing her by the shoulder, his fingers bit into her flesh.

'Get the fuck off me,' Ruby said, shrugging her shoulder free.

He licked his lips, his hand falling to her forearm. Smiling, he tilted his head to one side and stared deep into her eyes. She could smell the stale tobacco lingering on his breath, hear the click in his throat as he swallowed, but his eyes were icy-cold. She fought the urge to turn on her heel and leave. She hated being in such close proximity to Lenny. Every time they were together he had to lay hands on her, making no secret of the fact that he wanted to get her into bed. Had it not been for Nathan, he could have forced the issue, and Ruby could tell that there were plenty of times when he had been tempted. The sexual undercurrent was entirely one-sided, and Ruby despised him more now than ever.

She broke his grip, taking a step back. 'Touch me again, and I'm out of here. Then you can explain to your mum why I'm not investigating the case.' She placed her hands on her hips, the heat of her anger growing. She was a detective sergeant, and this visit was on job time. 'I'm the best person to clear Nathan's name because nobody else will be interested in his innocence. If you don't start treating me with a bit of respect, I'm off.'

'And you better listen to me,' Lenny said, jabbing his finger in Ruby's chest. 'Because if you don't get Nathan off, I'm gonna slit that pearly white throat of yours, and your daughter will be left without a mother for the second time. Do I make myself clear?'

His voice was like grease on her skin. Ruby found her temper rising. She glowered. 'You know what? I don't need this. I came here to help, and all you can do is threaten me. I'll take my investigation back to the station.' She wanted to tell him to go fuck himself, but she knew where to draw the line.

She strode towards the double doors, pushing them open. Just as she guessed, Frances had been waiting outside all along. But while Lenny had been upfront about his feelings for Ruby, Frances worked with a smile. It was almost like good cop–bad cop, except they were both on the wrong side of the law. They were working a routine on her. Ruby had done it herself enough times to know when she was being played.

'Sweetheart, where are you going? I've just sent down to the kitchen for tea.' Taking her gently by the forearm, Frances ushered Ruby back inside.

It was as if she held power over her. As much as she mistrusted Frances, Ruby respected her as a mother figure in her life. Frances and her mother, Joy, had been best friends since their teens, and she had grown up to the background of their kitchen table conversations. Both women's lives had changed beyond recognition but, in Ruby's mind, a part of them was still there, gossiping over a strong cuppa tea about ''er next door', and blowing smoke rings at the kitchen table.

It was the changing of the guards: as Frances entered the room, Lenny left. Taking a seat, Ruby reminded herself that she was the one holding all the power. Frances may have had servants to make her tea, but what she wanted more than anything was the safe return of her son. Checking her watch, Ruby reminded Frances that her time was limited. As the two women worked on a list of suspects, the tension began to drain away. Lenny had been there to issue a warning, and Frances could work now the game rules had been made clear. But threatening to leave Cathy motherless, was that really part of the plan? Surely Frances would not allow such a thing to happen. But Frances had taken over as a mother figure to Cathy, determined to take Ruby's place. Was she setting up Lenny to finish her off so she could bring up Cathy her way? With Nathan in prison, she would be free to do what she wanted. Ruby dismissed the thought. Frances would never want Nathan imprisoned, and Lenny would be too much of a loose cannon without him.

Still, her unease rose, and as she drove back to the station, she prayed for a quick resolution.

CHAPTER TWENTY-ONE

'Welcome to hell,' DI Downes muttered as Ruby took a seat yet again around the expansive conference table. Despite the fractious weather outside, humidity levels were high in the briefing room. The heating was controlled from HQ, and this week it seemed they were in 'all or nothing' mode. Ruby took a sip of bottled water, swishing it in her mouth to rid herself of the taste of her last cigarette. She usually counted the minutes until she could leave, but not today. Today they had plenty to talk about, and her mind was firmly on the case.

Mugs of tea and coffee were gratefully accepted as DC Owen Ludgrove offered up the contents of his tray. The next hour revolved around bringing the investigation up to speed. Due to the pathologist's report and a reliable alibi, Danny Smedley had been completely discounted as a suspect for Ellie Mason's murder. A shadow of doubt lingered in Ruby's mind as to his guilt with regards to the murder of Lisa Caldwell, but her concerns had fallen on deaf ears when she brought it up with her superiors. According to DCI Worrow their sights were firmly set on Nathan Crosby for Ellie's murder. With the CPS being so quick to charge Danny Smedley, there was no way Ruby was rushing into arresting Nathan now. Her immediate condemnation of Smedley had given her plenty to think about. She had warned probationers against blinkered vision many times during her career, but it seemed even she was not infallible.

She knew she would have to work hard to persuade her colleagues that Nathan was being set up. She could not afford to draw attention to their relationship in any way and found herself treading very lightly when discussing her meeting that morning.

'Witness statements have been obtained from members of the Crosby family as well as staff who were working in his home prior to when the evidence was found. Mrs Crosby is of the opinion that the organs were planted at her son's address.'

'Pfft,' DC Ash Baker groaned. 'And Nathan Crosby's as pure as an angel's fart! Pull the other one.'

A rumble of laughter spread through the room, and Ruby forced a smile as she waited for it to die down. 'Mrs Crosby has provided a list of ten names, people who may hold grudges against her family.' She looked around the room. 'It provides useful intel, if nothing else.'

'*Ten*? I would have thought the list would be a lot longer than that,' DI Downes muttered.

'Yeah,' Ash jibed. 'There are ten people in this room alone that'd like to see him put away.'

'Settle down,' DCI Worrow said, as the officers began to discuss it amongst themselves. 'I'm sure we'd all like to collar a Crosby, but Sergeant Preston is right, we can't afford to get blinkered. What about CCTV? I thought his home was pretty well covered.'

Ruby felt a flush of heat rise to her face. 'It is, Ma'am. Unfortunately, the systems were being upgraded that day. She's given me an invoice to evidence that the instalment was booked weeks ago.' But even with proof of the upgrade, Ruby knew how weak the excuse sounded.

Ash coughed in the background, masking the word 'tossers' beneath his breath. Another burst of laughter ensued, hastily silenced by DCI Worrow's glare. She turned her attention back to Ruby. 'I'm happy to leave those enquiries in your hands, you appear to have built up a rapport with the family. Let's make good use of it, and gather as much intel as you can.'

DCI Worrow was one of the few people who used her official title. She and DC 'Luddy' Ludgrove, although she was training him to call her by her first name. Another flare of heat bloomed in Ruby's cheeks as all eyes turned on her. 'Built up a rapport'? If only Worrow knew. 'Thank you, Ma'am,' she said while taking a seat, giving another member of the team an opportunity to speak. The intensity of DI Downes's stare prickled her senses, and her eyes fell on her notes, unable to return his gaze.

Later that day as she analysed the intelligence system, she was shocked to see just how many incidents Lenny Crosby had been caught up in since his prison release. It seemed that he had been on the offensive; rubbing a lot of people up the wrong way while his brother Nathan worked hard to distance himself from the shady side of the family dealings. The list of ten people came with a short explanation as to why each of them would be most likely to deal such a vicious revenge.

Jim Lennon: His nightclub was burnt down after he refused to sell it to Lenny and Nathan Crosby.

Vincent Malone: Badly beaten and hospitalised after he declined to serve Lenny Crosby after legal drinking hours. Threatened to inflict revenge on both brothers as they were together that night.

Mike Green: Threatened revenge on the Crosby family after his son was kneecapped for reasons undisclosed.

Stephen Green: Death threats against Nathan Crosby for reasons undisclosed.

The list went on. Ruby tutted as she re-read it – finding matching intelligence on more than half the names disclosed. The most frustrating thing was that the Crosby family business – the legitimate London Estate Agents – was doing so well that they no longer needed to be involved in drug supply. Drawn in by the power and respect, neither Lenny nor Nathan appeared able to let it go. For high-class customers, they offered a pure product for an upmarket price. But the clientele of A-listers was not the type to murder a young woman and hack out her lungs. Out of the list of ten people Frances had provided, none had entered Nathan's house. Yes, he had visitors and conducted some business at home, but it would have been noticed had they carried in a gift box with a set of internal organs within.

And what about Lenny, or Frances? Ruby chewed the end of her pen. They were in Chigwell that night – an account backed up by Cathy, who had been staying over too. Staff had alerted her as soon as the police turned up; information that was quickly passed on to Nathan, to keep him at bay.

Ruby had also asked about Leona, Nathan's ex-girlfriend, the daughter of a man that nobody dared cross. Frances had taken great pleasure in telling her that Leona was with Nathan on the night the organs were planted under his bed. But Ruby was quick to respond that she was already aware of this. Nathan's weekly visits to Leona's family home were a long tradition: playing poker with her father and his cronies to keep business flowing and relations on an even keel.

So where did that leave the investigation now? She scribbled down some notes in the pad on her desk. The only people who had keys to the property were Nathan and his staff. His family came and went freely, and certain areas inside the home were covered by CCTV, but not the bedrooms, for reasons of privacy. Windows were kept firmly closed, and the house was air-conditioned throughout. As she looked back on the notes she had made, she knew things did not look good. Ash was right; the timing seemed more than a coincidence. Was the plant organised to occur the same time the CCTV went down? But why on earth would Nathan's staff implicate themselves in such a crime? Tweedy Steve and the rest of the staff were well looked after. They had no problems with money or credit issues, although Ruby would be checking, just in case.

She tapped the pen against her bottom lip. It didn't make sense. Police would argue that the CCTV had been turned off by Nathan as he brought the box of horrors inside, a trophy piece from his kill. That seemed the most likely explanation of all. Except Ruby didn't believe it. The only small blessing was that he was in his club the night Lisa Caldwell was killed. If Ruby could connect the murders, she could prove Nathan had no part to play. She desperately wanted to speak to him, but what if Downes had put someone on her tail? Sod it, she thought, throwing her pen onto the desk. As soon as she got home she would contact Nathan and arrange to meet, regardless of the risk.

CHAPTER TWENTY-TWO

April

April stirred under the thin layer of blanket as the pinprick of light in her field of vision grew. She was slowly surfacing into consciousness, but the horrors of her situation had yet to sink in. For now, she was in a dream-like state, slowly taking in her surroundings without the cumbersome emotions of panic and fear. She had felt it before as a bad trip and presumed such was the case again. Her memory of events was foggy, intermingling with a physical coldness touching her bare skin. She had heard about things happening to working girls – bad things. But never once did she consider that this was to become her fate. So why couldn't she move her hands?

Her eyes were slow to open, still under the influence of the drugs she had taken the night before. Soon she would wake in a hotel bed, get dressed and carry on with her day. She wriggled her wrists, but something was keeping them pinned down. Her heart skipped a beat as her senses cleared. A shuffling noise rose from the corner, forcing her eyelids open. This was no hotel room. A chill swept across her body, along with a cold realisation: this was real.

She drew in a sharp breath, craning her neck from the padded chair. Her chest tightened as the smell of crumbling brick dust filled her nostrils. Slowly, the memory of her last actions returned. She had squeezed through a gap in the fencing to reach the derelict hospital and had come here on a job. . . But who? A vision of a man in a mask rose in her mind. Worn like a balaclava, it was the colour of thick bandages. The doctor. She remembered the tufts of wispy grey hair poking from the top as he turned to sedate her.

April felt a small pang of relief. She had agreed to this. In a few minutes, he would walk in and let her go. He had asked her to do something special – offering her a wad of notes for her cooperation. April had heard of things like these and knew girls who had taken part. 'It's easy money,' they had told her, 'making dosh while you sleep.' But April had seen their bruises and decided that was not the case. Snuff movies were enjoyed by a particular type of client that paid well over the odds; rape, torture, even murder were portrayed in the homemade pornos. Off-screen, the girls were sedated before the cameras began rolling. As they slipped into unconsciousness, the men had their way. April had been offered big money to play such roles and turned them all down. They liked her because she looked innocent, like the girl next door. The very thought of leaving herself so vulnerable and exposed made her flesh creep. So, when the doctor suggested he sedate her before sex, she presumed such was his wish.

He'd appeared horrified, assuring her this was not the case. He was ugly, he said, and he could not perform knowing how she would feel about having sex with such an abomination. Despite her assurances, he gained her sympathy by squeezing out a couple of tears. It would be just minutes, he promised, long enough for him to remove his mask and satisfy his needs. He was a professional; he knew how to control the dose; she would be out for just minutes of her time.

As he pressed two hundred pounds into her hand, she found herself agreeing to his request. Soon she would wake up two hundred pounds better off and no memory of what had taken place. It wasn't as if she didn't know him. She found herself feeling sorry for the strange old man so she agreed, and, now she had come around, she wondered where he had gone.

He had said nothing of removing her clothes or restraining her limbs. As she looked around the room, fresh fear found a hold in her insides and squeezed. She had been there for a lot longer than just minutes. The splinters of daylight that had been flooding through the boarded windows had disappeared. Above her, a rusted surgical lamp beamed down. The gentle hum of a generator purred in the background. And the smell. . . potent and sour. She had to get away.

'Hello?' she breathed, her words echoing around the desolate room. Craning her neck, she awaited a response.

A shuffling movement rustled a pile of newspapers in the corner. From the confines of her chair, April could still see the headlines of Ellie's death. The Snow White murder was emblazoned in black and white. Ellie Mason, wasn't she one of the doctor's clients too? April swallowed, her throat dry. Her heart was pounding harder now, so hard she could hear the swish, swish of the blood reverberating in her ears. She pulled on the thick leather bindings holding her wrists in place.

'Hey! Is anyone here? Can you hear me?' Her words were sharper this time, laced with a panic that was rising in her throat. All that was returned was the rattling of the wind through the battered panes, and the distant rumble of traffic that never went away. Yet she felt the chill of his presence nearby and, as she was caught in the grip of fear, she knew she had made a very big mistake.

CHAPTER TWENTY-THREE

Often in the darkest of times, officers pulled together to help each other through. One such example was known as the Wall of Shame. To the right of the office, sellotaped to the magnolia wall, were the latest campaign posters created by HQ and rotated on a monthly basis. This month it was a campaign against domestic violence. The month before it was burglary and robbery awareness. They were preaching to the converted as far as Ruby was concerned. The posters were targeted towards members of the public, and it made little sense to have them on the wall of their office, but every month DCI Worrow would check they were on display.

Officers were far more interested in the pictures on the wall across the way, which was positioned behind DC Ash Baker's desk. Ash was a dab hand with editing software and his comic tributes raised more than a smile or two. DI Downes was portrayed as Liam Neeson; his face superimposed on the famous scene from the movie *Taken*. However, in Ash's version, Downes was on the phone ordering takeaway food. Luddy was James Bond, complete with gun, suit and a licence to make tea. As for Ruby. . . often there were times she was afraid to look. The last poster displayed her as the famous Shoreditch flasher after she failed to notice the button on her shirt was undone during a drunken night out. But today there were no faces on display, merely landscapes, sunsets, and dolphins diving into the sea. They were the backdrop to motivational words printed in white on top – at least that's what Ruby thought.

'Are you trying to get promoted, mate?' she said, peering across Ash's desk at the posters on the wall.

'Ah, do you like them? Yeah, I know how much Ma'am Worrow likes that kind of stuff, so I thought I'd get with the programme.'

'Mmm,' Ruby frowned, taking a closer look. Silently her lips moved as she read each of the words in turn, each one widening her smile. 'Except, these don't contain motivational messages, do they?'

Her colleague's laughter softened the air as heads turned to watch Ash explain. 'I thought I'd kill two birds with the one stone and cut down on swearing in the office too.'

Ruby arched an eyebrow. 'I hate to break it to you, but the words cockwomble, bawbag and shitpouch look pretty sweary to me.'

Ash reached for an empty coffee jar, which had a slit cut in the lid. 'That's the beauty of it, we're allowed one swear word a day. Anyone that goes beyond that has to stick a quid in the jar. The money goes towards the tea club, so it's for a good cause.'

'Genius,' Ruby drawled. 'So what's the swear word for today?'

'Wazzock,' Ash said proudly. 'It's northern slang for idiot. Tomorrow we elevate to fuckwit, which means colossal idiot.'

'Uh huh,' Ruby nodded, her gaze falling on the end poster. 'I'm not sure our DCI will appreciate Friday, she's not so keen on the C-word.'

'You could have a point,' Ash said, the grin sliding off his face as he caught sight of her in the doorway. Turning back to his computer, he began clacking furiously on his keyboard.

Deep in conversation, DCI Worrow stood with DI Downes at the open door, barely giving them a glance before retreating to the safety of her office upstairs.

As Downes entered the room, he beckoned to Ruby to follow him into his office. Not a good sign, judging by his company seconds before. Ruby took the spare swivel chair, feeling like a naughty schoolgirl about to be told off.

Downes removed his suit jacket and rested it on the back of the chair. Taking a seat across from her, he tugged on his tie. It was flecked grey, the same colour as his eyes. Ruby wondered if someone was doing his laundry, as these days his shirts appeared freshly pressed. It was a vast improvement on the crumpled garments he had been wearing for the last few months. These days, his clothes smelt of fabric conditioner rather than whiskey, although it had been a while since Ruby was close enough to check.

'I've just been discussing that intelligence you submitted with Worrow,' Downes said, crossing his long legs as he sat back in his chair. 'She's very interested in your source.'

Ruby knew it was only a matter of time before he got on to her about it. Her superiors may accept her story of an anonymous tip-off, but there was no pulling the wool over Jack Downes's eyes.

'Yeah,' Ruby sighed, swinging the chair with the tips of her red high heels. Today she was coordinated, with red lips and nails to match. 'I've got some great contacts.' The seat was set far too high, but the lever had broken, making her feel more schoolgirlish than ever as she swung left to right. And God knows she never behaved herself at school.

Downes folded his arms, speaking in a tone which relayed he was unimpressed. 'Yeah, contacts. More like you've been hooking up with your old partner in crime.'

'Partner in crime, who would that be?' she said, trying her best to look puzzled.

'Sure you know very well. You've been meeting Nathan Crosby, haven't you?' He shook his head. 'Don't you think your loyalty would be better served to your job?'

'We talk to lots of criminals in the police,' Ruby said drily. 'I'm only doing what you asked me.'

'Don't be cheeky,' Downes said. 'It doesn't suit you.'

Ruby grinned. 'Oh, I rather think it does.'

'Look, I know I asked you to do some digging on the family, but there's a warrant out for Crosby's arrest. Orders from on high. You need to be bringing him in.'

'And I will. When the time is right,' Ruby muttered, wishing he wouldn't blow so hot and cold.

'Remember who pays your wages. Without the police, you wouldn't have a roof over your head.'

As he ran his fingers through his hair, Ruby could tell he had taken some heat from DCI Worrow. It must have annoyed him being told off by a woman half his age and with a tenth of his experience. But it was not her fault Worrow was keeping close tabs on him, and Ruby would not back down now. She thought of the scruffy flat that she could barely afford on her police wage, and the luxury accommodation that Nathan had gifted her months before. It elicited another smile, much to Downes's annoyance. It always wound him up that she had another side to her that he could not access, and she had no intention of making him any the wiser.

'You gave me the all-clear to do some digging, and I've risked my neck getting my hands on that intel report. I've sacrificed everything to get where I am, but you still question my loyalty.'

'Look, I don't doubt you mean well, I'm just saying you make me nervous. We've got a good team out there. I don't want your shady dealings dragging us down. If you know where Crosby is, you'd better call it in. Headquarters want a result, and they want it yesterday.'

So that was what this was all about: a knee-jerk reaction to publicity surrounding the murder. 'The last time I checked it was innocent until proven guilty. You're having a go at me for defending everything that this job is about. I'm trying to catch the killer – the real one. So I won't be making any hasty arrests to suit the powers that be.'

Downes frowned, his lips pursed tightly together. 'The order's been given. You're to arrest Crosby as a matter of urgency.'

Ruby rose. Her superiors could give all the orders they wanted. As a British police constable, the decision to arrest lay squarely on her shoulders. She was well within her rights to turn them down. They could always instruct another officer, who would happily comply, but Ruby was the only one likely to come close enough to do it.

'I'll make us a brew,' she said, taking his empty cup from his desk. She was parched. Despite their differences, she would harbour no ill feelings. He was just looking out for her in his own infuriating way.

'Fine,' he said as she opened the door to leave. 'Have it your way. But don't say I didn't warn you.'

'Understood, boss, I consider myself warned.' Nudging open the door, she left his office to join her team.

CHAPTER TWENTY-FOUR

Ruby and Nathan had many special places dotted around East London, and the range was one of them. A far cry from what was offered to firearms officers in the Met, their meeting place was nothing more than a derelict building with thick concrete walls and smashed windows. Soon the machinery would move in for its demolition, and Ruby found it sad that many of their old hang-outs had since been rebuilt to make way for redevelopment. Still, they could not take her memories.

She could feel the heat of Nathan's glare. His individual attention was afforded to the few people he trusted to meet alone. His ability to enter a room without making a sound used to drive her mad when they were together. It was a long-practised trait, expertly crafted over the years.

Thunderclouds rolled outside, casting a grey hue on the concrete walls as the last rays of the sun were absorbed. 'Nathan,' she whispered, carefully sidestepping the dirt and shingle underfoot. She cast a glance to the left, making out a bullet hole in the graffiti-daubed wall, and smiled as she remembered putting it there.

With a row of tin cans set up in front of them, Nathan was showing her how to shoot for the first time. Giddy with excitement, she giggled while he wrapped his arms around her from behind. He whispered in her ear, his warm breath sending shivers down her spine as he told her off for not concentrating on the gun.

'This is a deadly weapon,' he said. *'It's no laughing matter.'*

She cleared her throat, aiming the revolver at the tin can ahead.

'Don't hold it like a cup and saucer,' he said, adjusting her grip. *'Put your support hand to good use; keep your thumbs together. Now, wrap it around here, like this. It'll help with the kickback.'*

Ruby shifted her hands into position.

'Now, aim and shoot,' Nathan instructed.

Taking a deep breath, Ruby squeezed the trigger, jerking as the weapon recoiled. A wisp of smoke rose from the barrel of the gun. It had felt heavy and clunky in her hand, and she wanted to throw it to the ground. Nathan made it look so easy. It was louder than she expected, and the power of the weapon had jerked her hand, hurting her wrist and making her gasp.

Nathan gently released the gun from her grasp, clicking on the safety latch. Soft laughter escaped his lips as he stared at the bullet hole in the wall. 'Jesus, Ruby! Did you have your eyes closed or something?'

'I might have,' Ruby said, flushed with embarrassment. 'I'm rubbish at this, aren't I?'

Nathan smiled. 'You'll get better.'

And she did. After six weeks, she was confidently handling the firearm. It was a comfort to know it was something she could fall back on. Being caught with a gun could put her in prison, but Ruby justified it in her mind. Her job was becoming increasingly dangerous and, if officers in the US were allowed personal protection, then why wasn't she? She had always felt ill-equipped for her role, but knowing she had a gun close at hand helped her sleep at night. It was her personal protection and, if it came down to it, she would make good use of it.

✱ ✱ ✱

Glass cracked underfoot, a product of the smashed windows. Stepping out from the shadows, Nathan stood before her.

'Alright?' he said. Like her, he seemed glad to see a friendly face. Dressed in his black jacket, combats and Dr Martens boots, he looked more like a member of the SAS than a criminal on the run.

'How are you?' she said, taking a step towards him.

'Be a lot better when you find out who's responsible for these murders.'

Ruby wished she had some good news to impart. Persuading her colleagues to widen their search for a suspect had been like wading through treacle, and it pained her to laugh at their jokes about who would get to bang him to rights first.

She crept through the empty building, Downes's words echoing in her memory as he commanded her to bring Nathan in. Their belief in Nathan's guilt always came back to the same thing: if he were innocent, he would not have run away. The fact there had been a scalpel involved made them all the more assured in their decision. Nathan's dad, Jimmy Crosby, was no stranger to the knife back in his day. They didn't nickname him the butcher for nothing. Ruby had wanted to say that Jimmy was dead and gone, but she kept such information to herself, loath to raise suspicion.

Nathan tensed as a police siren speared the silence.

'It's OK,' she said, 'I wasn't followed.'

'You sure about that?' Nathan said, his hand hovering on the pocket of his combats.

Ruby nodded, her heart skipping a beat. He was armed, and that could spell trouble. 'I'm trying to clear your name, but it keeps coming down to the same thing. People are asking why you're on the run.'

'So I'm public enemy number one with Shoreditch's finest on my case.' He spoke with a thin smile. 'Any closer to finding the real killer?'

'I've been in touch with your mum. We're going through a list. . .' She turned away from the intensity of his gaze. 'It's just that some of the stuff – putting someone in hospital because they refused to serve you?' She shook her head. 'It's grim reading.'

'That had nothing to do with me. Lenny's a liability, more now than ever.'

'Then why can't you leave him behind? He's not worth your loyalty. It's because of him that you're in this mess.'

Nathan's voice softened, and he placed a hand on Ruby's forearm. 'He's my brother, the only one I've got. Aren't you any closer to sorting this out?'

'Oh no, I've been twiddling my thumbs all morning,' she said, regretting the words as soon as they had left her mouth.

Nathan's eyes narrowed. 'Is this a game to you, or do you agree with all the rest? That I deserve to be put away, one way or the other?'

Like two pieces of dry flint, Ruby and Nathan began to produce sparks. It was always the same when they were both under pressure. They were too alike, with neither one of them wanting to back down. She exhaled a terse breath, unable to contain her annoyance.

'I've been working 24/7 on this case. It wasn't a game to Ellie Mason when she had her organs ripped from her chest.'

'I know, I know,' Nathan said. 'She wasn't much older than Cathy.' He took Ruby by the hand. 'Promise me you'll keep an eye on her while I'm away. Don't let me down.'

Ruby's response was instant. 'I'm there for you, you know that. And I don't need your family giving me the heavy hand to do it.'

'Lenny.' Nathan groaned. 'Has he threatened you?'

'Does the Pope pray?' Ruby said, her mouth rising in a wayward half-smirk. 'I can take care of Lenny, but I don't appreciate your mum getting in on the act.'

Darkness shadowed Nathan's face. 'Don't answer back to him. It's not like the old days, I've seen what he's done to people for a lot less.'

'Maybe I've been wrong,' Ruby said, in an effort to change the subject. 'I shouldn't have dismissed Danny Smedley so quickly. Maybe he's committed Ellie's murder and sold her organs on to someone to use against you.'

'The old days. . .' Nathan muttered under his breath, withdrawing into himself as he recalled a memory. He returned his attention to Ruby. 'You're wrong, it's not Danny Smedley.'

'But it could be,' she said, tapping her lower lip with her fingers. 'He might have an accomplice – someone who has it in for you.'

'It's not Smedley because I know who it is.' Swearing under his breath, he ran his fingers through his tousled hair. 'Why didn't I think of him sooner?'

'Who is it then?'

Nathan's face tightened. 'Perhaps it's best if I sort out a confession first.'

'You're setting your men on him? Is that what it is? Because if anything happens to the suspect, you'll never be free. You've got no choice, you have to play this by the book.'

'Alright, I'll tell you, if you just listen!' Nathan said, grasping her by the arms.

She could see it in his eyes. He was building up to admit his involvement in something she would not want to hear. 'Just spit it out, will you. Who did this?'

Nathan's attention was on the flash of headlights outside. 'You set me up,' he said as police cars screeched to a halt in the yard.

Ruby gasped in horror as DI Downes launched himself from one of the cars below. 'What? No, I didn't. He must have followed me and called for backup.'

Stepping back from the window, Nathan pushed his hand in his pocket and drew out his pistol. 'I'm not being taken in,' he said, his face conflicted. 'Not today.'

CHAPTER TWENTY-FIVE

April

Her bones aching, April took a sharp breath as she returned to consciousness once more. She recalled her last memory; the doctor pushing a thin syringe into her vein as the walls of the room closed in around her. The blanket had fallen to the floor. The leather chair was cold beneath her body as she writhed beneath the doctor's touch. Staring at the damp spores on the ceiling, she had not wanted her last memory to be of the doctor's face but she could not block out the smell of his breath, wet and raspy, his grimy fingers sinking into her flesh as he pinned her down. Gradually her struggling had subsided as the liquid drug clawed her back to the darkness once more.

Goosebumps rose on her naked flesh, and she felt the tug of foreign objects in her skin. Her eyes followed the small clear tube embedded in her arm to the pouch of clear fluid dangling from a rusted metal hanger at her side. Lower down, she felt the drag of something cold between her legs. Sharp panic brought her thoughts into focus. It was a urine catheter. She'd had one once before when she was giving birth to her baby. Just how long had she been here?

She craned her neck forward, turning her gaze to the full-length mirror at the end of her bed. Her mouth dropped open as she stared. There, under the gloom of a single lamp, her reflection offered up a ghoulish display. Dry air scratched against the hollow of her throat as she tried to scream. Her chest heaved. A pale-skinned red-haired woman stared back at her in dismay. She had sculpted eyebrows, and her eyelashes, which felt heavy as she blinked – they were red too. Her eyes focused on her mouth, a plump pink Cupid's bow. She pursed them together and was rewarded with a sudden stinging sensation. What had he done to her? She blinked away the tears forming in her eyes. She could cry later; she had to get away. April twisted in the chair, trying to drag her thin wrists through the tight leather straps. Clawing at the arm rests with her fingernails, she noticed the clear sparkly polish as it glittered under the surgeon's light. Was there an inch of her body that the doctor had not interfered with?

Her stomach tightened in a spasm, not from hunger but something else. Her body was still coming down from the drugs. She emitted a groan, as a slice of pain ripped through her, wanting to draw up her knees but noticing for the first time that her ankles were restrained too. Panic induced a beaded sweat, which gathered on her forehead. Just what had he planned for her? Was this a kinky game? Were there cameras? Had he been having sex with her while she was unconscious? But she would have felt it. And her body was devoid of the bruises she had suffered in the past when men had forced themselves on her. Was he taking pictures?

Her attention was drawn to the tray of surgeon's tools, and the scream she had been holding made its escape. It was a loud and furious cry, filling the room and sending the creatures gathered under the newspapers scattering like billiard balls across the floor. The sight of so many rats would once have terrified her into submission, but there were far worse things in store. Wriggling against her bindings, she wanted to topple the chair. A slice of fear stopped her in her tracks. She was too scared of what the rats would do to her on the floor. In the distance, a train shuddered past. She could hear the carriages cutting through the night air. Carriages filled with people she could not reach. Her sense of desolation grew. She had to fight if she wanted to get out of this alive.

Ignoring the pain in her wrist she continued to wriggle her left hand, each effort punctuated by short, quick intakes of breath. April clasped her thumb and little finger together, narrowing her knuckles as she worked them through the tight space. Her heart skipped a beat as her hand slipped through the unforgiving leather strap. She shook it quickly until feeling returned, then yanked out the tubes invading her body. Fluid slapped across her breasts as one jerked forward like an impotent snake, but she didn't feel it because she was intent on undoing the buckle of her right wrist. With shaking fingers, and both hands free, she undid the straps on her ankles, her ears trained on the corridor outside. Any second now he could return.

Wrapping the blanket around her, she slid from the surgeon's chair. But her legs felt hollow, and it took three steady breaths until she could advance on the table of instruments before her. Rats squeaked their annoyance. Stepping forward, she wrapped her fingers around the scalpel. Shock began to pervade her body. Picking up the blanket, she told herself she would get out of this; she would slice the face of anyone that dared come near. Crumbling plaster bruised the soles of her feet as she hobbled across the cold floor. There were no clothes to be seen, yet something told her she was not the first person to be brought back to this space. Was this where Ellie spent her last moments?

Slowly she ventured into the corridor, seeking the light that would guide her outside. The air was cold and sharp in her throat as she tried to accustom her eyes to the sudden darkness. Staggering, she left behind the sounds of the humming generator and nesting rats. Her grasp around the scalpel tightened as she stepped cautiously down the corridor. In the distance, the faint orange glow of street lights beckoned from afar. The sounds of her jagged breath echoed around her, but it was impossible to slow it down as adrenalin quickened her heartbeat in preparation for escape. As she turned the corner, blanket gripped in one hand and scalpel in the other, she did not see the dark figure reach out until it was too late. The pain was instant as he bent her wrist backwards, forcing her to drop the blade to the floor. Her cries were extinguished as a knee came up to her stomach, winding her until she was bent over in two. Weakly, she kicked and punched as the doctor hoisted her onto his shoulder. She pounded his back, kicking the hands wrapped tightly around her thighs.

'Get off me,' she cried, tears streaking her face. Screaming for help, she shook and wriggled until he was forced to loosen her to the floor. 'Oh my God,' she gasped, catching sight of herself in the mirror for the second time. 'What have you done?'

Silently he stared, wordless and unrelenting. And then it came. The high-pitched squeaking she had heard in her dreams. Except it wasn't a dream at all: it was the rats. Soon the room was filled with the pitter-patter of rodent claws as the slick black rats gathered around her, dancing at her feet. April emitted a strangled cry, tears coursing down the edges of her cheeks. Unspeaking, the man watched her behaviour as if observing a creature in the zoo. The nipping, the scratching, she could barely stand it, as the rats clawed at her ankles and legs. It was only then that she noticed she was standing on crushed glass. She squinted in the dim light as the broken shards gleamed on the floor, cutting into the soles of her feet and adding to her discomfort. Blood oozed from her skin, sending the rats into a frenzy as they sniffed and scratched at her ankles and feet.

'Help me,' she cried, pleading with her tormentor.

Slowly, the doctor approached. Instinctively she opened up her arms to him as he offered to pick her up from the floor. Anything was better than this hell, she thought. They would eat her alive if she stayed in that spot for too long. Tired and weak, she had little defence, and she sobbed in his arms as he gently cradled her naked body. She was having a nightmare, she told herself. None of this was real; soon it would be over. She hiccupped as the sobs subsided, barely noticing the needle as it withdrew from her arm. Gratefully, she fell back into the recesses of sleep.

CHAPTER TWENTY-SIX

'No,' Ruby said in a harsh whisper. 'It wasn't me, I swear.' Her breath quickened as the scenario unfolded before her. Heavy footsteps pounded their way into the building. Nathan stood, unmoving, his firearm trained on the door.

'Put the gun away,' she said. 'You're going to get yourself killed.' Any second now DI Downes would burst in. She could not bear to imagine what would happen next. 'Please, take the roof. I'll tell them you didn't show.' There was less than a six-foot gap between the roof of their building and the one beside it, and, in their youth Nathan used to jump from one to the other with ease.

Nathan's eyes flicked from the door to Ruby, his face stony. Shoving the gun into the groove of his combats, he threw her a disbelieving look before climbing out of the window and taking the fire exit to the roof. The pressure of the murder allegation had taken its toll. For the first time she saw a glint of fear in his eyes. He could wriggle his way out of most things in life, and now he wholly depended on her. She composed herself, leaning casually against the brittle window frame as a team of firearms officers burst into the room.

'He's not here,' she said to Downes, her face taut. 'He didn't show.' She wet her lips, tasting the dust that had risen after Nathan made his escape.

Ruby glared at Downes over the roof of the car as she flung open the passenger door. It made sense for her to accept his offer of a lift to the station given she had got there by taxi. The cavalry had gone ahead, disappointed by the no-show. After being briefed by Downes that Ruby was setting up the meet to arrest Nathan, they had no reason to doubt her words. But Ruby was too incensed to worry about repercussions and as Downes drove through the city to Shoreditch, she continued her sideways glances until she could bear the silence no longer.

'Why did you do it, Jack? Why did you follow me?'

DI Downes rammed the car into gear, his face illuminated by the headlights of oncoming traffic. 'Because I'm trying to save your neck. I told Worrow that you were there to flush him out. So unless you want to be nicked for perverting the course of justice, leave the talking to me.'

'The fact I'd leave anything to you implies some kind of trust and that doesn't exist between us anymore,' she said, her words tight.

✳ ✳ ✳

Satisfied that Nathan got away unseen, Ruby returned to the office, keeping her door firmly closed. She had hoped that Downes would have the sense to leave her alone, but as soon as he trotted downstairs from his meeting with DCI Worrow, he headed straight for her door. Ruby stared at her computer screen, wishing he would go away. She did not want to speak the bitter words lacing her tongue. Besides, she was caught red-handed and knew she had no right. True to his word, he was most likely smoothing things over with DCI Worrow to prevent any flack later on. They were under real pressure for a suspect arrest, and every failed attempt at capture was a bitter blow. Had she and Downes had a normal working relationship, she'd most likely be grovelling for forgiveness by now. But they were more than just sergeant and DI: he was her best friend. And only now, when anger seared through her like hot coals, did she realise just how close they had become.

'Sulking now, are you?' he said, standing over her as he waited for an answer.

Bitterness bloomed in Ruby's chest. She wanted to explain that her motives were good. That if he had trusted her, just this once, she would now have the name of their prime suspect. That was what angered her the most. He had ruined everything. There was no way the Crosbys would cooperate with the investigation now. 'I think it's best if you give me a few minutes alone.' Ruby's voice was strained, and she swallowed back the response not fitting for her DI.

'Well, tough. We're having this out whether you like it or not,' Downes said, turning and closing the window blinds. From the corner of her eye, Ruby could see him deliver a hard stare to those who were not minding their own business in the office outside. Downes's neck was tinged pink – a sure sign that DCI Worrow had grilled him for letting Nathan Crosby slip through his fingers.

'You've got no right to be angry with me,' Downes said, 'when all I've done is look out for you.'

Ruby turned to face him. Carrying the heat of her anger, her expression was enough to make him raise an eyebrow in response.

She realised she was shaking, and she leant against her desk, clasping the edges of the wooden frame until her knuckles turned white. 'You used me,' she said, her words thick with emotion. 'This friendship we've developed, please tell me it's not just been about Nathan.'

'What are you on about?' Downes said, his voice rising to match Ruby's.

'You've wanted to collar him for years. All this time you've been getting close to me so you could fulfil your ambition of nicking a Crosby before your retirement.'

'For feck's sake, what's gotten into you?' Downes said. 'You couldn't be more wrong.'

'I don't believe you. I think you're only too happy to pin this on him. The only reason you're progressing the case with Danny Smedley is because you can't have Lisa and Ellie's murders linked.'

'Those murders are nothing alike.' Downes ran both hands through his hair. 'And may I remind you that you're the one that got Smedley charged. I told you to wait but, oh no, you had to go charging in there and arrest him.'

'Yes, well. . . I may have got that wrong.' She bit her bottom lip.

'You're the most exasperating copper I've ever met. You've so much potential, and all you do is defend a bunch of gangsters, putting your job at risk. And you say I'm using you?' Downes laughed incredulously. 'Open your eyes, will you? One of these days you're going to land yourself in prison, and there won't be a thing I can do about it.'

'Nathan was just about to give me the name of the killer,' Ruby said. 'If you had held off just five minutes longer, we'd have him in custody by now.'

'If I'd got there five minutes sooner, you mean. You're chasing ghosts. The only killer is the one you let slip away.'

Ruby straightened, her hands bunched into fists. 'Why can't you admit that, just this once, you got it wrong?'

'You need to calm down,' Downes said firmly. 'I'm your superior officer. Have you forgotten that?'

'Calm down?' Ruby shouted. 'Don't you realise what you've done? How long do you think it's going to take to get back to the Crosbys that I served Nathan up? Can you imagine their reactions? You've put my neck on the line. If anything happens to me, it's all down to you.'

Downes laid a hand on her shoulder. 'Ruby, I. . .'

Ruby shrugged it off as she turned away, her voice cold and measured. 'Please. As my DI, I apologise for my disrespectful behaviour. Now can you *please* give me some time alone, before I say something else that I shouldn't.' She bowed her head, the weight of her troubles heavier now than ever. She listened as Downes approached the door, opened it slightly.

'You can come around to mine... at least until this all blows over.' His words were laced with a hint of regret.

'I don't think such behaviour would be fitting. As you said, you're my superior officer,' Ruby said, the heat leaving her voice. 'I think from now on we should keep things on a professional basis only.'

CHAPTER TWENTY-SEVEN

'I'm telling you, mate, the job's fucked,' a low voice said. The words were followed by mumbling agreements as the group of officers groaned about forced overtime and cancelled rest days.

Ruby smiled. Last month they were moaning because overtime had been binned due to budget cuts. You did not join the police if you wanted an easy life. It was all-consuming, with room for little else. The failed marriages in her division were a testament to that.

'What do you think, Sarge?' PC Jules Forrest turned to her. The young officer was sporting a black eye, no doubt the real source of his annoyance. She had come to know him in the past few months during their shared smoke breaks.

She stubbed out her cigarette. 'It's the nature of the beast, I'm afraid, and it's not likely to change.' Slipping a compact from her pocket, she quickly applied a layer of red lipstick before heading back inside. It was her warpaint, and she hoped it displayed a confidence she did not feel inside.

* * *

Ruby took her usual seat at the end of the well-worn briefing table. Years of meetings were etched in the wood, evidenced as coffee stains and inky pen marks. She mentally counted heads as detectives filed inside. Overhead, the lights flickered on, the thunderous weather doing little to illuminate the room.

DCI Worrow stood to lead the briefing. As always, the detective chief inspector was immaculately turned out. Her pale skin held a delicate lacing of make-up, and she spoke with authority as she commanded the attention of her team. Speaking in short, stiff bursts, she sounded as if she was reading from a police procedural book. Only last week Ruby had caught DC Ash Baker joking about how she spoke to her boyfriend during sex. Despite her reservations, Ruby still stood up for her, because life in the police force was hard enough for women without their male counterparts turning against them.

'We believe that Ellie Mason was held captive for at least two of the three days she was reported missing. As you see from the autopsy report, this was not a frenzied attack. Ellie worked as a prostitute, but as far as we're aware she did not entertain clients at her flat. CSI have made a detailed examination for blood, fibres, prints, hair and semen – there's no evidence to suggest she was held captive at that address. The fact that rat droppings were found in her hair seems to cement this theory. One of our top priorities is to find the site where she was held.'

'What about the Crosby house, Ma'am?' DC Ash Baker said, raising his pencil. 'Has that been searched?'

DCI Worrow's face tightened at the sound of the Crosby's name. 'Thoroughly. The family has been most cooperative. DS Preston is liaising with them. Do you have any updates for us, Ruby?'

Ruby straightened in her chair. 'Apart from their statement? Not yet. They're still maintaining that Nathan Crosby is away on business and they're unable to get a hold of him.'

'Indeed,' DCI Worrow said. 'It's a shame that lead of yours fell flat. He'll have to return at some point, so it's best we build as strong a case as we can for when we arrest him. Keep them on side. You've obtained some useful intelligence on their shady dealings. Keep chipping away.'

Ruby nodded. She had been desperately trying to get in touch with Nathan since he abandoned their meet, but he had gone completely off the radar. Lenny and Frances had refused to answer her calls and, when she turned up at the address, the electric gates had remained firmly closed. A quick Facebook message to her daughter, Cathy, had ascertained that Ruby was well and truly in the doghouse with Lenny; given the mood he was in, it was best she kept away. At least Cathy was OK. It was worth the extra expense of Wi-Fi just for their late-night chats. It seemed an odd set-up for mother and daughter, just speaking online, but Cathy was a grown woman. Ruby knew it would take time to gain her daughter's trust, and a brief chat on Facebook or Skype was better than nothing at all.

Her attention returned to briefing as Worrow spoke of the search so far. They did not have the manpower to search every derelict building and outhouse in East London, and Ruby had visited enough rat-infested flats to know the search might never reach a conclusion. To her, the answer lay in Ellie's client list. Why else had she been found dressed up, unless it was a fairy-tale fetish of some kind? Now that Ellie's computer had been seized, Ruby could only hope that answers lay within.

'I want local hospitals and custody suites checked,' Worrow said. 'Ellie was streetwise. I know the autopsy suggests there wasn't a struggle, but the fact her fingernails have been cleaned and bleached makes me think she may have fought back. Check for anyone that may have been booked in with defence wounds. It may well be our suspect. Ellie may have been left alone for a period of time. I want all our local sex offenders spoken to, and intel gathered on recent prison releases. Danny Smedley may not be responsible for this one, but he may not be working alone. Who did he befriend in prison? Anyone handy with a scalpel?' Worrow continued with her taskings, ensuring all team members had plenty to keep them occupied, along with their existing workloads.

'What about house-to-house?' Worrow asked. 'Any suspect descriptions?'

'It's all very nondescript,' DC Ludgrove said, having exhausted local enquiries in the area where Ellie's body was found.

Worrow glared at Luddy. 'So you're telling me that someone has dumped a body of a young woman dressed as Snow White on top of a tombstone in broad daylight and nobody has noticed anything unusual?'

'If they have, they're not talking,' Luddy said, a flush rising beneath his shirt collar. 'A couple of people said they thought it was kids messing around.'

'And they've no description whatsoever?'

'No, Ma'am.' Luddy shook his head. 'There was mention of someone pushing a wheelchair, and we found indentations in the grass. It's possible that's how the body was transported.'

Ruby raised an eyebrow. This was fresh evidence. 'They were definitely pushing it?' she said. 'It wasn't an electric model then?'

'Yes, that's what they said. There was no mention of a Snow White costume, though; the person in the wheelchair was covered in a blanket apparently.'

'Check local CCTV again. See if you can catch our wheelchair pusher in the vicinity,' Worrow instructed.

Ruby tapped her pen against her notepad. A wheelchair lent further credibility to her theory of someone who had access to hospital equipment. The killer was handy with a knife. Had the Crosby family links to people in the medical profession? And if so, who?

CHAPTER TWENTY-EIGHT

The text came with a tone so insistent that Ruby knew who it was without reading the name: Frances, the one-woman powerhouse, who had immediately responded to Ruby's request to meet. She tutted as she stared at the text, an invite – no, command – to meet for lunch. God, that woman, she had no clue how the police worked. Most days, lunch comprised of dropping crumbs over a keyboard as she bit into a tuna sandwich. As if she had time to meet in some swish hotel restaurant for tea and cakes. The best she could do was to grant her twenty minutes in the local café.

On the junction of Shepherdess Walk and City Road, the Shepherdess Café was walking distance from the station. It was one of the few places left that delivered an East End vibe. A proper London café as far as Ruby was concerned. She grinned at the thought of Frances, with her perfect blonde hair and designer clothes, sitting with her legs crossed in her local café. But then Frances had not always been that way. She had grown up in an East End terrace, just like her.

Frances surprised her by accepting the offer straightaway.

Less than an hour later Ruby found herself sitting across from Frances, staring into her mug of tea. Bitterness and resentment laced Ruby's thoughts. They had a common interest: Nathan. If only Frances had been a better mother, brought them up with some sense of normality, then they would not be in a mess like they were today. It all stemmed from his violent background – instigated by Nathan's father, while Frances stood on, failing to protect the two people that needed her the most. Because of that people were dying. A revenge attack on innocent victims because of something the Crosbys did years ago. And so it went around and around, a nightmarish carousel of violence and hate. Just how many more people had to get hurt?

'You look tired,' Frances said, looking entirely at home as she folded her arms across the table. It was just how she used to sit when she and Ruby's mother chatted in the kitchen of their East End terrace years before.

Frances, in comparison, was glowing. Ruby eyed her suspiciously. She had probably been for a facial that morning, and a spot of light shopping. She had never worked a day in her life; at least, nothing that would bring in an honest income. It was another reason why Ruby was hesitant to move into the luxury flat that Nathan had bought her – the last thing she wanted was to become like her. Ruby cut her thoughts short. Frances was a mother and still held concern over her son.

'I've been working round the clock,' Ruby said wearily. 'Have you heard from Nathan?'

'No, have you?' Frances took one look at her builder's brew tea and pushed it away. Her taste had apparently refined over the years.

Ruby frowned. If there was one person in the world Nathan kept in touch with, it was his mother. 'No,' she said, the grip on her own mug tightening. 'Are you worried?'

'Worried enough to come here and speak to you. He's not answering his phone, and he usually checks in every day. I've spoken to Tweedy, and he hasn't heard a word.'

Ruby's shoulders dropped an inch with relief. So, Frances knew little of her encounter with Nathan. But why hadn't Steve anything to report? Tweedy Steve was the closest friend that Nathan had, and the three of them had known each other since school. Apart from her, he was Nathan's closest confidante. The fact he hadn't spoken to him launched a little rocket of worry. 'Are you sure?' she said. 'It's not been long. Maybe Nathan asked him to keep quiet.'

'No chance.' Frances pursed her lips at the very possibility of being lied to. 'I'm afraid whoever's trying to set him up has hurt him. Everyone knows Nathan's gone underground. Maybe that's what they wanted all along, so the police wouldn't treat his disappearance as suspicious. Have you any idea where he might be?'

'I've no clue. Nathan doesn't tell me that sort of stuff because he doesn't like to compromise me.' That wasn't entirely true as Ruby had been compromised plenty. But she wasn't going to mention the last time they met – when the police came rolling up onto the scene. It was most likely why he did not interest her with his location now.

'I see it all the time,' Frances said. 'People in my world, they just disappear into thin air. Sometimes you hear of them talking down the boozer, saying they know what happened to this person or that. . .' Her voice trailed away and she stared, unblinkingly, at Ruby, tapping her pink varnished nails against the freshly wiped table as she waited for answers.

You live by the sword, you die by the sword, Ruby wanted to say, but could not bring herself to utter the words. This was Nathan they were talking about and, in his case, she would make an exception. 'Surely he's got too big a reputation for people to try it on? They know what they'd be unleashing,' she said, 'and nobody wants a war.'

'Exactly. Which is why it would have to be done without fanfare,' she said. 'If they can't get to Lenny, they'll get to Nathan. A Crosby is a Crosby in their eyes. He could be dead and buried, or worse.'

Ruby's brow furrowed. What could be worse than that? Then she recalled the method of disposal the Crosbys were rumoured to use: freezing a body and shoving it through a wood chipper, dissolving it in a bath of acid, burning it and burying the blackened bones. But she could not think like that because, to her, Nathan was still alive. He was too strong a character just to disappear. 'I'm sure he's OK,' she said. 'We have to stay strong. Has Cathy said anything?'

Frances's face displayed momentary annoyance at the mention of her granddaughter's name. 'We're trying not to tell her too much, but she has a way of finding things out.'

'Do you want me to talk to her?' Ruby said, knowing Frances was doing everything she could to keep her and her daughter apart. Frances did not know about their late-night online chats, and how they were slowly building up a relationship from afar. But it was like walking through treacle. Without Nathan by her side, it was as if she had lost a limb.

'There's no need. I think it's better that she focuses on her studies right now.' The two women sat across from each other united in their concern.

'As soon I hear anything I'll let you know. We've got hundreds of lines of enquiries, but our manpower's limited.'

'If you need anything my end I'm more than happy to sort it out,' Frances said in a condescending voice. 'Lenny has plenty of contacts.'

Ruby fought back a shudder at the mention of Lenny's name. 'The eyes of the world are upon us,' she said, peering over Frances's shoulder to check nobody was listening. 'I think right now it's best we play this by the book.' She returned her gaze to Frances, unable to shake off the feeling of being watched.

'As you wish,' Frances said, unzipping her designer handbag to pay for their teas. 'Anyway, I must be off. I've got a spa date with Leona. You remember her, don't you? That lovely young girl who's dating Nathan. She's beside herself with worry.'

Ruby gave a wry grin. She was well aware the couple had parted. Was Frances desperately trying to keep Leona and Nathan together? Sending a message for Ruby to step out of her way? Just how far was she willing to go to keep them apart?

'Thanks for the tea,' she said, unwilling to play her games anymore.

She walked to the station, aware of heavy footsteps keeping time behind her. A swear word laced her tongue as she swivelled on her heel, expecting to see Nathan's brother, Lenny. But it wasn't Lenny; it was DI Downes, and his presence set her scowl even deeper.

'Have you been following me?' she said, her voice whipped away by the gathering wind.

'Be grateful it's me and not DCI Worrow,' Downes said. 'She's been asking me where you are.'

'God!' Ruby shouted, her nerves frayed after holding in her temper during her meeting with Frances. 'This is the only vocation where you get told off for doing your bloody job. Most people go home after work. I put unpaid hours in, and get penalised.'

'It's hardly that. I just wanted to make sure you weren't meeting Nathan Crosby again.'

'What a shame you were wasting your time,' Ruby said. 'He's disappeared off the radar.'

'Good riddance,' DI Downes said, quickening his step to keep pace with her. 'I'd like nothing better than a sinkhole to swallow up the lot of them.'

Pedestrians bustled past, too caught up in their own lives to care about the argument taking place on the pavement. Ruby stopped dead, oblivious to the passers-by. 'Does that include me? And my daughter? You know, for a while I was stupid enough to think you actually cared.'

'Listen, I've had a shitty day and. . .' His words were drowned out as an iconic red bus rumbled past; a symbol of London, the beating heart of the streets Ruby vowed to protect.

'Yeah, yeah, I know,' she said, hands on hips. 'So you thought you'd take it out on me. Change the record. I've worked flat out this week. I don't expect any thanks but I don't appreciate being shadowed every time I step outside to do my job.'

Downes emitted a thin laugh. 'Thanks? All I've done this week is constantly ask myself where your loyalties lie. You're only putting in the hours to clear your boyfriend's name.'

Ruby could not believe what she was hearing. 'We're not twelve, Jack. Nathan's not my boyfriend, but he *is* the father of my child. What would you have me do? And why does it always come down to you questioning my loyalty?'

Taking her by the elbow, Downes leaned into her, lowering his voice so only she could hear. 'Because there should be no question. You serve the Crown, you're not on the Crosby's payroll, at least not that I'm aware of.' Ruby tried to pull away, but Downes only tightened his grip. 'You work for the Metropolitan Police and supervise a team of officers who would walk over hot coals if you asked them to. That sort of power is not to be taken lightly. Do you really want to drag them into the mire as you fight to protect the Crosbys?' He dropped his hand.

Ruby's cheeks were inflamed, but she had to have the last word. 'Actually, I'm fighting to safeguard the lives of young women out on the streets but I'm sure as hell not going to stand by and allow you to send Nathan down for something he didn't do. Now, if you'll excuse me, I've got to get back to work.'

She strode on, leaving Downes shaking his head as he stood on the pavement. Why couldn't he leave her alone to get on with things? She wanted the same as everyone else, to see the killer brought to justice. So why did she feel so torn in two?

CHAPTER TWENTY-NINE

Discounting immediate family, Nathan trusted his whereabouts to very few. Ruby knew that warnings had been issued to ports and airports, so there was no way that he would risk going abroad. Besides, family commitments dictated that he would not be far from home. If there was one thing Nathan was, it was loyal. His ability to stick by his wayward brother was a testament to that. It was why Ruby found herself taking the short taxi ride to Tweedy Steve's two-bedroom maisonette in Collingwood Street. Out of all Nathan's employees, he was the only one she afforded any trust so Ruby wasn't buying the fact that Tweedy had little knowledge of Nathan's whereabouts. With a heart to match his six-foot seven stature she was confident he would not slam the door in her face. But she had not come here for a reunion. Nathan's home was like a fortress, with high-security fencing and CCTV. Nobody knew it better than Tweedy Steve. The only people allowed free access were family and staff. It was one facet of the investigation that police weren't focusing on enough. Who planted the evidence and, with no sign of forced entry, how did they get inside?

It was with some relief that she accepted the mug of steaming hot tea laid before her as Tweedy allowed her to take a seat.

'Sorry,' he said, 'I've run out of sugar.' His long auburn beard was shaped into a point – the side effect of absent stroking. He would have looked positively devilish had she not had first-hand experience of his kind heart.

'That's OK, it's about time I gave it up,' Ruby said, blowing the steam off the top before taking a sip. At least there was no dubious froth on top. It would not have been the first time she had been offered spittle-laced tea. She glanced around the kitchen-cum-living room. It had a mannish smell of aftershave and takeaway food and was a typical bachelor pad. Not as swanky as Nathan's luxurious abode, but clean. Ruby knew from previous flat hunting that it contained two decent-sized bedrooms and a bathroom far superior to her own. She glanced at the PlayStation connected to a flatscreen TV – knotted wires snaking from two controllers onto the worn tweed sofa. She smiled. Furnishings, clothing, his love for all things tweed was one of his likeable quirks. Game cases lay open-mouthed on the coffee table next to two empty mugs. He could have a girlfriend around, but she doubted this was the case.

''Scuse the mess, I wasn't expecting company,' Tweedy said, giving his beard a compulsory stroke. 'Now, what can I do you for?'

'It's a palace compared to my place,' Ruby said, noticing the yellowed bruise fading on his cheekbone. She knew better than to ask of the origin; bruises were a side effect of his job. The only thing that puzzled her was who on earth would be brave enough to punch this giant of a man, or crazy enough. Thoughts of Lenny sprinkled her mind, and she dismissed them as she took another sip of tea. 'I'm sure you know why I'm here. We're close to finding a suspect for this case, but I can't get a hold of Nathan. Last time we met, he was about to give me a name.'

'Hardly surprising he's done a flit after what happened,' Tweedy said. 'The cops aren't gonna be banging on my door in a minute, are they?'

'Oh, c'mon, that had nothing to do with me. My DI, he traced my location and called for backup. Then he told the DCI it was all my idea.'

'Bit of a weird relationship you've got with your DI,' Tweedy said.

'Mate, you don't know the half of it. But he's at a post-mortem today, so you don't need to worry for now.' Given the hours she had been working, she was entitled to an hour off during the day, and DI Downes was less likely to call the cavalry if he thought she was at home catching up on some much-needed sleep. She had been furious at the intrusion but had eventually accepted that he had every right – it was his job. The fact he was willing to cover up her real association with the Crosbys had saved her from some very awkward questions from DCI Worrow and above. Ruby took another sip of her tea. 'I don't have long. Can you ask Nathan to come out so we can talk about this?'

Tweedy's brow raised. 'He's not here.'

'*Call of Duty*? *Grand Theft Auto*?' Ruby nodded towards the empty game cases. 'I thought you only liked footie games.'

Tweedy gave a non-committal shrug.

'And you're a bloke. You wouldn't give yourself two cups to wash up when you can just reuse the same one.'

She stood, pushing back her chair as Nathan entered the room.

'Always the detective,' he said, his hazy blue eyes bright with amusement. 'I wondered how long it would take before you started grilling him. You really should come and work for me.' Dressed in black jeans and a Lacoste V-neck sweater, he crossed his legs as he leant against the window frame, keeping an eye on the traffic below.

'I thought I was,' Ruby said, happy to see a rare smile. 'Aren't I the only one fool enough to try and clear your name?'

'How's Cathy?' he said, his gaze sending tingles down Ruby's spine.

'Worried about you, but fine. She's starting to open up to me a bit more.' Ruby smiled. She had come to enjoy their late-night Facebook chats. 'Why? Haven't you been in touch with your mum?'

Nathan shook his head, his smile waning. 'We had a bit of a falling out.'

'Over me?' Ruby asked, knowing full well it was. She could see it now; Frances telling Nathan that something would have to be done about her, and Nathan threatening all sorts as he defended her honour. But Nathan did not offer up a response, and time was too precious to waste on chit-chat. 'You should get in touch, let her know you're OK. She's worried about you.'

'She'll live,' Nathan said, his response suggesting he was in no hurry.

'You seem a lot brighter today. I take it you've got a suspect for me.'

'Babe, I'm about to hand you the killer on a plate,' Nathan said, throwing another glance out the window. 'That should get you some brownie points with your DCI, and wipe the smirk off Downes's face.'

'So why the hesitation? You could have told me the last time we met. Why delay?'

He took a step towards her. 'Because I wanted to explain. Sit down.'

'This is where I bow out,' Tweedy said. 'I'll be in my room. Try not to come to blows.'

Ruby's eyes widened. 'What's that supposed to mean? You're worrying me now.'

'He's kidding,' Nathan said, beckoning her to join him on the sofa. 'Come. How long have you got?'

'Loads. I've just come off a crazy long shift. Downes sent me home for a kip before he left.'

Snuggling up with Nathan in Tweedy's spare room briefly touched her thoughts. It was a delicious image, but one she could not afford. If Nathan was offering up Ellie's murderer, then she knew where her priorities lay. It was time to find out the killer's identity, and she had not a second to spare.

CHAPTER THIRTY

Entering the Ten Bells public house was like stepping back in time. There was a reason it was the doctor's favourite haunt. Until 1988, the public house was known as the Jack The Ripper in homage to one of the most famous serial killers to prowl the streets of London. On the corner of Commercial Street and Fournier Street, the pub's first floor offered a generous view of the East End. Although the exterior had been modernised, upstairs held a decorative charm harking back to Victorian gin palaces, making the doctor feel very much at home. He had always felt he had been born in the wrong era. Fantasising about days of old, he sipped his port, staring at the nineteenth-century decorative tiling gracing the walls.

It was good to get out – take a break from the young lady who had been taking up all of his time. Touching the tips of his ears, his long black scarf provided ample concealment. A pair of tinted glasses and a black woollen hat completed the ensemble. He had been cooped up in that derelict building for far too long.

Attracted to its murderous history, he had frequented this East End pub long before he fulfilled his fantasy of killing prostitutes of his own. The area was diverse enough that his looks drew little attention, and he enjoyed his time there, musing about the infamous killer and how his legend had lived on. His thoughts led to ripper victims Annie Chapman and Mary Kelly. Both prostitutes, they frequented the pub during the autumn of terror, which took five women's lives. There were many theories as to who had been responsible but the possibility of a surgeon appealed to Doctor

Tanner the most. Crossing his legs, he ignored the cocktail drinkers and trendy music as he immersed his thoughts in the past.

Later, as he stepped out onto the streets, he was grateful for the light smattering of rain. It afforded him the excuse of using an umbrella, which shielded him from the attention of the people he was trying to avoid. He would finish off his visit with a stroll down Brick Lane.

The paradox of beauty and death had always fascinated him, and the variety of artwork on display often took his breath away. Every sense was assailed: the smell of street food and curry houses; the hustle and bustle of the streets – vibrant, colourful images which stayed with him long after he had left. Each visit had something to offer, as freshly painted works of art lined buildings, walls and warehouses – an inspiration and a joy to behold.

But to Doctor Tanner, there was no better canvas to work on than one that carried the essence of a soul.

The son of a mortician, he had grown up amongst the dead. Schooled from home, he was seldom in contact with the living and, when he wasn't helping his father with the embalming process, he was assisting his mother in applying make-up to the recently deceased. His mother took great care with her subjects. Gently she positioned them, her thumb on their chin as she applied a coat of lipstick to disguise the blueness of their lips. The soft powdering of blusher, a careful application of mascara, everything about her was warm and gentle – just like the princesses that occupied the fairy stories she read to him as a child. But as he lay in bed, his thoughts had floated to the bodies of the deceased, prepared for their eternal sleep. Doctor Tanner sighed as the memory infiltrated his consciousness. He missed those days when he would sneak downstairs to the funeral parlour after their grieving families had gone, to read them one last bedtime story. How he had wanted to transform them into something better, as his mother had done, make their lifeless bodies the very embodiment of art. But the death of his parents hardened him, and his fascination turned to violence as he was left to face life on his own. With them, his uniqueness had been celebrated, but after their joint suicides, he was cast out into the world, a world which did not welcome someone like him.

CHAPTER THIRTY-ONE

The answers that Ruby had waited to hear were finally within her grasp. Sharing the sofa with Nathan, she half-expected the door buzzer to ring as police demanded entry to Tweedy Steve's flat. But no such interruption was forthcoming and she focused on Nathan's voice as he drew breath to speak.

'He used to work for the family business. "No questions asked," Mum used to say. You remember our old GP, don't you?'

'Doctor Tanner?' Ruby said, their first encounter with him still fresh in her mind.

They were just children, Ruby and Nathan, playing together on the kitchen floor as their mothers chatted at the table. Their ordinary day was transformed into pandemonium as Ruby's father dragged Nathan's dad into their living room, leaving a trail of blood leaking from a stab wound that looked sure to finish him off. Dr Tanner was quick to arrive. The lean, beak-nosed young man was adept at stitching up wounds and curing ailments. Ruby mentally did the math. He must be in his early sixties now.

'Are you saying it's him? He's the murderer?'

Nathan nodded in response.

His unwillingness to elaborate made Ruby sigh. Must she tease out every piece of information? She would need more than this if she was to secure a conviction. 'But why? Is he still on the payroll?'

'God, no! It's another reason why I didn't think of him straight-away. I thought we'd seen the last of him years ago. Especially after. . .' The words died in his mouth, and as he leaned back on the sofa, Nathan seemed reluctant for them to find a home in Ruby's consciousness.

'Don't hold back,' she said. 'After the stuff I've dealt with, you can't shock me.'

Nathan shot her a doubtful look, and Ruby knew he was right to do so. She may have seen it all, but things were different as far as he was concerned.

He stretched his arms on the back of the sofa and, with his index finger, began to twirl Ruby's hair. It was something he had done since they were kids. The warmth of his fingers against the nape of her neck made goosebumps rise on her skin. Exhausted from lack of sleep, she allowed herself to briefly close her eyes and fall into the steady lull of his voice as he spoke about Doctor Tanner. The stress-laced tone from their previous encounter had evaporated. He seemed assured that he had the right man. Ruby guessed Nathan had done his homework and was willing to stay in hiding a few days longer so that he could gift her a positive outcome. She blinked, pushing away the sleep that was threatening to overcome her, despite the urgency of her task.

'Sorry,' she said, inhaling a deep breath as she sat forward. 'I'm bloody knackered. Can't you give me the details so I can get back to the station and get him nicked?'

'All in good time.' Nathan rose, walked to the fridge and took out a can of Red Bull. 'Here, get this down you.' He cracked open the can.

Ruby took a sip, the cool, fizzy concoction refreshing her senses. She waited for Nathan to continue as he sat beside her. Being in such close proximity was playing havoc with her thought patterns. As his knee touched hers, she edged back in her seat, forcing herself to concentrate on the real reason for her visit.

'You were saying about Doctor Tanner?' she said, feeling self-conscious beneath his lingering gaze.

'My old man offered him a job and helped him train as a surgeon. It wasn't enough that he was on call to stitch up Dad's cronies, he had to get him involved in the torture side of things too. He had a flair for it, but he enjoyed it a bit too much.'

'I remember him. He used to give me the creeps. It was the way he used to look at me like he wanted to peel off my skin to see what was underneath.' Ruby shuddered at the memory. 'When did he stop working for you?'

'He didn't bloody report to me,' Nathan said, his mouth set in a grimace. 'Lenny kept him on until a couple of years ago when he was fired. I reckon that's why he's really killed those girls. He thrived on hurting people. Someone like that, they don't change.'

'Why was he sacked?' Ruby said, sensing his hesitation. They were finally getting to the crux of things, and she did not want him to stop now. She took another mouthful of Red Bull then focused all her attention on Nathan.

'Do you remember that eight-year-old kid that went missing? Hannah Marshall, the one that was found in the woods?'

Ruby slowly nodded, wondering what Hannah had to do with Ellie Mason. They had many missing children on their books at that time, but Hannah had stood out because she was also a victim of parental neglect. Social services had been ready to place her in care when she disappeared from her home. Her parents had claimed abduction and, with concerns that she had been murdered Ruby's team had become involved. Ruby had never been so relieved to find a missing child. Three days later Hannah was discovered in woodlands, pale-faced and shaking, but unwilling to speak a word. Whatever trauma she had been through, it was enough to keep her experiences locked deeply inside. It had always bothered Ruby because Hannah's wispy blonde hair had been dyed brown, and she was found wearing brand-new clothes.

'Her parents still claim it wasn't them that took her,' Ruby said, lost in thoughts of the young girl.

'It wasn't, it was Tanner.'

'How can you be so sure?' Ruby said.

'Because it was me that left her in the woods.'

'What?' Ruby whispered, shock robbing the strength from her words.

'Tanner was renting one of our properties, and I decided to pay him a visit. I wanted to warn him off. Tell him we had no use for him anymore. Things had changed, and I didn't want a vulture like Tanner around my gaff.'

'And Lenny agreed to this?'

Nathan nodded, gesticulating as he spoke. 'From the confines of his prison cell. He didn't like him any more than I did.'

Ruby nodded. How could she forget that Lenny was inside when it happened? Perhaps deep down a part of her wanted to blame him for whatever bombshell Nathan was going to drop next.

'When I got there, Tanner didn't answer and the windows were all boarded up. I had a spare key, so I let myself in. I found Hannah unconscious in one of the bedrooms.'

Ruby inhaled a gasp. 'No! Really? Why didn't you call the police?'

'*Me?* Call you lot and say I've got your missing child in one of my properties? I couldn't risk it. I got her dressed, covered her with a blanket and left her in the woods. I guess that's why she couldn't remember much because she'd been unconscious the whole time she was gone.'

'She would have known who took her in the first place,' Ruby said, imagining Nathan scooping up the little girl and taking her out of harm's way. 'So you were our mystery informant.' She touched his shoulder, and he shifted on the sofa, turning to face her.

She wanted to hug him for keeping the little girl safe. It was just like Nathan to keep his heroics quiet, shying away from the admiration she was willing to bestow.

Lacing his fingers between hers, Nathan drew the back of Ruby's hand to his mouth and softly planted a kiss. It was a tender act from a man who had spent half his life immersed in violence.

Ruby swallowed, fighting to keep the rush of emotions in check. She'd spent years trying to tame their sexual chemistry. Seconds ticked by as unspoken words passed between them. She knew what he was thinking because he had said it a thousand times before. Why couldn't she just leave all this behind? Give up the police and spend her days with him? But they would only hurt each other in the end.

'I got someone to make the call,' Nathan said, finally, releasing her grip. 'I kept watch until she was picked up.'

Ruby nodded, trying to gather up her broken thoughts as tiredness and emotion overwhelmed her all at once. 'There weren't any signs of abuse. She was unharmed, wasn't she?'

'Only because I got to her in time.' Nathan's frown grew at the recollection. 'It was risky. I could have been caught with her in the back of the van. But I couldn't think what else to do. Back then I didn't trust anyone I knew to look after her. It was obvious what Tanner was planning.'

'I'm surprised you didn't kill him for that,' Ruby said.

'You know me by now, babe,' Nathan said. 'If there's one thing that makes me see red, it's kids being abused. He probably told her he was a doctor. She trusted him enough to get in his car. I set out to fix things so it wouldn't happen again.'

'You ambushed him? What did you do?' Ruby said, cold dread rising inside her.

'The only thing I could do. I disfigured him for life.' A hint of a satisfied grin touched his lips. 'By the time the acid hit his skin, I knew no kid would ever walk away with him again.'

Ruby winced at the ugliness of the words. 'And now he's killed Ellie as revenge? Why her, Nathan? Did you and Ellie have a fling?'

'Ellie? No, she worked in Lenny's escort agency. I gave her the sack when she was caught sampling the gear. I guess the doctor treated her at some point. The girls. . . Lenny made them have regular check-ups to make sure they were clean.'

'Hmm,' Ruby said, the sound of women being objectified making her hackles rise. 'What happened to him after the attack?'

Nathan shrugged. 'His face was a mess.' He caught Ruby's disapproving glare. 'But I don't regret any of it. If I hadn't turned up that day, he would have killed her for sure.'

'But acid, that's so brutal. Have you ever used it before?'

'What do you take me for?' Nathan said.

'Seriously?' Ruby said, her voice rising. 'You're telling me you've thrown acid in someone's face, and then asking me not to judge you for it?'

Nathan got to his feet. 'See, this is why I didn't tell you straight-away. You've always been a bit of an ostrich. You're fine dealing with other people's problems, but when it's a little bit close to home, you hide away. This is life in all its ugly splendour. Now, what are you going to do about it?'

Ruby stood. There was only one answer to that question. 'I'm going to make an arrest.'

CHAPTER THIRTY-TWO

Humming as he worked, the doctor dropped the bloodstained cotton into the bin at his feet and plugged the wound. It was just as well the young woman was dead for this part. He had been patient as the fatal overdose had taken hold, listening steadily with his stethoscope as the sluggish lub-dub, lub-dub of her heartbeat faded away. He could have saved her, changed his mind and administered a drug that would have reversed the effect. He had glanced at the syringe containing the antidote as he bent over her body – feeling God-like as he held the power of life and death. It was an experiment to see if he could invoke some last-minute compassion, and bring her back from the brink of death. But to him, she was there for his pleasure alone. It made it easy for him to carry out his work. Devoid of a heartbeat, the incision produced a gentle flow of blood instead of the sudden violent spurt that would taint his good work.

It was not as if he were angry with the woman, or harboured any hatred towards her. His was an addiction not easily cured. His fascination with the human body had developed significantly since his youth. Given his background, it had been easy to depersonalise those he treated. He knew it was wrong. Society taught him this was so. But there were so many people in the world. Would anyone mourn the loss of those living in the gutter? Everybody died, and these girls were the scourge of society, the most easily forgotten of them all. He was merely accelerating the inevitable, and she would leave this world immortalised as art. He was doing her a favour. He smiled. This would be his finest work yet.

Beneath him the rats were squeaking, the scent of blood tantalising their senses. 'Later,' he said, irritated by the interruption. A cool breeze broke through the crack in the window, chilling the sweat on his brow. He was so close to completion, and his back ached from carrying out his work. Allowing her to surface from the temporary coma had been a necessary evil. How else was he going to get her to walk on the shards of glass? He had observed from the shadows, trying to predict her next move in his game of cat and mouse. It had been foolish to leave the scalpel where she could find it, but he was not accustomed to his subjects fighting back. She should have been too drugged and dazed to think about grasping an implement of any kind. Just a few steps, that was all she had to take to make her feel like she was walking on knives. In the end, she had been grateful to fall into his arms and for him to make it all go away.

He returned his attention to the wound. Satisfied he had stemmed the flow of blood, he rinsed his hands in the small basin on the table and patted them dry. He had barely noticed that the record had stopped. As he set it back in motion, the sound of Beethoven's Symphony No. 5 filled the room. The dramatic contrast in instrumentation invoked an intense rhythmic energy, and he inhaled a deep breath, allowing the stress of the day to ebb away. Colours rose, splashes of reds, blues and purples as the music came to a crescendo. . . then calmed as the melody ebbed and flowed. It was said that Beethoven felt he had been sent by God: 'Music is a higher revelation than all wisdom and philosophy,' he once said. Such was the doctor's sentiment when it came to his art. His focus returned to the body: she was almost ready. Trailing down the back of the surgeon's chair, her red-blonde hair was kinked into a natural wave. Shaved and bleached, April was unrecognisable from the girl who had come to his door. How long would it take the press to figure out which fairy tale she had stepped from? His fingers traced over her corpse as he imagined the headlines. With great beauty comes great sacrifice. His work here almost done, his mind wandered to his next work of art.

CHAPTER THIRTY-THREE

Ruby paused in the corridor, staring up the stairs that would lead her to what they called the 'ivory towers' – the floor frequented by her DCI and higher-ranking superior officers. Her eyelids grew heavy as she tried to work out what to do for the best. It was late afternoon and tiredness had seeped through to the marrow of her bones. She leant on the stairwell as she tried to conduct her thoughts. She could go straight to DCI Worrow and give her a sanitised version of Nathan's revelation. If she was lucky, a warrant for Doctor Tanner's arrest could be issued today. Worrow was more likely to take the arrest seriously than DI Jack Downes. But there was a firm chain of command and skipping ranks could be taken as a personal insult. She sighed, her footsteps echoing down the corridor to his office. Her mind was too foggy to pre-empt what she was going to say.

The memory of Nathan's kiss still lingered on her lips. Just as she said goodbye, he had taken her by the arm, gently pulling her back inside and pinning her against the door. After gazing at her face for what felt like an eternity, he had pressed his mouth upon hers, hungrily seeking the knowledge that she still loved him, despite everything he had done. Her reciprocation had left him in no doubt. He had changed in their time apart. Perhaps it was time away from his family that had brought him back to her. She wondered if cracks were forming in the foundations of the Crosby empire. Silently she wished that Nathan would leave it all behind. Helping him clear his name would be a small step towards earning him the freedom that would help him begin again.

She found Downes in the kitchen, frowning, as he held a spoon of sugar over one of the many empty mugs on the tray.

'Blimey, got you on the tea run, have they?' she said, amused at the sight. 'Luddy takes one sugar, no milk. Ash has coffee with three sugars, black. Eve has no sugars, milky tea. The rest will be happy with a builder's brew.' She smiled. She was slowly winning her team around to the joys of tea.

'I thought you were working a split shift,' Downes said, spooning coffee and sugar into the mugs as instructed.

It would not be the first time she had split her shift in two, catching up on an hour's sleep during the day to keep her clear-headed for what was to come.

Ruby dropped two teabags into the biggest mug. 'I've got a lead. I think that takes precedence over sleep, don't you?'

Downes stiffened. 'When did this come in?'

'It's hot off the presses,' she said. 'Here, let me help you with that.' Grabbing her mug from the tray, she pushed open the door. Having beaten her tiredness and come out the other side, she was buzzing from the development. She couldn't sleep now if she wanted to.

Within five minutes refreshments were handed out to weary workers, and Ruby was sitting across from Downes at his desk. A well-thumbed copy of *Auto Trader* lay splayed next to a folder marked 'staff appraisals'. Ruby averted her gaze. If there was one time she could do without an assessment, it was now.

'Well?' Downes said. 'What have you got?'

'A suspect,' Ruby said, her heart picking up an extra beat. This was important. She needed to convince him she was on the right track. 'His name is Doctor Tanner, and he fits the profile down to a T. He's handy with a scalpel and has a huge grudge against the Crosbys, Nathan in particular. He's done this sort of thing before.'

Downes sat up, his expression brightening. 'Where's your proof?'

'I've got enough to get him in.' She filled him in on the missing child up to the point where Nathan left her in the woods. It did not take long to bring him up to speed. 'I'm sure that if I speak to the child and tell her that she's nothing to worry about, she'll identify Doctor Tanner as the man that abducted her. Then we should have enough to search his home. Hopefully, obtain some evidence of Ellie's murder.' Ruby imagined Nathan, his fury rising at the sight of the little blonde-haired girl, helpless and alone, in Tanner's property.

Downes rubbed his chin. His shirt sleeves were rolled up to his elbows, the tie knot loosened around his neck. 'It's a bit thin. I presume your informant hasn't provided you with a statement?'

'No, but I've spoken to Nathan on the phone,' Ruby lied. 'He's got an alibi for his whereabouts in the twenty-four hours after Ellie's death. See? He couldn't have put her organs under the bed.' She held Downes's stare, which imparted that he wasn't buying a word. 'He's away on business, but I've told him he still needs to come in.'

'Hmm,' he said. 'I'm surprised it took him this long to arrange it.'

Downes was not easily fooled. They both knew that the Crosby family could buy an alibi anytime they wanted. However, this time Nathan was telling the truth, and his ex-girlfriend, Leona, was only too happy to provide him with an alibi that confirmed he was in her family home during the time in question.

Downes crossed his legs, his ankle resting on his knee. His foot twitched as he spoke. A restless body and a restless mind. 'So you're telling me that this doctor holds a grudge against Nathan Crosby because he took the child the doctor abducted? That was years ago. Why's he acting on it now?'

'There's more to it than that. A lot more.' She paused, loath to implicate Nathan in any wrongdoing. If they arrested Doctor Tanner, he could turn on Nathan and implicate him in the acid attack, something that would carry a lengthy prison sentence. But he would have to prove it first. 'It's off the record,' Ruby said. But alarm bells were ringing in her mind. The status of their relationship had changed, and she did not know if she could trust DI Downes anymore.

'I can't work with one hand tied behind my back,' he said, sensing her discomfort. 'We're police officers, we don't pick and choose which criminals deserve to be prosecuted and which ones don't. If they've committed an offence, they're coming in.'

'Fine,' Ruby said, 'We'll get the doctor in for questioning on the kidnapping charge after we speak to the little girl.'

'So that's all you're telling me?' Downes said, his face creased in a frown.

'Yes,' Ruby said, relieved that Downes had made up her mind for her. 'I don't think it's in the public interest to delve any deeper.' She rose, steadying herself as a fresh wave of tiredness weakened her legs. 'I'd best instruct the troops, see what we can dig up on Doctor Tanner with a view to progressing the investigation.'

'Steady on, I'm sure we can work around this. What else have you got on Crosby?'

But Ruby carried on as if she had not heard him. 'I'll instruct the team, put together a package and we can go from there.'

The chances of Doctor Tanner being at his registered address were slim. Nathan would have had it checked out as soon as the thought entered his mind. His absence was a small blessing. Had they harmed Tanner then any evidence of his murderous crime may have gone down with him. It was a race against time to find him. She could only hope that he would not strike again.

CHAPTER THIRTY-FOUR

As Ruby entered her flat, she felt a chill descend. It was not from the growing fog outside, but the fact her flat was pitched in darkness. She had switched on the living room light when she left, and now the gap beneath the door revealed nothing but darkness. Leaving the light on was a habit born out of unease. She saw the way some of the residents had looked at her, and their sideways glances suggested they knew what she was. The police were not welcome in her tower block, though her association with the Crosby family afforded an ounce of protection – unless they were the ones chasing her. Her heartbeat sped up a notch as she shoved her key in the lock. Sure the door was secure, but the Crosbys never let a little thing like a lock and key stop them. Thoughts of seeing Nathan fired a spark of hope within. Would he be angry for her perceived betrayal, or perhaps he just wanted to spend the night? She hoped it was the latter. She slid her hand over the light switch, her body stiffening at the sight of a figure by the window. As the light bulb flashed on, she emitted an involuntary gasp: it was not Nathan, but Lenny. By the menacing look on his face he was not best pleased.

'Oh, it's you,' she said, reluctantly closing the door behind her. 'What are you doing here? Is Nathan with you?' Her eyes darted around the room then back to her unwanted guest. She was relieved to see the only thing in his hands was a bag of cheese and onion crisps. A small act of assertiveness – eating the little food she had left. She knew the Crosby family would be angry at Nathan's narrow miss with the law. But what had he told them? Was Nathan losing faith in her already?

'Of course he ain't here. As if he'd risk getting nicked a second time,' Lenny said, scrunching up the half-eaten bag of crisps and throwing them on the floor.

'That wasn't my fault,' Ruby swallowed, cursing herself for the nervousness in her voice. 'I was followed.'

Lenny took a step towards her. 'And why would you be tailed unless someone knew you were meeting him?'

There was no way Ruby was putting DI Downes at risk for doing his job. She may have been mad as hell with him, but if she squealed that Downes was responsible, there was a chance they would invoke their own form of revenge. Lenny was on edge, who knew what he was capable of without Nathan to rein him in?

'It's not exactly a big secret anymore,' Ruby lied. 'I've tried to keep our relationship under wraps, but since Cathy came on the scene. . .'

'Ah yes, Cathy. Another member of the family you've abandoned.'

Ruby flinched as he spoke about her daughter in that way. Lenny always had a knack for pressing her buttons. 'Isn't it about time *you* were straight with *me*?' she said, unable to resist turning the onus onto him. 'Why didn't you tell me about Doctor Tanner? You wouldn't like to keep Nathan on the run, would you? So you can put the family business back where it used to be?'

Lenny set his jaw as he walked towards her. Her heart hammering, Ruby stood her ground. She was fed up being scared of the Crosbys. All the same it did not do to rile him. Making Lenny angry was like poking a stick at a nest full of hornets.

He grabbed Ruby's jaw, his fingers digging into her skin as she tried to push him away. 'Just because family loyalty means nothing to you, don't mean we're all the same.'

Ruby squirmed beneath his grip, drawing back her foot to kick him in the shin. But Lenny pre-empted her movements, slamming her hard against the door. The back of her head rebounded against the wood, and he used the full force of his weight to immobilise her. The smell of cheese and onion reeked on his breath. Her stomach clenched as she froze, her eyes trailing down to his spare hand. Lenny always came tooled up, and one false move from her could land her in serious trouble.

'If you were any other bird I'd be teaching you a lesson right now, just for getting Nathan into bother.' Lenny's eyes glazed over, a smile curling on his lips. 'He might believe your story of being followed, but I don't.'

Ruby held his gaze, one hand on his chest and the other on his forearm. 'But I'm not just any other bird, am I? I'm the only person that can get Nathan out of this mess. If you're as loyal to your brother as you say you are, you'd best start working with me.' Squaring her shoulders, she looked him firmly in the eye. 'What is it with you every time you come round here? Can't you have a conversation without copping a feel?'

It was enough to make him release his grip. Lenny ran his fingers through his hair, suddenly unsure of himself. Ruby knew she presented a whole set of problems in his black-and-white world. It was true: if she was anyone else God knows what he would be doing to her right now. But Ruby fell between the cracks and for now she had been offered some protection. She was also one of the few people who had the guts to answer him back. She sidled past him to the cabinet. Pulling out two glasses from the cupboard, she eased the cork off a bottle of spiced rum. Sitting at the coffee table, she beckoned him over.

'I need whatever you've got on Doctor Tanner, because it sounds to me like he's our suspect.'

Standing over her, Lenny sniffed the contents of the glass before taking a sip. 'Whatever Nathan did to him happened years ago. We've pissed off enough people between then and now. It could be anyone.'

'No, you're wrong,' Ruby said, wishing he would sit down. 'The autopsy report said the killer is skilled with a scalpel, possibly a surgeon or doctor. Granted, it could be a nurse, or even a vet, but from what Nathan has said, Tanner knew the girls personally. He has a vendetta, and he's not afraid to spill blood.' She thought about the torture he was rumoured to have induced on his victims while Lenny watched on. 'The stitches were clean when they sewed Ellie Mason back up. But it's the whole fairy-tale thing that got me thinking. Maybe he's got a fetish, dressing them up because there's not much beauty in his life.'

Lenny blurted out a laugh. 'Like *Phantom of the Opera*, you mean? Mum's been to see that twice this week, driving me effin' mad she is, singing it around the house. God, you want to hear her when she hits those high notes.'

Ruby couldn't help but smile. In that split second it was like old times. It never ceased to amaze her how Lenny could change from being frightening to amicable in a matter of seconds. He was well respected in the circle he mixed with, and some would even say popular. Ruby thought back to when they were children. Her telling him stories as she tried to move the sullen look from his face. Quite often she did, but sometimes his face came with bruises, and no amount of silly jokes could dissolve the heat from his anger then.

'This has got to stay between us. If this leaks to the press it'll compromise the investigation, and I need a strong case for when it gets to court. Oh, and there's something else too,' she said, her thoughts tripping over each other. 'Nathan pulled a gun yesterday. He could have got himself shot. You've got to tell him to keep his cool until I sort this all out.'

'You needn't worry about me. I didn't build my reputation by being a grass,' Lenny said, tapping his foot against the tea-stained coffee table. 'And I don't need you telling me what to say to my family.'

'You do when he's inches away from getting shot. There were armed officers present, they don't mess around.'

Lenny looked grim-faced as he knocked back another swig of rum. 'Is that everything?'

Ruby snapped out of the image she had been playing in her head since her encounter with Nathan. She had pictured him getting shot so many times it was almost as if she were recalling a memory. He had come too close to the law this time, perhaps this would shake some sense into him. Ruby sighed, casting her gaze upwards to the man before her, the man who would never let his brother go.

'The coroner found rat faeces in Ellie Mason's hair. Whoever took her went to a great deal of trouble to mould her into a certain type of image, but she must have been left alone at some point. It had to be somewhere rats could have nestled up to her. This doctor, did he have pet rats?'

'What? No,' Lenny said. 'He was a respectable-looking geezer. . . for a nonce.'

Ruby screwed the lid back on the bottle of rum. 'Is there any way you could have got that wrong?' she said, knowing how Lenny hated being accused of making mistakes. Why had Doctor Tanner moved on to women if he had intended to sexually abuse the child? Hurt her, yes, perhaps even kill her, but was she a potential abuse victim or someone on whom he could practise his skills?

'A bloke kidnaps a kid and leaves her naked and unconscious on his bed, what do you think he was gonna do to her? Read her a bedtime story?'

'Alright, I get your point,' Ruby said, with a hint of irritation. 'Just have a think. Let me know if you can come up with any old acquaintances, places he frequented, cars he drove.' Canned laughter blared from the television in the flat next door. Her neighbours were nocturnal creatures, they held little consideration for the people around them. 'What was he like when he worked for you?' Ruby said. 'Doctor Tanner, what can you tell me about his personality? Had he any family?'

'Personality? Thought he was something special. Pretentious git,' Lenny snorted. 'As for his family, his parents gassed themselves when he was a kid. At least, that's what my old man said. They were a weird bunch by all accounts.'

Ruby masked a yawn with the back of her hand. 'He always struck me as strange.' She blinked back her watery eyes. 'How's Cathy?'

'I didn't come here for a family reunion,' Lenny said, his face clouding over as he rested his empty glass on the coffee table. 'Just sort this out.'

Ruby craned her neck as Lenny headed for the door. His stride was sharp, determined.

'And if I can't, what happens then?'

'Let's say it won't just be Nathan's neck on the line.'

'What do you mean by that?' Ruby rose from her chair.

Lenny bared his teeth in a ghoulish smile. 'Get this case solved and you won't have to find out.'

Ruby bolted the door as Lenny left, shoving a chair against the handle. It would not stop him coming back, but it would slow him down. Precious minutes to give her time to react.

✳ ✳ ✳

The baseball bat that lived under her bed now lay nestled beneath her duvet. Lying in bed, she took small comfort from it as she resurrected their conversation. She had barely slept over the last few days and needed a clear mind for work. A bubble of fear rose inside her, defying her vow to stay strong. She pulled the duvet tightly around her as a blast of icy air filtered in through the window. Nathan's absence felt like a physical ache in her chest. What she would give to be in his arms, feeling the warmth of his body as he wrapped himself around her.

That night her nightmares produced rat-infested tunnels and a darkness so thick she could barely see her hand. In the distance, a light appeared, framing the doctor she once knew, and the glint of a scalpel in his hand.

CHAPTER THIRTY-FIVE

Shrouded by dark thoughts, Ruby cried out as she awoke. Her heart was beating faster than was good for her. The day's events had plunged her into a series of nightmares as her brain tried to comprehend recent events. Sweat trailed down her back as she unfurled the sheets from around her feet, while the memory of her nightmares replayed in her mind. Although she disagreed with Nathan's methods of dealing with perceived paedophiles and murderers, she could understand a knee-jerk reaction. But this had been planned, cold and calculating. Why hadn't he just called the police? She knew why: because on the street where she grew up, police were not your friends. It had been easy for her to blame their violence on Lenny, and perhaps Nathan was right, she *had* been burrowing her head in the sand all these years. It was time to face up to who Nathan really was.

As she lay back in bed, the doctor's face came into view. Pale and cunning, he leered at her – no hint of remorse behind his beady black eyes. Just what had he planned for that little abducted girl? And as for all the people he had tortured… Some would call the acid attack karma. The pain must have been immense as his flesh melted away. Was that why he had waited for his revenge? Ruby had read stories of acid burn victims in the news. They were inspiring people who had turned their lives around, devoting their time to helping others as a result of their experiences. Not so with the doctor. 'There's good and bad in everyone,' her mother used to say. Mum… She was overdue a visit, but once again work had dictated her routine. Her mind ticked over as she tried to process it all.

Going through her phone, she replied to the spate of Facebook instant messages from Cathy. She could see her father in her, her quick temper and those stormy eyes that carried a depth of emotion. Her hair was growing now, her dark waves touching her shoulders. Her frame was still too thin for Ruby's liking, but it was not for her to say given they were still building their relationship. Asking her to stay indoors, Ruby urged her daughter to keep herself safe until the killer was behind bars.

As she dressed for work, Ruby took comfort in seeing how uneasy Nathan had been as he recalled what he had done. Deep down he knew it was wrong. Now it had come back to haunt him, with innocent victims paying the price. Violence breeds violence, and Ruby had to break the cycle before it claimed another victim.

The phone rang in her hand, making her jump to attention. It was Downes.

'Are yous awake?' he said, the urgency of his voice hastening her departure.

'Walking out the door now, boss. What's wrong?' she said, fiddling with her keys. She would take the stairs. The lift would only cut her phone signal, and right now she needed to know what was going on.

'Meet me at the Britannia Leisure Centre. We've got another body.'

Ruby stood by the edge of the pool, hands deep in her blazer pockets as the police diver broke the surface of the water, the feeling of déjà vu creeping over her skin. It was not that long ago she had been following enquiries with the manager about Lisa Caldwell. Danny Smedley may be remanded in prison, but as far as Ruby was concerned, the streets were far from safe. And now Ruby's officers were urgently reviewing missing person reports to ascertain the identity of their latest victim. This was the doctor's work; it had to be. Why else would the body be dressed in a costume from a fancy dress store?

As crime scene investigators gave the diver the thumbs up, he made his way towards the body to gently bring her in. Her long wavy hair swayed in the water, the unnatural tint of red a warning signal to those who approached. Around her wrist was a seashell bracelet and, together with the silver halter-neck top and fishtail netted skirt, it formed an image that made Ruby's heart turn over. 'The Little Mermaid,' she whispered.

Downes agreed with her findings with a sombre nod of the head. But this story had a far from happy ending, and the fact a theme was arising made it even worse: they had a serial killer on their hands. Ruby held her breath as the diver gently turned the body over. She knew what was coming, it wasn't just the tinge of blood haloing the victim's head that gave it away. Ruby had studied the grimmest version of the most popular fairy stories. Devoid of the saccharine-sweet ending, they were enough to keep anybody awake at night. And now the doctor had belched out a second victim, which meant he was on the prowl again.

Ruby leant over the side of the pool, breathing in the distinct chlorine vapour. The victim was a similar age to Ellie, who had been posed as Snow White. With the same pale skin and artificial lashes, there was no doubt in Ruby's mind that they had met their deaths at the same cruel hand. In keeping with the story, fresh cuts criss-crossed the soles of the young woman's bare feet.

'Can you open her mouth for me, please?' Ruby said, taking her phone and activating the torch.

'What are you looking for?' Downes said, leaning over her shoulder.

'The Little Mermaid sacrificed a lot to become human. Not only did she feel as if she was walking on knives, she also lost the ability to speak.'

As the diver slowly opened the girl's mouth, Ruby shone the light inside. Her worst fears were realised. 'Thank you,' she said, rising to allow him to recover the body as per procedure. 'It's just as I thought.' Her voice was low and steady as she spoke. 'The bastard's cut out her tongue.'

Reeling from the discovery, she left DI Downes to speak to the driver while she turned to grab some fresh air. As she reached the door a glint of silver caught her eye. Could it be? She recognised the frayed watch-strap immediately. But surely it couldn't be the same one? Pretending to do up her shoelaces, she stooped for a closer look. She was in the middle of a crime scene and disturbing evidence went against every police code. Yet, her fingers reached out and picked it up just the same. Ruby's heart fell like a stone. This was not just any watch; it was the echo of a memory. The words on the back were as clear as when she had them engraved twenty years ago. *To Nathan, love you forever, Ruby.*

CHAPTER THIRTY-SIX

'You've got it wrong,' Mrs Mead said, her fingers twisting the tightly bound tissue on her lap. 'That's not my April. She's not a prostitute, she's a model.'

'I'm sorry,' Ruby said. She had witnessed the whole gamut of emotions with this case.

Having travelled to Essex to break the news, she found that April's mother was clearly in denial. Who could blame her, Ruby thought. And on top of everything else, she hadn't even known she was a grandmother. It had not taken long for her team to find April on their system, given they had her fingerprints for a previous arrest for soliciting. She was better known for a number of domestics she'd had with her ex-boyfriend, who was now in prison serving time for assault. April had been treated as a high-risk victim of domestic abuse in the past, and details of her baby were on their system too. According to her friend, who reported her missing, she was giving up prostitution to go and live in Essex with her. But when she did not show up at the train station, alarm bells began to chime.

'I can't imagine how incredibly difficult this must be for you and your family, but we've checked her fingerprints as they're already on file. Mrs Mead. . .'

'Joan,' the woman sniffed.

'Joan. Were you aware that April had a baby in care?' Ruby had already spoken to social services and clarified that she had not been informed. The decision to keep her mother in the dark was April's. As an adult, she was entitled to make her own choices but

Ruby felt this act of secrecy was bound to deepen the wounds of grief suffered by her mother.

Joan frowned, the lines in her forehead instantly ageing her. 'A baby? No, no, no. This just proves you've got it wrong. I'd know if I was a grandmother now, wouldn't I? This is just stupid. How on earth would she have a baby without me knowing?'

'When was she born?' April's sister, Lara, asked.

Ruby sighed. It was tough enough breaking the news of April's death without adding this bombshell into the mix. 'She's six months old. She's been fostered, but April was working with social care with the view of getting her back.'

Silently, Lara's lips moved as she counted back the months. 'June. I remember she was acting all funny back then. We wanted to come and see her. Do you remember, Mum? But she wouldn't have it. She said she was going away on a photo shoot. I knew by her voice that something was wrong.'

'No,' Joan said. 'We saw her last month. She didn't look like she'd had a baby. I don't believe it.'

'It's been a terrible shock,' Ruby said, handing her a piece of folded notepaper. 'Here are the details of the social worker. She'll be in touch soon about Charley. You can call her in the meantime if you like.'

'Charley? Is that her name?' Lara said, fresh tears springing to her eyes. 'We used to argue over the name because I liked it too. We planned everything together when we were kids – our dream wedding, what we'd call our children. Do you remember, Mum. . . *Mum*?'

But Joan was staring into space, her face chalky white. Ruby guessed that somewhere in her mind she was turning over the fact that her daughter was never coming home. She had seen such behaviour many times. Overcome by grief, April's mother had withdrawn from the world that brought such pain. At least she had her family around her. Ruby couldn't understand why April had not called on them for support when it came to giving up her daughter. At least Joan didn't ask her for details about her daughter's death. She knew the time would come, but for now, she had not been able to take any more.

Ruby stood, just as there was a knock on the door. She hoped it was a family liaison officer. She would take the heat of their anger and frustrations, and Ruby felt nothing but admiration for her.

'Right, guys, what have we got?' Ruby asked as she faced her team. She had grouped them together just as she returned from her visit to Mrs Mead, and they had been given numerous tasks to add to their existing burgeoning workload.

'April's flat is being searched right now,' DC Ludgrove piped up. The youngest member of the team, Ruby had been impressed with his performance so far. A young man with no children or partner to answer to, his time was generously given to the job. 'She's been working through an online escort site as far as we know. Her computer's being seized for examination.'

'Good,' Ruby said. 'I want that examined as a priority.' She sighed, knowing the tech department were snowed under with requests. 'In the meantime, find out everything you can about the site she worked for. Contact them directly, see what information you can get by asking nicely. I want a list of her clients on my desk. Usually, with these sites users pay by credit card, and a percentage goes to the escort, along with cash in hand for any extras on the side. They'll have names and addresses. See if you can match any of those clients with the intel we have on Ellie Mason.'

She turned to DC Ash Baker. 'I want you to. . . Ash, are you OK?' she asked, watching the colour visibly drain from his face. She had meant to catch up with him about his wife's situation.

'Sorry,' he said, rubbing his chest. 'Just some pains, it's probably indigestion. I'll be OK in a minute.'

'Come into my office,' she said. 'I'll get you a drink of water.' She turned back to the heads still bobbing from behind their computers. 'C'mon, guys, you know what you have to do. We're under the cosh here.' There was one task she would have to carry out herself. It was too much of a coincidence that both Ellie and April were working girls. She needed to contact the Crosbys and find out if April was ever on their books.

'Here, let me open the window, let in a bit of air,' Ruby said, allowing a blast of petrol-polluted air to waft inside. She turned back to Ash, whose expression was tight and drawn. 'You look awful. Do you want me to call you a doctor?'

Ash shook his head, keeping his eyes on the floor. His hand had dropped away from his chest, and his fingers were now tightly interlinked. It was something she had seen before, and it could only mean one thing.

'You're not in any pain, are you?'

'No, Sarge,' he said. The use of her title raised another flicker of concern. This wasn't good, not good at all.

'What's happened? Is it your wife? Your daughters. . . do you need to go home?'

Ash tugged at his tie, loosening the knot. 'No, the wife's fine. She's settling in, and the kids are at my sister's.' He sighed, waving away her offer of a drink of water. 'It's just that. . .'

Ruby caught the slight tremble in his bottom lip as the words seemed to get stuck in his throat. She rose to close the blinds. It was a signal to her fellow workers that she was not to be disturbed. Pulling her chair up next to his, she spoke in soft, comforting tones. 'C'mon, mate, it can't be that bad, can it?'

'It is.' Ash swiped away a tear from the corner of his eye, but it was instantly replaced by another. His face bloomed pink, and Ruby laid her hand on his shoulder.

'Mate, it's me. If you need to speak to me in confidence. . .'

'Oh God, I can't believe I'm about to tell you this.' The words came out in a long exhale. 'But it's going to get out at some point.'

Ruby craned her head to one side. 'You're talking to the Queen of Fuck-ups. I'm sure it won't come as any great shock to me.'

Pulling a tissue from his pocket, Ash blew his nose. 'You don't understand. If this comes to light, I'll lose my job. I'll lose everything.'

Ruby straightened in her chair. 'Consider this conversation off the record. The sooner you tell me what it is, the sooner we can figure out what to do.'

CHAPTER THIRTY-SEVEN

'Ruby, what brings you to my door?' Downes said, looking past her to the adjacent townhouses across the street. He had a right to be surprised. Ruby was well aware that several of his neighbours were senior police officers. This was her first visit to his home, and the last thing she wanted was to give them something to talk about.

'It's work related,' she said. 'Can I come in?'

Downes drew back the red varnished door, risking one last cautionary glance outside before closing it behind her. 'You do know this is meant to be your day off, don't you?'

Ruby threw him a wayward grin. Rest days were a memory to her, and it wasn't going to change. Not with Doctor Tanner on the loose. More and more officers were being drafted in to help with the murder investigation, but she could not rest. Her personal connection to the case meant she was not going to squander time off by sitting at home and watching TV. 'This is important,' she said, slipping off her boots before entering the living room. 'I'm not interrupting anything, am I?'

The top two buttons of his shirt were undone, revealing a smattering of chest hair. A pair of pink Mr Men socks peeped out from beneath his faded jeans.

Ruby smiled.

He caught her grin and returned it. 'No, I was heading in myself a bit later on. A man can get fed up with his own company. Will I wet the tea?'

Ruby's eyes fell on the family photos that graced the cream stone fireplace. Happy and smiling, they reflected better times as Downes posed for the picture with his wife. She realised he was watching her, and tore her eyes away. With the smell of vanilla scented candles and the freshly polished surfaces, it was almost as if his wife had just stepped outside. This feminine home was not what Ruby had expected at all. She smiled, trying to hide her surprise. 'Sorry, what was that?'

'Tea?' Downes said, plumping up a fluffy cushion for her to sit down.

'No, thanks, I don't have time,' Ruby said, enjoying the feel of the plush cream carpet between her toes. It was a huge contrast to the cheap linoleum and thin red carpet gracing her floors. And, unlike her flat, Downes's home was spotlessly clean. 'Sorry to come out of the blue, I didn't want to be overheard.' She wrung her hands, remembering her vow to keep things strictly professional from now on. 'This isn't about me. It's Ash. He needs help, and I don't know where else to turn.'

'Right,' Downes said, his brows furrowed. 'What sort of trouble has he got himself into?'

'Do you know about his wife being sectioned?' Ruby said, hoping a potted history of his family background would present a buffer for what was to come.

Downes nodded.

'Right. Well, he's been suffering from depression. The last couple of years have been tough on him.'

'He's always laughing and joking at work,' Downes said. 'Did you see those posters on his wall? Jesus, there were words there I've never heard of in me life!'

'He's good at covering things up,' Ruby said. 'The poor guy's been through the mill.'

'We've all got our crosses to bear,' Downes said, his gaze landing on the photograph of his wife.

It was true. Ruby had had her own share of family problems, her mum's dementia being one of them. Moving her from their cosy shared home into Oakwood Residential Care had been tough. Now, her budget living accommodation was just within her means. She hated her flat but was happy to sacrifice her comfort if it meant her mother received better care. And she was not the only person who had been under stress: Downes had lost his wife to cancer the year before. For both, work had been a lifeline in some very choppy waters. It still was. She gave up trying to soften the blow of what was to come.

'Well, there's no easy way to tell you, so I'm just going to get on with it,' she said, clearing her throat. Downes and Baker went back a long way, and she hoped he would not hang him out to dry when the going got tough. It was something their superiors had a habit of doing.

'You know that I've instructed officers to come back to me with a list of April Mead's clients?'

Downes shook his head, a low groan escaping his lips. 'You're not telling me that. . .'

'Yes, I am,' Ruby said. 'He's been using her services on and off for the last couple of years. Not just April either, he knew Ellie Mason and some of the others too.'

'For feck's sake,' Downes said. 'If the papers find out about this. . . Worrow's gonna do her nut.'

'I know,' Ruby said, not wanting to stop in case she changed her mind. 'And there's more. April and Ellie used to work for the Crosby escort service. They were both fired within the last year.'

'So there is a connection,' Downes said. 'Which means they'll be scrutinising their clients even more. Did Ash use the girls when they worked for the Crosbys?'

'Yes, apparently he booked them online. He said he didn't know who they worked for.' Ruby sighed. 'It's not good, is it?'

'Flamin' idiot! Why didn't he come to me with this?'

'I guess he thought I'd soften the blow.'

Downes began to pace, running his fingers through his hair. 'You could look at this another way, the Crosbys are bumping off their ex-staff because they know too much. They work on discretion and have some influential names on their books.'

'Come off it, Jack. They're young girls. They wouldn't have the brass neck to go up against the Crosbys.'

'Well, they certainly won't now. Especially not with the last one having her tongue cut out. That's a warning to keep quiet, not a so-called fairy tale.'

'God! I wish I hadn't come around here now,' Ruby said, slinging her handbag over her shoulder as she rose to leave. It had been a bad idea coming here. She thought of Nathan's watch, and what Downes would say if he knew of its presence. Having discovered it planted at the murder scene, she had risked her career by hiding it in the old biscuit tin beneath the floorboards of her home. Whoever had left it at the pool had damaged the strap to make it appear as if it had fallen from his wrist. But Nathan had not worn it in years, and the leisure centre was not a place he frequented. Its appearance served to confirm just how far the killer was willing to go in order to set him up for the murders. But she had little time to dwell on it, as Downes beckoned her back to the sofa.

'Sit down, will ya. I'm only thinking out loud.'

Ruby frowned. 'Can't you see? Doctor Tanner would have treated those girls. They kept regular appointments with him because they weren't allowed to practice without a clean bill of health.'

'We need a list of Crosby's escorts. Do you think they're up for it?'

'Let me take care of that. What are we going to do about Ash?' Ruby said.

Downes puffed out his cheeks as he exhaled. 'With DCI Worrow heading the investigation? God, she'll have his guts for garters!'

Ruby nodded, knowing how hot she was when it came to police integrity.

'We can't stop the inevitable, we can only delay it.'

'I'm worried about Ash's mental health,' Ruby said. 'His mum's gone back home, and he's been left all alone. If I could persuade him to accept some help, maybe it would put him on a steady footing for what lies ahead.'

'Right,' Downes said, thoughtfully. 'You think he's that bad?'

'Yes. No. I don't know.' She exhaled a terse breath. 'He said something about being worth more dead than alive, but when I asked him about it he turned it into a joke. You know what he's like, always messing about.'

'Hmm... Has Ash used a credit card to pay for April's er. . . services?'

Ruby nodded.

Downes dragged his fingers through his hair. 'What a. . .'

'I think cockwomble is the word you're looking for today,' Ruby said, unable to stop the grin spreading on her face. She couldn't help it. Black humour was how police dealt with the darkest of times.

Downes returned her smile. 'What are we like, eh? How about a drink, a proper drink?' he said, eyeing the decanter of whiskey. It glinted from behind the doors of the glass cabinet next to a collection of crystal ornaments. The fact it was locked away told Ruby all she needed to know.

She was not going to provide him with the excuse he needed to open it. His drinking was something that had bothered her up until recently, and the last thing she wanted was for him to slip into the abyss again.

'No, thanks, I've got stuff to do. Can I use your loo before I go?'

Downes paused for the briefest of moments before nodding. 'It's straight upstairs.'

With its shiny chrome and dazzling tiles, the bathroom was just as immaculate as downstairs. Ruby reflected as she washed her hands – there was something not quite right about this house. It had bothered her since she came in. She opened the mirrored bathroom cabinet. To the left was an array of men's razors, shaving foam and deodorant. But Ruby's attention was on the right, her eyes dancing over the hair removal cream, Impulse deodorant and make-up remover. She frowned. What use would Downes have of these? The couple didn't have any children. She touched the bristles of the pink toothbrush stiffened from lack of use. A build-up of toothpaste had accumulated on the side. A small folding hairbrush contained soft blonde hairs within the bristles, the same colour as his wife's hair. Everything was as she'd left it over a year ago. A pang of sadness overcame her. There she was wittering on about work when he had problems of his own. She couldn't help but peek through his bedroom door as she stepped out on the landing. Like the rest of the house, it contained what she presumed were his wife's belongings. Clothes, shoes, they were all there… *What am I doing?* she thought, feeling guilty for her intrusion.

Ruby tried to appear nonchalant as Downes showed her outside. 'I hope you didn't mind me calling unannounced,' she said one more time. 'I just thought I'd pre-warn you so you can take Ash aside and have a quiet word. You know, to prepare him for what's ahead. I've spoken to him about counselling, maybe you could recommend it too.' She smiled, making a scissors motion with her fingers. 'We could come at him from both angles, the good old pincer technique.'

But Downes looked strained. 'You did the right thing. Speak to Luddy, have him arrange for the list of April's clients to go directly to me. If he asks why, just say it contains sensitive information.'

'Will do,' Ruby said. 'I'll have the names of the rest of the girls on the Crosby's books by today. That is, if they'll let me in. I've been in the doghouse since you turned up.'

Downes gave her a sheepish grin. He made no effort to dissuade her this time. 'Do you want me to come with you?'

Ruby snorted. 'Don't be daft! I'll see you back in the nick. If I get anything juicy, I'll give you a ring.'

'Make sure you do,' he said. 'I don't want any more dead bodies turning up on my patch today.'

'Oh, and boss?'

'Yes?'

'I like your socks.'

CHAPTER THIRTY-EIGHT

'How can you live in this place?' Lenny said, staring out the window of Ruby's flat. It offered a view of a high-rise building, and a graffiti-stained playground that parents were too scared to allow their children to visit. Her tower block had seen its fair share of police raids, drug busts and gangs but none were as dangerous as the man taking in the view.

She had not expected a response to her text so soon, much less one asking to meet at her flat.

'Isn't it about time you sorted yourself out, got yourself a decent gaff?'

Ruby cocked her head to one side, gazing at him with a level of mistrust. Something had changed. Lenny was talking to her like he did in the old days, back when they were teenagers. Growing up next door to each other, he was always bossing her around. Something had shifted when he got out of prison, but now Ruby felt movement again. Was this his way of making an effort? Was he so scared of losing Nathan that he'd decided to work with her rather than against her? Whatever the reason, she did not trust him one iota.

'Why did you ask to come here?' Ruby said, ignoring his question as she tried to pre-empt his next move. 'It doesn't look good for you to be seen at my address. Not when Nathan's mixed up in this investigation.'

Lenny offered a thin-lipped smile. 'Don't worry yourself, love. I've been avoiding the filth half my life. You think I can't get into this shitty flat without being seen?'

'Yeah, well we don't all live in the lap of luxury.' Ruby tightened her jacket around her. Heating was an extravagance, and she only had it on for a couple of hours at night. 'We're coming very close to nicking a suspect for the murders. That should take Nathan out of the frame. But I need a clear connection between the girls. I've been told Ellie and April were fired from your escort agency in the last year. Can you give me a list of your girls and their clients? In particular, any who knew Doctor Tanner.'

'They were all under his care,' Lenny said. 'In more ways than one from what I've heard.'

'This is crucial evidence,' Ruby said, trying to keep the topic away from sex. 'Tanner's our prime suspect. I'll see to it that you won't be implicated in any wrongdoing.'

Lenny raised his eyebrows. 'Too right you will. You'll get what you need. One of my staff will come to the nick, he'll give you what's relevant. Will that do you?'

'Yes, it will.' She wanted to question him about the acid attack, but her desire for him to leave was stronger. Had Nathan carried it out himself or arranged for someone else to do it? It shouldn't have made any difference, but the question kept her awake at night just the same.

He closed her flimsy curtains, an act of intimidation that Ruby instantly recognised. 'So tell me, how far along are you in this investigation of yours? You're taking your time, ain't you?'

'And you're my boss now, are you?' Ruby said in a droll voice. Lenny spoke to everyone as if he owned them, and she resented him viewing her as another part of his property.

'I don't care for your tone.'

Ruby sighed. All they did was bicker, and it was getting her nowhere. She glanced at her watch. Turning her police radio anticlockwise, she unclipped it from her shoulder harness. After their last meeting, she had not come unarmed. Her cuffs and gas nestled against her ribcage under her jacket. It was a message to Lenny that he would not lay hands on her again. She pressed her finger on the power button, tapping in her collar number until it came to life. She checked her channel and turned it down until it emanated a low buzzing noise: she was back on the radar, which meant control could track her location by GPS.

'Thanks for helping out but I've got to get back to work now, see how the investigation's progressing.'

Lenny, who had been scrutinising her every movement, folded his arms. 'You'd better progress it, because if my brother ends up behind bars. . .'

Ruby fished the car keys from her pocket, trying to remind herself that, despite his hard man act, Lenny was as worried about Nathan as she was. She thought of ten-year-old Lenny, and how he had absorbed his father's blows to protect Nathan from his wrath. Lenny, who had broken a broom over his father's back as he throttled his mother on the floor of their kitchen. The consequence of that act was a broken nose that would alter his features for ever.

But a lifetime of being shielded by his brother had left Nathan with an obligation he could never satisfy. She turned to face Lenny as she waited by the door for him to leave. 'I know you're worried, but I'm working as hard as I can. There's also a matter of these young girls getting slaughtered on my patch. Lisa, Ellie, April. . . Something tells me he won't stop there.'

'Those slags are of no interest to me,' Lenny said, straightening his tie as he walked towards the door. 'Just remember, time is ticking. I expect results soon.'

'Yeah, you and my DCI,' Ruby said, her final parting shot as he let himself out.

Taking a deep breath, she chastised herself for answering back but it was too hard to stop the spark of defiance slipping out as she spoke. Besides, if she didn't stand up to Lenny she would be for ever under his thumb. Why had he met her here at her flat? Was it to check up on her or was he just worried about Nathan? She gave up trying to second-guess the man she had grown up with, with his fractured background and unstable mental ability. She could torture herself for hours trying to understand his motives.

She crept around the flat as she freshened up to return to work. The ghost of his presence still lingered, making her uneasy. She would forgo the sandwich she was going to make, and eat on the hoof. She needed to get into the sanctuary of her office. At least there would be no unexpected surprises there. Pulling back her curtains, she threw one last glance onto the streets below. In another couple of hours twilight would be closing in; the twinkling lights filling the skyline and drawing in the predators that prowled the streets. She frowned, her fingers resting on the cracked windowpane. The killer was out there right now, his breath heavy as he planned his next move – but where? There were over eight and a half million people living in London, and over two hundred thousand of them in Hackney alone. But she wouldn't let the figures put her off. He was walking her pavements, and she would not rest until he was behind bars.

CHAPTER THIRTY-NINE

'You lot are spanking the overtime, aren't you?' Ruby said. The team was running at full strength, except for Eve, who was over four months pregnant, and Ash, who was visiting his wife. A quick call had ensured he was OK. Ruby's stomach growled, reminding her she had not eaten. Turning on her heels, she shoved her hands in her trouser pockets and fished out some change. 'Anyone want some chocolate from the machine?'

'We've eaten,' Luddy said, 'I. . . er. . . left you a sandwich in your office. Cheese and pickle, your favourite.'

'Homemade?' Ruby flashed him a smile.

Luddy nodded. 'Yup.'

'Ooh, you little beauty! And for afters? Any of your mum's famous homemade shortbread?'

'Of course, she made a biscuit tin full. I kept you a slice – it's all on your desk.'

'Tell your mum thanks from me. That'll go down a treat.'

Shoving her change back in her pocket, she made a round of teas and coffees for the workers before tucking into her food. Luddy was single and lived at home with his mum. He lived and breathed the job, and Ruby imagined Mrs Ludgrove had heard all about the office politics and their individual quirks. His colleagues used to take the piss out of her sending in food – until they tasted it and hounded him for more. Luddy said it made her feel useful, feeding the troops, and nobody in the office complained. She made a mental note to collect a few quid for a bunch of flowers – it was the least they could do. Ruby's eyes flicked to the framed photo on her crumb-laden desk. Her own mum would be having dinner now. Guilt bloomed inside her. She needed to set aside some time to pay her a visit; it had been days. She took another bite of her sandwich, finding it harder to swallow this time.

After catching up with her most urgent tasks, she joined her team. 'I just wanted to say thanks for coming in on your day off. I know we're all under pressure right now, but look after yourselves, OK?' Her team listened attentively as she brought them up to speed on Doctor Tanner. Choosing her words carefully, she disclosed his links with the historic child abduction and his employment within the Crosby escort agency from which Ellie and April had both been fired.

'But what about Lisa Caldwell?' Luddy piped up. 'There's nothing to link her death to this doctor, is there?'

'Not yet, and DCI Worrow seems convinced that Danny Smedley's our man,' Ruby said, glancing around her to check she wasn't in earshot. 'But don't discount the fact they could be linked. I want you to bear in mind that Lisa could have been a trial run.' She hated to term the young woman's death in such a flippant fashion, but such a term was a common one in police circles and immediately understood. It was not uncommon for criminals and deviants to bolster their confidence and build up to what was to come. Handbag snatches often led to sexual assaults; domestic abuse to murder. It was possible that Lisa Caldwell was nothing but practice for what was to come.

'Who's eaten all the shortbread?' DI Downes said, making Ruby jump.

'Boss, I didn't see you come in. I'm just briefing the team on what we have to date.'

Downes pulled out the freshly written statement nestled under his arm. 'This has just come in, marked for your attention. A list of women who worked in the same brothel as Ellie and April – all under the care of Doctor Tanner.' His glance fell on Ruby. 'Our very helpful witness believes that Tanner was also paying the women for sex, right up until he disappeared off the radar.'

'Which was. . . ?' Ruby asked, trying to tease out the information. It seemed that Lenny had come good and delivered the information as promised.

'Which was in the last couple of months. Tanner's not at his flat and neighbours haven't seen him.

'I've also had some results back from the post-mortem. We've been allocated a decent budget, allowing us to rush tests through. Traces of cotton wadding were found within the mouth cavity of our last victim, April Mead. This isn't cotton wool that you'd buy over the counter, it's a very particular type of wadding used during surgery to plug wounds.' He glanced around the room to ensure he had everyone's attention. 'The same cotton wadding was found in Ellie Mason's chest cavity. They've traced the origin, and it was sold by a pharmaceutical company that went out of business two years ago. Whoever used this would have had access to surgical supplies not available to Joe Public.'

'Guv, does this mean Nathan Crosby's no longer a suspect?' Luddy piped up. With his crumpled shirt and pallid complexion, the sixteen-hour shifts had taken their toll. But it could not extinguish his enthusiasm as new leads filtered through.

'No, he's still coming in when he surfaces,' Downes said. 'But I want you to dig up what you can on Doctor Tanner today. You'll be given tasking sheets and I want your updates before next briefing. For now, he's our number one priority.'

Ruby exhaled with relief. Hearing DI Downes say it out loud lifted her spirits, making her forget all about the disturbed sleep and Lenny's recent threats. 'I'd like the team to put some feelers out for the child Tanner was alleged to have abducted, guv? Contact social services, see if she's up for speaking to us again.' Nathan's bombshell that Tanner was responsible for the child found in the woods had opened up a new line of enquiry. If she could positively identify him as her abductor then his arrest would put a stop to the killing spree.

'You can, but if she's in the system they're not going to release her details quickly. You'll need to go through their legal team, and that takes time. Let's focus on putting a package together for Tanner's arrest. We've got enough with the witness statement and autopsy results for now.'

The fact her team were on the hunt for Doctor Tanner was good enough for Ruby. She would make it her business to speak to the girls listed in the statement personally. At last, pieces of the investigation were beginning to gel. She loved this part of the enquiry when their efforts started gaining momentum. She thought of the victims, and how they had died beneath a cruel, merciless hand. He was not stopping, not unless she stopped him first. The hunt was on.

CHAPTER FORTY

It was three thirty. In an hour and a half, London would fall into rush hour. Soon, grim-faced commuters would be pouring from work, while cars, taxis and double-decker buses would drive bumper to bumper, stalling Ruby's journey. If she was going to hit the streets, she had to do it now.

Immersed in viewing CCTV, DC Ludgrove jumped as she tapped his shoulder.

'Are you game for a trip out?' Ruby said, casting her eyes over his desk. To his right was a wad of well-thumbed paperwork and beside it a pad imprinted with hastily scribbled notes. Fresh from the briefing, she knew his workload was high, and the physical paperwork was nothing compared to the masses of statements, exhibits, and crime scene photos uploaded online. But she reasoned with herself that if they got a quick result, his enquiries could be cut in two.

'Sure,' he said, appearing relieved to get the opportunity to leave the office for a while. She laid out the list in front of him. The names had already been brought up during briefing but she went over them again to refresh his memory.

'There's nothing to link Lisa Caldwell to the escort agency, but I figure if we concentrate on Tanner's association with Ellie and April then we can build evidence of a case and go from there. You never know, he might admit to Lisa's death if he's banged to rights for the others.'

Luddy nodded. 'So we're only looking at women that Tanner knew who worked in the agency?'

Ruby nodded; she would have loved to have had the manpower to investigate all their leads at once, but time was precious and they had to prioritise. 'Ellie Mason was the most recent person to leave, followed by April Meade. There's nothing to say he won't target the girls currently working for the Crosbys, but given their reputation in the community, it's doubtful.'

'Then why are they fair game once they've left?' Luddy said. 'Surely, if the girls are acquainted with such a force, that should offer them some protection?'

'It doesn't work like that,' Ruby said. 'Lenny Crosby sees the girls as his property. Think of it as owning a fleet of cars: once you trade them in, you're no longer interested. He's the same with his girls. Once they leave he doesn't care what happens to them. That's why I think Tanner's only targeting girls who have left – they're easy targets.'

Luddy grabbed his black suit jacket from the back of his chair. 'Either that or the Crosbys bumped them off because they knew too much.'

Ruby felt a prickle of annoyance. Luddy had an inkling of her friendship with Nathan after the last high-profile incident. If he of all people was thinking this, what were the rest of the team saying? 'It's not Nathan Crosby. Haven't you been listening to briefing?' she snapped.

'Sorry, Sarge, it was just a thought,' he said, straightening his jacket and fixing his collar.

'Call me Ruby,' she muttered, taking a folded piece of paper from her trouser pocket. 'Now, we've only got two names on this list: Sharon Connors and Mandy Prentice. Mandy was the last to leave so my guess is that Sharon is next. Initial searches have brought up nothing for Mandy. She could have got married, moved abroad, or—'

'Or already be dead,' Luddy said.

'God, you're a bundle of laughs today, aren't you? Hopefully, Mandy's alive and well. I do know where Sharon is though. So, if you're up for it, I'd like to pay her a visit.'

'Sounds like a plan,' Luddy said, his words echoing down the corridor as they headed out to the car park. 'Hang on, wasn't there a team set up to speak to the working girls?'

Ruby nodded, impressed by his knowledge. 'Yes, I've spoken to the liaison officer. Sharon's down on her list as being spoken to – for all the good it did. All of our street girls have been on high alert since the murders, and even more so now that two of their own have been killed. Unfortunately, their addictions overrule any reservations. For most of them, it's business as usual. Given Sharon's told the officer where to shove their help, I'd like to approach it in a different way.' She threw him a grin. 'Don't look so worried, it shouldn't take long.'

Luddy glanced from left to right before lowering his voice. 'Something tells me this visit isn't by the book.'

Ruby shrugged. 'I'm not asking you to do anything that'll get you into trouble. I can go on my own. . .'

Luddy grinned. 'You're joking me, aren't you? Anything to get out of the office.'

Ruby smiled. Once the most cautious of the group, Luddy was developing an adventurous streak. She was a bad influence.

'Good,' she said, unable to stop the smile spreading over her face. 'I'm going to the loo. Here are the keys of the motor. You're driving, I'll see you out there.'

A quick pit stop was needed at their local convenience store. A box of chocolates, milk, bread, soup, ham and tomatoes were contained in her shopping bag, along with a six-pack of beer.

'Bit of an odd time to do your shopping,' Luddy said, casting an eye over her grocery bags as Ruby shoved them in the footwell of the car.

'They're not for me.' Clicking her seat belt into place, she did not elaborate further. Buying alcohol on duty was strictly forbidden, but it was a small rule that Ruby was willing to break if it helped her carry out her plan.

Minutes later, they were at their location. 'I recognise this street,' Luddy said as he turned the corner. 'It was in briefing.' Boarded-up shops lined the road, their windows daubed in purple and red graffiti tags. Frayed from the wind, a tattered British flag hung from the window of the occupied flats above. On the pavement below, a man in a beanie hat and combat jacket sat slumped with eyes open, high on whatever cocktail of drugs was racing through his veins. Ruby could not imagine what it must be like to have drug users and prostitutes walking the streets outside your home all day.

'It's where the toms hang out,' she said. 'Uniform is patrolling a few times a day, but they're still out here. Look…' She pointed to a hard-faced brunette hanging around the corner. 'Ten flippin' degrees and she's wearing a T-shirt and skirt.'

Her elbows clamped to her side, Sharon Connors peered at their car as it approached, most likely in the hope of business.

'Pull in next to her, and wind down your window,' she said to Luddy. 'And for God's sake, relax. I don't want her running off.' Ruby cast a sideways glance to see his knuckles tightening over the steering wheel. He would make a terrible undercover officer; Luddy always wore his heart on his sleeve.

As the car came to a halt, Sharon approached. She stuck her head in through the window of their vehicle.

'You're bleedin' Old Bill, aren't ya?' she muttered. 'I'm not on the game, I'm waiting for a friend.'

'Sure you are,' Ruby said, as Sharon spun off the same old line. That was what they always said. It was unfortunate that she recognised them – it meant having to go straight to plan B. 'Get in the car.'

Sharon hesitated, her eyes flicking left to right. But Ruby had caught sight of her ridiculous heels. She would not be running anywhere in that get-up.

'C'mon,' Ruby said, 'I just want a word. You must be freezing your tits off in this weather.'

'Get lost! All you give me is grief.' Sharon swivelled on her heel far more eloquently than Ruby would have given her credit for.

But Ruby wasn't ready to give up on her just yet. 'Stay here,' she said to Luddy, before jumping out of the car. Taking three sharp strides, she grabbed Sharon by the forearm, tightening her grip as the girl squealed in annoyance.

'Gerroff me!'

Ruby gave her a shake, almost sending her toppling into the gutter. 'What's it gonna take to get it through your thick skull that you're in danger?' She tapped the side of Sharon's head three times, and the girl flinched as she pulled away. But Ruby was quicker and caught her by the wrist. 'We've tried it the nice way, now we do it my way.' Dragging her over to the car, she opened the back door.

Luddy's eyebrows shot up in anticipation of Ruby's next move.

'I ain't going with you,' Sharon said. 'Get your filthy copper hands off me!'

'Just chill,' Ruby said, bundling her into the back. She slid in beside her, grateful she had thought to check the child locks were in place before they left. 'I'll pay you for your time, twenty quid for twenty minutes. Now, do you want the money or not?'

'What choice do I have?' Sharon bleated, pulling at the car door handle, which wouldn't open. Folding her arms, she flounced back on the seat, her lips in full pout. 'If I don't go with you, I'll end up being nicked. Isn't that right?'

'Totally,' Ruby said, with a satisfied smile. 'So what's it going to be?'

'Forty quid,' Sharon said, still pouting.

Ruby snorted with laughter. 'Pull the other one. I'll give you twenty and no more.' She turned to Luddy. 'Drive on if you will. Oh, I've always wanted to say that.'

Luddy turned on the engine and the weathered Ford Focus grumbled into life. Lately, there had been a ticking sound, and Ruby made a mental note to report it, but for now her aim was to get Sharon to safety.

'Where are we going?' Sharon said, peering through the smudged window. Needles of rain began to tap the glass, and she shrank back in her seat and wrapped her arms around herself.

'You'll find out soon enough,' Ruby said, turning up the heating dial.

But by the time they reached Ruby's flat, Sharon was swearing like a drunk.

'She's got an impressive repertoire,' Luddy smirked as he parked up outside Ruby's block of flats. 'Her and Ash would get on just fine.'

Ruby imparted a tight smile, knowing that Sharon and Ash would get on a bit too well. Had he used her services too?

Sharon didn't like surprises, Ruby could see that; the irony was that she was laying herself open for the biggest surprise of all by touting for business on the street where a murderer prowled.

Luddy had been to Ruby's flat just once before, and his expression spoke volumes as he walked through the door. But it was easy for him, brought up in a nice semi in the suburbs. He had a somewhat privileged background, unlike Ruby, who had to fight for everything she got. It was healthy to live where she did, she told herself. Helped keep her feet on the ground.

'Blimey,' Sharon said, her annoyance temporarily forgotten. 'Is this your place? It's worse than mine.'

'Have a seat, this won't take long.' She took the shopping from Luddy. His face paled, suggesting his enthusiasm for bending the rules had melted away.

Ruby prodded at the remote control until the television came to life. Her thirty-storey block of flats was a concrete mammoth. Satellite dishes sprouted from the side like mushrooms, with the occasional hanging basket softening the outlook. Ruby had only invested in Freeview, and she flicked on some random music station playing hip-hop loud enough to drown out their conversation. It competed with the usual thump, thump, thump of drum and bass from next door.

'Sandwich?' Ruby said, quickly making one up from the groceries she had just bought. 'Here,' she placed it on the cigarette cratered coffee table. 'It might do you some good.'

But Sharon sat with her eyes on the door like a rabbit captured for sport.

'Time we got down to business,' Ruby said, taking a seat beside her.

She turned to Luddy, who was still hanging around near the door. Hands deep in pockets, he bounced on the soles of his feet. His discomfort was painful to watch. Ruby decided to put him out of his misery. 'Can you wait in the car, mate? This won't take too long.'

Slowly, Ruby checked her appearance in her compact mirror, running a line of lipstick over her mouth. She smacked her lips together, smiling to check that none had trailed against her teeth. She liked red – it made her feel empowered, in control.

As Luddy left, Sharon raised an over-plucked eyebrow. 'What's the real reason you've brought me here? You want me all to yourself, is that what it is?'

'I've got a proposition for you,' Ruby said with a sigh.

CHAPTER FORTY-ONE

'You live with your boyfriend, don't you?' As far as Ruby knew, Sharon didn't have a pimp on board ready to beat her up if she didn't meet her quota. But her boyfriend was more than capable of manipulating her into heading out to the streets.

Sharon looked at her with a measure of distrust. 'What's it got to do with you?'

Ruby reiterated everything she knew about Doctor Tanner and how she believed that Sharon was next on the list.

But Sharon simply stared lifelessly into space. 'I've already told you lot, I can take care of myself.'

'Don't you get it?' Ruby said, unable to believe what she was hearing. 'Lisa, Ellie, April… they're all dead. You're next. There's no such thing as a safe punter any more. I'm working as hard as I can to get this guy off the streets, and I don't want your death on my conscience.'

Flopping back on the sofa Sharon stared up at the ceiling, allowing her tears to streak down each side of her face. 'It's alright for you, with your good job and copper friends,' she sniffed. 'I'm an addict. You don't know what it's like.'

Ruby exhaled an exasperated breath. Was she speaking a different language or something? She was trying to keep her alive. 'Believe it or not, I care about your sorry arse, and not because of what I can get out of you. I know you don't work the streets for fun, you do it because you have to.' Ruby knew about Sharon's background after a lengthy chat with the liaison officer. 'That fella of yours. . . how can he let you put your neck on the line? Do you think that's what a caring relationship involves? I care more about you than he does, and I barely know you. Why else would I be risking my job to keep you somewhere safe?' She checked her watch, tutting at the time that had ran away since her arrival. 'This is the plan. You're staying here tonight, away from your boyfriend. You can text him if you like, tell him you're down the station helping us with our enquiries.'

'I can't stay here. In your place? Why?'

'Because it will keep you safe.' Ruby pointed out her window to the streets below, where a monster prowled. 'Tanner's out there looking for you, I can feel it.' She returned her gaze to Sharon. 'I've bought soup, chocolates and even beer. Chill in front of the TV, veg out. I'll be back soon in a few hours and we can talk about it then.'

'I need a fix, that's what I need. Get me some gear. Please. There's a dealer the next floor up, just get me what I need and I'll stay.'

The fact that there were dealers living in the same block of flats came as no surprise. Ruby had turned a blind eye to their activities in the hope of a quiet life. There was no way she was going to approach them now. Besides, she didn't need to. If she wanted drugs, she knew where to get them. But her risk taking would only stretch so far.

Ruby dipped her fingers into her trouser pocket and pulled out twenty pounds. It was all she had, but enough to get Sharon through the night. 'I'm leaving this on the coffee table,' she said. 'If it's gone after you leave I won't say a word. But please, wait for me to get back so we can talk about this together.'

Staring at the cash, Sharon bit her bottom lip so hard it turned white.

'Sharon, focus. Do you want to live, or are you playing with your life because you just don't want to be here anymore?'

The answer was instant. 'Of course I want to live. What sort of a stupid question is that?'

'Because you're playing Russian roulette.' Ruby folded her arms. 'There's one bullet and, say, six chambers. Each time you go out on the streets represents a chamber in a gun. So you spin the chambers, and each time you tout for business you put that gun to your head and pull the trigger. Think about it, you're playing with your life.'

'I don't want to hear it,' Sharon said, blinking back the tears filling her red-rimmed eyes.

But Ruby continued. She had to hammer her message home. 'And it's not an easy death. He doesn't gently lull women to sleep, he tortures them. Why doesn't that frighten you? Because if you want to end it all, there's a lot nicer ways to die.' Ruby's belief that Sharon was suicidal seemed to make her think.

'I want a new life,' Sharon blurted, her words strained. 'I know Billy's no good for me. It's just that he's got me through some tough times in the past. But maybe you're right. If I can get myself out of this, then he will too.'

Finally, she's starting to see sense, Ruby thought, although she wasn't naive enough to believe that all was well. 'You have to be strong enough for the both of you, otherwise how's he going to feel if you end up dead?'

'I know, I know,' Sharon said, giving her a sideways glance.

But Ruby was not finished with her yet. Picking up her bag from the side of the sofa, she slid out a photo, moving the sandwich aside to place it on the coffee table before them. 'This is Ellie after that monster finished with her. He left us a message, this freak, operated on her while she was alive – and she would have felt every slice of pain.'

Sharon clamped her hand over her mouth, 'I knew her,' she whispered between her fingers. 'I knew her.'

'And you knew April, too, didn't you?' Ruby said, placing her photo beside Ellie's.

Sharon retched at the sight of April on the mortuary table. April with her mouth open, devoid of a tongue.

'He cut her tongue out. Can you imagine being awake and not being able to fight? He keeps them for days, suspended between life and death. I can't comprehend going through that sort of pain for five minutes, never mind three long days.' Ruby paused for breath. 'These girls were just like you. April was due to move to Essex to be near her family, but she took just one more punter.' As the tears trickled down Sharon's cheeks Ruby could see her words had the desired effect. She didn't know if April or Ellie *were* alive when Dr Tanner worked on them, but she had to be graphic to show Sharon where she was going to end up. 'When I get back, we'll talk about getting you into a women's refuge. I can get you safeguarding. I can. . .'

'I shouldn't have shouted at you,' Sharon said, wiping her nose with the back of her sleeve. 'You were only trying to help.'

'The shouting I can deal with,' Ruby said, 'but if you report me for bringing you here then I'll be removed from the investigation. Nobody knows the case like me. I'm willing to put my neck on the line to catch this monster. Do you understand what I'm saying? Because he's coming to get you, I can guarantee that.'

Sharon offered up a small smile. 'I won't dob you in, I ain't no grass.' She wiped her eyes, but no amount of rubbing could shift the dark shadows beneath. She stared at Ruby. The hatred she harboured had dissipated, replaced by a quiet respect. 'I don't think I'll ever get those pictures out of my head,' she said, swallowing back tears. 'Are you sure they suffered?'

Ruby nodded. She could have been kind, but the truth had to be brutal. Just like the world outside. It was the only way to open Sharon's eyes.

Sharon lowered her head, her limp hair hanging around her face. 'Catch him, yeah? Get the bastard and make him pay.'

'I will.' Ruby stood up to leave. 'Help yourself to food,' she said, noticing the sandwich had remained uneaten.

'There's only one thing I need,' Sharon said, snatching the twenty-pound note from the table in the living room. Plucking her phone from the sofa where Ruby had left it, she began to make a call.

CHAPTER FORTY-TWO

Luddy was leaning on the bonnet of the car, his face a mixture of fear and admiration. 'How did it go?'

'She thought I brought her here because I wanted her body,' Ruby smiled sadly. 'But I've managed to persuade her to stay just for safekeeping.'

'Well, there's an image,' Luddy said, grinning as he hopped into the car.

'Eww! You make sure you just keep it there.' She pulled across her seat belt after sliding into the seat beside him. 'I don't want anyone else knowing, I just need to keep her safe until I get back from work.' Sharon had proceeded to call her boyfriend and tell him she was safe. With the promise of a fix on her return, he seemed satisfied with the explanation.

The car engine produced its familiar knocking sound as it turned over, and Ruby reminded herself for the second time to book it in for repair.

'Sharon's not going to listen, you know,' Luddy said, bringing Ruby back to the task in hand. 'If there's one thing I've learned about working girls, it's that they don't trust people enough to accept help. People have let them down most of their lives. She'll be gone when you get back.'

Under normal circumstances Ruby would have teased Luddy about his so-called knowledge of street girls. But it wasn't funny, none of this was. She sighed, hoping she had not put herself on a path of forced retirement. 'Well, if it keeps her out of danger for a couple of hours then I'm happy,' she said. 'Now put your foot down, or we'll be caught up in the traffic. Downes will be wondering where we are.'

But there was no breaking the speed limit as far as Luddy was concerned, and he took the journey to the station with his usual caution. He pressed the brake pedal as the car rolled up to a set of traffic lights, glancing at Ruby as he waited for the lights to turn. 'What are you going to do if we find Mandy? Hunt her down and bring her home too?'

'Three's a crowd,' Ruby said, 'and there's not enough room in my flat. I thought we could bring her to your house instead.'

Luddy paled. 'You are kidding, aren't you?'

'Wouldn't your mum approve?' Ruby said with a grin. She nodded towards the traffic lights, which had turned green. 'Of course I'm kidding, you numpty. Now put your foot down, we've got work to do.'

CHAPTER FORTY-THREE

Noses twitching, the furred creatures stood on their hind legs, their beady black eyes following the doctor as he walked. Nightly, he strolled in the derelict hospital, led by the street light filtering through the insect-littered windows. He passed the rows of bed frames standing sentry in the wards. Each one interspersed by wall lamps, their rusted necks craned towards the doorway as if watching him pass. On the walls, faded cartoon characters guided him through the winding corridors and abandoned wards – but their smiles were macabre, their teeth sharp. Sometimes, as he passed, he could almost hear their whispers as they conspired against him. But then the air was different at night. That was when the shadows came to life and the walls began to breathe. Glass splintered underfoot as he returned to his surgery. The haunting smell of antiseptic filtered through his nostrils, but it was the memory of a scent from days long gone. He did not see the crumbling plaster, the missing ceiling tiles, nor smell the sour rodent urine laced with rotting brick. His mind brought him to a happier time – when he was respected and of value to the world. And now he was sure that time would come again. He froze, his feet temporarily stilled as he strained to hear a siren wail. Was it police or ambulance? In London, such sounds were part of the cacophony of city life.

People noticed less in the city. Plugged into the latest technology, like automatons, they filtered from work to the tubes. But he still drew the attention of those engaged with the world. Children would squeal and point, recoiling as he cast his one good eye in their direction. They were the most perfect creatures of all. But these days they were also the most guarded. Yet here he was, reduced to snatching dirty whores off the street. He licked his lips, a smile rising on his face. But then he did turn them into such pretty little girls.

His armpits damp with sweat, he unbuttoned his military coat and hooked it onto the rusted drip stand. He did not need it for his latest victim because he was no longer afforded the luxury of time. His newest victim had presented the greatest challenge, and he had come close to being discovered. It was a long time since he had made a house call, but they were next on the list. With the police investigation gaining momentum, they were hardly likely to come to him.

He smoothed the blanket over the sleeping form, his raspy breath cooling his parted lips. Excitement blossomed inside him. Escaping the tower block unnoticed had not been easy, but the drug he administered had been enough to make his latest guest appear drunk as they wobbled on their feet. In that estate, such behaviour did not raise an eyelid. All the same, it was a blessing that he had use of a lift because he couldn't have dragged them all the way down the flights of stairs. Like an addiction, his compulsion was demanding and would have forced him to try just the same.

The pleasure he derived from creating his works of art dissipated all too quickly, leaving him thirsting for more. He clamped a hand on his chest, slowing his breathing and taking comfort as his heart relaxed into a steady beat. Why was he putting himself through all this? The answer lay in the full-length mirror before him. He forced himself to look at his reflection: it was a face where pain and anger were laid bare. He glanced at his milky left eye through the vision of his right. They had not just taken his sight, they had taken everything. His revenge would not be complete until each of his victims was struck off the list.

He glanced down at the sleeping form, taking in its potential. He had art to present to the world, but sometimes it felt like the world wasn't listening. But many artists felt that way, tortured and undervalued. He was following in the footsteps of the greats. It was such a shame that fame had not come until their passing. Perhaps it would be the same for him. It gave him comfort to know that he would continue living long after his body had crumbled to powder and bone. He placed a hand on his victim's warm brow as if he could absorb their energy for what was to come. They were sleeping now, at peace with their pathetic life. He glanced at his watch: it was time to get to work.

CHAPTER FORTY-FOUR

'Tweedy,' Ruby said, with more than a hint of concern. She had come in the front way, not expecting to see her old school friend standing in line. 'What brings you here?' A sliver of panic rose within as she wondered what was so wrong that he had to drag himself to the front counter of Shoreditch police station to ask for her.

She ushered him into a side room. Devoid of CCTV cameras, it was a functional square block. Windowless, it held a table and chairs, a computer for taking statements, and a black panic strip, which ran horizontally against the walls.

'I was in the area, thought I'd pop in. . . see how things are going.'

Tweedy dragged out the hard plastic chair from beneath the table. Its rubber feet screeched against the flooring as he shoved it back to allow for his girth. He was casually dressed, wearing his usual tweed jacket and jeans. His jumper rode up as he sat down, exposing a generous midsection. One of the hazards of being six foot seven, Ruby thought. The small box room was free from the distractions of the busy main desk, and at least it afforded them some privacy. All the same, she felt uncomfortable with his presence at her place of work, particularly when he was there to discuss Nathan Crosby.

Her eyes were drawn to the slice of light under the door, blotted by the shadow on the other side. She frowned, glancing at Tweedy and then nodding silently towards the bottom of the door. This was not a safe environment to discuss incriminating details.

She was not the only one who looked uncomfortable. Tweedy rubbed his beard, a light sheen of sweat lacing his forehead.

Ruby tried to keep her tone light, but inside her stomach was twisting as she tried to figure out the reasons behind his impromptu visit. 'Obviously, I can't discuss details of the case. . .' She reeled off the textbook response just in case anyone was listening. 'But the investigation's progressing at a decent pace. I expect we'll be making an arrest very soon.' She leant forward, her voice barely audible. 'Is Nathan OK?' she whispered, followed by a louder: 'I trust everything is OK with you, nothing to add since your last statement?'

'No, all's good here,' he said, stuffing his hands deep in the pockets of his tweed jacket. 'I only wanted an update.'

'As soon as we've made an arrest I'll inform you.' Ruby glanced back at the door. Whoever was listening in was still out there. 'I have to ask you,' she said, shaking her head before he returned the response, 'have you heard from Nathan Crosby at all? We're very keen to eliminate him from our enquiries.'

A conspiratorial smile touched Tweedy's lips. 'He's away on business. He has an alibi for that day, hasn't he?'

'Oh yes, he has. As I said, it was just to go over a few minor things. We've a lot of enquiries to get through. I'd like to clear this up sooner rather than later.'

'For sure. From what I've heard, he'll be back in a couple of days. His property business has been manic. One of the district managers walked out. He's hiring a new guy, and he's meant to be shit hot. But that's Nathan for ya. You can't keep a good man down.' He looked at his watch. 'Anyway, I'd best shoot off. I don't want to keep you any longer.' As he pushed back his chair, the shadowy figure hastily slid away like a fleeting ghost just as dawn was about to break. Ruby wondered who had been listening in on their conversation. 'Know of any good places to eat around here?' Tweedy said, laying his hand on the door handle.

Ruby smiled. Like her, Tweedy had grown up in the East End. It may have changed in the past few years, with food chains replacing the restaurants that could not afford the increase in rent, but regardless of the change, he knew this place like the back of his hand. 'Sure. Do you like Nando's?' she said, playing along.

'Sounds good. Can you point me in the right direction?'

'It's just around the corner. I'll show you out.'

Ruby scoped the reception area as she left. Apart from desk staff sitting behind the glass counter, the once busy space was now empty. Taking a breath of evening air, they walked past The Eagle pub as they made their way down the street. Satisfied she was out of earshot, she glanced up at Tweedy as she spoke. Even in her heels he towered over her. 'Bloody hell, mate, what brought you to the nick? You do know we had an audience in there, don't you?'

Tweedy gave her a sheepish grin. 'Sorry, um. . . Nathan wanted an update. He's itching to go home.'

Ruby frowned. If Nathan wanted an update, he could have called her on their private phone. 'You gave me a fright. I thought something had happened to him.'

'God, no, he's fine. I'll be glad when things can get back to normal. He keeps beating me in *Call of Duty*.'

'Hmm,' Ruby said, giving him the eye. She was still not convinced he was telling the truth. 'Are you sure there's nothing else?'

'I hear you're going after Doctor Tanner,' Tweedy said, changing the subject.

'I am. Why?' Ruby raised her voice against the steady stream of traffic and pedestrians.

'I just wanted to say, well, to warn you, just be careful. I meant to say it when you were down last, but you were gone before I realised, and Nathan probably didn't think to tell you.'

'Tell me what?'

'He was a nasty piece of work. I'm surprised he managed to stay out of trouble this long. I stayed out of that side of things because

I don't have the stomach for it, but the doctor was very handy with a scalpel, if you know what I mean.'

'I know he was employed for more than bandaging up cuts and bruises,' she said.

'Yeah, there was that,' he said grimly. They were both referring to torture – the side of the business that Lenny employed to bring people around to his way of thinking. 'Tanner was an evil bastard, cunning. Liked to set people up. Sometimes he'd loosen people's bindings then wait around the corner and slit their throats as they tried to escape. I just wanted to let you know what you're up against. Don't underestimate him. He was a slippery fucker, quick on his feet.'

Hands in her trouser pockets, Ruby arched an eyebrow, giving Tweedy a look that said she could take care of herself.

'I know you're capable, but he's a trap setter. Don't go bundling in or you'll get hurt.' He sighed, his words trailing away on the exhale. 'I wouldn't want that on my conscience.'

'What do you mean, on your conscience?' Ruby said as small alarm bells began to activate in the back of her head.

Tweedy's gaze swivelled up the street and back to Ruby. 'What? Oh, nothing, just that I'd blame myself if I hadn't warned you. Anyway, it's time I was off. See ya round, yeah?'

'Sure. Thanks, mate, take care.'

She returned to the station, lost in thought. Tweedy was her friend, she shouldn't doubt him, but someone had planted the evidence in Nathan's home – and someone knew more than they were letting on. As she approached the front counter, she was pleased to see the face of Bob, a member of staff she had known since her probationary days. His small stout frame took up residence behind the glass, and with his balding head and greying beard, he reminded her of a garden gnome. She leant on the counter; she had to ask. 'Sorry, mate, but do you remember who was waiting to use the statement room while I was in there? I think someone else had it booked, but, you know what I'm like, I just went straight in.'

Bob raised his bushy grey eyebrows. 'Ah, I see. I did wonder why he was standing there. It was DI Downes. I told him the other room was free, but he said it was OK.'

'No worries, I'll speak to him now.'

Possibilities raced through her mind as she took the stairs to her floor. Why was DI Downes listening in, and how did he know Tweedy was there? Unless. . . she paused, chilled by the thought that greeted her. Unless Tweedy wasn't there to meet her. She made the presumption and ushered him into the room – but what if she was wrong? From the second they began talking, he seemed on edge. She had put it down to him being in a police station. But what if she had interrupted another meeting? One between Tweedy and her DI?

CHAPTER FORTY-FIVE

For the next couple of hours, Ruby threw herself into her work. She hated delegation but for now, she was happy to relinquish the hundreds of lines of enquiries to the various officers who were experts, specialising in their field. DI Downes and DCI Worrow were coming into their own, working together as a strong team. They had a band of dedicated officers, and enquiries were being rushed through. But she could not stop the creeping sense of unease. Someone close to her was lying; she just had to work out who.

Her priority was arresting the killer. As much as she wanted to clear Nathan's name, she was doing it for the victims first. That first night she had found Lisa Caldwell lying naked on the grass – hair splayed, lips slightly parted – she could not get her image out of her mind. And then there was Ellie, one of life's unfortunates, ending up cold and lifeless on a graveyard tomb. As for April. . . her unnatural red hair floating in the water, mingling with the blood of the cavity from which her tongue had been ruthlessly plucked. Ruby blinked tightly, the memories like wisps of smoke floating into the ether, but she needed them to drive her on to solve the case before he killed again.

She busied herself with reading through the online enquiries to date, tutting as each one drew up a blank. It seemed as if Doctor Tanner was a ghost – everywhere at once, yet impossible to find. Officers had updated the result of their investigations in turn and lines and lines of enquiries flooded her computer screen. Tanner's flat had been empty for so long that the electricity supply had been switched off due to unpaid bills. The benefits he once claimed were no longer being drawn, and his debit card was found, unused, on his kitchen table by searching officers. A warrant for his arrest had been granted, and he was not someone who would slip through a crowd unseen. But still, there were no signs of his existence. The newspapers were less than understanding, only too keen to point the finger of blame.

DCI Worrow had updated the system too, asking the question: what was he doing for food, heat, money? After researching his bank statements, officers revealed that Doctor Tanner had drawn out a large sum of cash right before this all began. The bank CCTV corroborated this information as he was seen making the withdrawal. Yet his passport was still in his flat and, apparently, he did not drive. CCTV was being interrogated, but such vast areas took time to download and view. Time was a luxury they could ill afford.

The next urgent line of enquiry was to safeguard the people on the list. The thought of Sharon being at her flat gave Ruby's stomach another excuse to churn. Sharon hated the police, and could just as easily pick up the phone and make an accusation against her. But would she hang her out to dry for trying to save her life?

Tomorrow she would continue the search for Mandy, one of the girls on Crosby's list. An ex-prostitute, she had dropped off the radar. A public appeal had been denied. Thanks to the press, the fact the murderer was targeting prostitutes was known to all. Ruby seethed as she had read them. The portrayal of the working girls as opposed to university student Lisa had left her stunned. Mandy would not appreciate her former life being splashed in the tabloids. Ruby could see the screaming headlines now. *Former prostitute on serial killer list.* And even if they used her first name in the appeal, how many Mandys were ex-prostitutes from the city centre?

She thought about her last case, and the grim basement reserved for the victims. How many basements were there in central London?

How many homes with bunkers since the war? Local hospitals had been checked, along with their spare rooms, mortuary and basements. Derelict buildings were next on the list. And then there were graveyards, sewers and more. Ruby took a deep breath as her emotions swelled. It felt as if she were staring out to sea as she sat in a tiny lifeboat waiting for a tsunami to engulf her. She thought of Sharon waiting in her flat. What if she wasn't there? What if Lenny paid her another visit and found her guest lying in her bed? What on earth would she say to that? As the last of the lights in the office were extinguished, she knew she could not delay it any longer; she had to go home.

Standing at the office door, Ruby glanced back at her desk, wondering if she would be there tomorrow, or up to her neck in disciplinary proceedings. She switched off her desk lamp, gathering up all her resolve to deal with what was waiting at home.

CHAPTER FORTY-SIX

As Ruby approached the front door of her flat, she pressed her ear to the wood. People like Sharon were unpredictable, capable of turning on the one person who tried to help because nobody had ever offered anything for free. She checked under the door for shadows. Such was her mistrust that it was becoming a habit. But all that seeped out was the orange glow of the lamp she had left turned on. She smiled to herself as she wondered if the music Sharon had left blaring on the TV had irritated her neighbours that day. Inconsiderate sods, she thought, pulling out her keys. It gave her a certain satisfaction to feed them a bit of their own medicine. Pushing open the door, she stood to one side before kicking off her heels and padding inside.

Releasing her breath, she glanced around the room. 'Sharon?' she called out, her disappointment growing as she realised she had gone. Shards of glass littered the linoleum floor, the remnants of the glass of milk she had poured her before she left. Ruby shook her head, slipping into a pair of old flats as she grabbed a dustpan and brush.

Ruby sighed. She had kept her safe for a while, but there was nothing more she could do. Her heart sank as she stepped inside her bedroom, and she wished that for once she had thought things through. What if Sharon had found her firearm? What if. . .? Her mind raced ahead, cursing her stupidity. How could she let herself get so emotionally involved in a case that she was taking potential victims into her own home? Yet, she knew that she would do it again if it meant saving a life. DC Ludgrove would be loyal; he would not dob her in, but he would never let her forget it either.

Judging by the crumpled bed, it appeared that Sharon had tried to sleep. Ruby's nose twitched as she pulled back her duvet, drawn by a sour smell. Swearing under her breath, she recoiled at what greeted her – a pool of vomit that had seeped right through to the mattress beneath. So Sharon had tried to sleep, but her body had turned on her, driving her to seek out the drug she could not do without. 'I shouldn't have given her the money,' Ruby muttered under her breath. But she knew if she didn't, Sharon would be spending another night on the street. Throwing back the duvet, she headed for the living room, unable to face cleaning up the mess after a full night on shift. Plucking her mobile from her bag, she read the text on her screen.

Had to bail. Needed a fix. Sorry about the bed. X Sharon

Ruby sighed as a wave of tiredness swept over her, the emotional and physical demands of the case making themselves known. She would have to throw out her mattress or at least bleach it within an inch of its life. Either way, she wasn't sleeping on it tonight. She stood with her hands on her hips, staring at the battered sofa that had come with the flat. There was no way she was sleeping on that. She could not go to the flat Nathan had bought her in case he was there. The last thing she wanted to do was to alert police to his hiding place a second time. She picked up her phone and made a call.

'Wotcha,' Downes said, answering the phone after just one ring.

'I was wondering. . .' Ruby said, pinching the bridge of her nose between finger and thumb, '. . .if you have a spare bed for the night. My flat's been broken into.' The cover story was necessary in case Sharon did a U-turn and made a false allegation that she had been dragged there against her will.

'Are you OK?' Downes said.

She pulled open the fridge and looked inside. 'I'm fine, but someone's eaten all my food and puked in my bed.'

'Merciful hour! A proper modern-day Goldilocks, aren't you? Have you called it in?'

It would have sounded comical were it not such a desperate situation. 'Nah, I'm pretty sure it's some kids on the block. I gave them a telling-off for smoking weed the other day. It's my fault for not locking it properly.'

'Yeah, but all the same—'

'Calling it in will make things difficult,' Ruby interrupted. 'Nothing's been taken.'

Silence fell as Downes absorbed her words. 'Sure, come on over. Have you eaten? I was just going to order a takeaway. My treat.'

'That'd be lovely, thanks.' It was just as well considering Ruby had given the last of her cash to Sharon. All that was left in her fridge were some tomatoes and a half pint of milk. As well as taking her money, the cheeky cow had taken her groceries too.

'Don't delay,' Downes said. 'I'll order it now so come straight round.'

Ruby knew that Downes would be glad of the company, although she hoped he would not see it for more than it was. All she wanted was to sleep, and she rolled her most unattractive pyjamas into her bag. As much as it pained her, she quickly grabbed some bin bags and shoved her bedding inside. The least she could do was leave them out for the binman. The flat smelt bad enough without coming back to that. There was one more thing left to do before she could leave. It took less than a minute to check her secret hiding place beneath the floorboards in the corner of her room. She exhaled with relief as she found her secret stash still in place. Sharon would've had to be a mind reader to find it. All the same, she had been stupid leaving her alone in her flat. The only good thing about it was there was nothing of value to steal. She pushed back the spare floorboard until it clicked into place. Rolling back the frayed red carpet, she inhaled the dusky smell of old cigarettes and dirt-trodden shoes. She sat back on her knees, pushing her hair back from her face as she wondered what had brought her to stay in such a godforsaken place. But there was no time to feel sorry for herself now.

She approached the front door, flinging it open until the inside handle dented the plasterboard on the other side. Gathering up all her strength, she kicked at the panel, just enough to make it appear that a break-in had taken place. Satisfied her story appeared plausible, she picked up her things and left.

CHAPTER FORTY-SEVEN

By eleven o'clock Downes's finest malt had worked its magic, making all the stress of the past week just float away. She had not meant to drink, but one glass led to two, and they were both mellowed, enjoying each other's company and the fact they were not sitting at home, alone. In the background soft jazz played, a testament to Downes's eclectic taste in music.

'I've missed this,' Downes said, stretching lazily on the sofa. He rested his sock-covered feet on Ruby's lap in the way that only close friends could. In jeans and a T-shirt, he appeared a younger version of the man who rushed around the office muttering under his breath. 'Is it safe to say we're back on an even keel?'

The ice cubes clinked in her tumbler as Ruby swirled the honeyed liquid. 'I'd like to be,' she said, her eyes still fixed on her glass, 'but how can I trust you if you're waiting to trip me up?' She sighed as she took in his puzzled expression. 'I know you were ear-wigging on my meeting with Tweedy Steve.'

'Jesus, Ruby, have you got eyes in the back of your head?' He threw her a roguish smile, his expression turning serious as he caught the uncertainty in her eyes. 'Everything I do is out of concern for you. I go to sleep, and all I can see is your face. I can't. . .'

'What? Can't *what*?' Ruby said, the last shred of annoyance dissipating.

Downes shook his head. 'I'm an old man, I shouldn't be getting myself tangled up with the likes of you. I just think it's time you sorted yourself out and ploughed your energy into your job.'

'But that's not up to you, is it?' Ruby said. 'I decide what's right for me.' Silence fell between them and her tone softened. 'But you're right, it's time I figured out what to do.'

'Ach, you can't ever leave the job. It's in your blood. And as much as you throw a blind eye to the Crosbys' shady dealings, I know it sickens you inside. These are the very people we're fighting the war against.' Jack leant forward and, picking up the decanter, topped up their drinks. 'Maybe you're right, you'll have to make a decision. I just hope for your sake that it's the right one. That team of yours would walk over broken glass if you asked them to. Can you say the same about the Crosbys?'

They fell into silence, their thoughts heavy. Ruby sank back a mouthful of her drink. 'Do you really think Nathan's responsible for those girls' deaths?'

Downes shrugged. 'I've been working long enough in this job to be able to look at it dispassionately. You've got the biggest heart, and if it was me in trouble you're the first person I'd want in my corner. . .'

'But?' Ruby said.

'Sometimes you need to step back and focus purely on the evidence. Nathan's no stranger to violence, and I'm worried that all this fairy-tale stuff is diverting you from what's really going on.'

'But the doctor. . .' Ruby said, too tired to be annoyed.

'The doctor worked for them in the past, and he's doing so now,' Downes said. 'Can't you see? They placed the evidence under Nathan's bed to distance themselves from his crimes. It's very clever when you look at it, but a ploy nonetheless.'

'I'm not going to argue, I just feel so guilty sitting here in comfort while there's a murderer on the loose.' She swallowed, the remnants of her drink feeling bitter in her mouth.

Downes clamped a hand on her knee and briefly gave it a little shake. 'Don't you worry, we'll get Tanner in. Worrow will have my balls as earrings if we don't.'

Ruby chuckled. Despite their disagreements, it was great to be back on good terms again.

The minutes ticked by. Downes hummed to some incomprehensible jazz tune Ruby had never heard of.

'How are you? Everything alright?' she asked, trying to play down her concerns. Jack was a proud man. He did not accept help easily despite the fact he spent half his life dictating to her.

Jack's humming stilled. 'You saw, didn't you? The stuff belonging to the missus – you saw it when you were snooping around upstairs.' The words were said with a strained smile.

'I wasn't snooping,' Ruby took another sip of whiskey. 'I was looking for some painkillers in the bathroom cabinet when I came across her stuff. And then when I came out of the hall, your bedroom door was open and. . .'

'And you thought you'd take a little peek inside to see what I was hiding. Did you think I had another woman or something?'

Ruby shook her head; apparently too quickly for Downes's liking, given his frown.

'Because you didn't think an auld fellow like me would be able to pull again?'

'Because I thought you were too much in love with your wife to let her go,' Ruby said sadly. 'And that's nothing to be ashamed of. Not many people experience such commitment in their lives.'

'But you're about to tell me that it's time to move on?'

'No, if having your wife's things in the house gives you comfort then where's the harm?'

'It's been over a year,' he sighed, his eyes taking in the ornaments that were obviously chosen by her – the collection of crystals, the matching ballerinas, the floral curtains with matching pelmet that went out of fashion years ago. 'I had the electrician round the other day. People just presume she's still alive.'

Ruby cupped the back of his hand. 'Well, they will do, won't they?'

'I tried. Bagged up all her stuff for charity and put it in the hall. Every day I told myself that I was too busy to donate it. But when I went to bed at night the room just felt so bare. The only thing that could get me to sleep would be a few drinks. . .'

'And a few drinks turned into a bottle a day?' Ruby asked.

'Yeah. I became so dependent that I couldn't get through work without it and, well, you know the rest.'

Ruby remembered how his drinking habits had worried her. The smell of whiskey on his breath, the flash of the silver hip flask, and the packet of mints he'd consume during the day. Then there were his bad tempers and crumpled clothes. It had taken a lot of willpower for him to detox and find his way back.

'So one day you had a dig at me for drinking at work. Something just clicked. I came home and threw out all my booze, unpacked Debbie's stuff and put it all back.'

'But you're OK to drink now?' Ruby said, feeling guilty for coming round.

'I'm not an alcoholic but I was heading towards it, so, I've made a pact – I only drink in company.'

Ruby shrugged. 'I guess it's better than being permanently pissed.'

Downes returned her smile. 'I'm not going to risk my pension so close to retirement. I'll leave all the risky stuff to you.'

'Why, Jack Downes, I'm sure I don't know what you mean,' Ruby said, her eyes twinkling as she spoke.

'I think you keep me young,' he said. 'I wake up in the morning, and I think, what's she going to get up to today?'

Ruby laughed. It was the first time that Downes had ever acknowledged her rule breaking as anything positive. 'Spice of life,' she said, wondering if he'd be still laughing if he heard about what she'd got up to with Sharon. He shifted position and cosied up beside her, taking the empty glass from her hand. His skin was warm and comforting to the touch. Ruby's heart jolted in her chest; she knew what was coming next.

'We don't have to part ways here, you know,' he murmured. 'There's a spare bed all made up, but if you prefer. . .'

Ruby knew what he meant but when work wasn't occupying her thoughts, her head was consumed with Nathan. Lately, she had renewed hope that they could get back together and Nathan might be able to play it straight. She was not going to do anything to jeopardise that. She straightened her posture. Downes was good for her, and she would have enjoyed a night of comfort in his arms. Strong and rugged, he was just the medicine to finish a bad day. But it wouldn't have felt right, not anymore.

'Thanks, but I'm shattered,' she said, truthfully, rising from the sofa. 'If you want, I can come back after work and help you pack away Debbie's things?' It was the best she could come up with. . . extending her friendship when she had nothing left to give.

Jack nodded. 'Sure, that would be grand. You can help me sort what's of use and what's not.'

'Here's to new beginnings,' she said, taking her glass and raising it one last time.

'New beginnings,' Downes said.

CHAPTER FORTY-EIGHT

A half-drunk mug of tea, a tortoise shaped paperweight and a box of staples… each item held down the piles of paperwork which flapped under the gust of icy wind blasting in through Ruby's office window. She wriggled her toes as she released them from the confines of her heels, enjoying the sensation of cool air on her skin. What she really needed was to go for a run, to push herself to the limit until her lungs burned, forcing her thoughts to become clear. But now, as she stared at the information on her computer screen she wondered how she was going to talk her way out of this one.

'Are ya ailing for something? It's like the Antarctic in here,' Downes said, making her jump.

'I just needed some air to clear my head.' She reached over and pulled the window shut, silencing the flapping paper and returning her office to normality. Or, at least as normal as it could be given what she had just discovered.

'You might want to take a look at this.' Ruby pointed to the latest witness statement that had been uploaded to the system. 'It turns out that Frances Crosby agrees with my theory. She's provided us with a list of regular clients – sanitised to some degree – who used their services.'

Downes peered over her shoulder, squinting, as he scanned the list of names.

'Some of these are well known. Is this document restricted?'

'Yep. Visible only to you, me and DCI Worrow.'

She allowed the words to sink in as Downes scanned the list. She could feel his breath on her hair, and worry crawled over her like an errant spider as she waited for a reaction.

'Ashley Baker,' he said, finally. 'Have you checked the phone number?'

The list comprised names and phone numbers, with little else. But that was all that was needed to link DC Ash Baker with the victims to date. 'Yeah, and it matches the one on his file. It'll take DCI Worrow all of two minutes to cross-reference it when she twigs. The only good thing is that the troops on the ground won't know.' Her team were working to breaking point. Something like this was bound to affect morale. She cursed Ash's stupidity, and cursed herself for not picking up on his depression sooner.

Downes exhaled sharply. 'Fuck!'

A knock on the door brought Ruby back to her senses, and she minimised the computer programme, trying not to look as if she had stumbled across some terrible secret. 'Yes?' she said, shoving her bare feet back into her shoes. It was Ash, the last person she wanted to see given what they had been discussing just seconds earlier. She prayed that Downes would not say anything, not yet.

Ruby imagined Frances Crosby gloating over the ripple effect that her statement would have caused. She had hinted often enough how they had infiltrated the police, and now the evidence was seared on the back of Ruby's eyelids. Ash's name and phone number in black and white. Was Ash Baker the prostitute killer? The question flashed up before her, taking her by surprise. Her thoughts sometimes did that. It was the side of her personality that wasn't afraid to ask the question, the side that trusted nobody, not even her own colleagues.

'Alright?' Ash said, a concerned tone touching his voice. His eyes flickered to the computer monitor and back to Ruby. He must have known they were talking about him when he walked in.

'Fine, sorry,' she said, sweeping back an errant lock of hair from her eyes. 'I was miles away. What is it?'

'I was just asking if either of you wanted a cuppa tea. Luddy's on the phone to the CPS, and I offered to get a round in.'

A tray of teas and coffees always preluded a call with the Crown Prosecution Service. Such consultations could take an hour or more to get through. The team's cases didn't just begin and end with the one they were working on, there was a never-ending backlog that demanded their attention too. There was never such a thing as a clear desk in the police, and an empty email inbox was unheard of. As Ruby declined his offer, she dismissed the thought that had taken her by surprise. Of course Ash had nothing to do with the murders. She had her suspect, now all she had to do was to find him. But a hint of doubt still lingered. She had been wrong once, could she be wrong again?

'Is everything OK?' Ash asked, pausing in the doorway. Ruby glanced at Downes, whose mouth was set in a thin hard line.

'Yeah,' Ruby said, forcing a smile, 'just a discrepancy with the overtime figures. It's sorted out now.'

Ash chortled. 'Good, because I'm skint.'

'Skint? You should be loaded, all the overtime you've been doing. What are you doing with it all?' Downes said.

Ruby stiffened; she knew it was a dig. This needed to be handled properly. The last thing she wanted was a showdown between them.

But if Ash noticed the challenge in Downes's voice, he did not acknowledge it. 'Goes like sand through your fingers when you have kids.' His words trailed away as he closed the door behind him.

'That was close,' Ruby said, plopping down in her chair. 'Best not to say anything until we've worked out what to do with it.'

Downes exhaled loudly, and Ruby could see that the burden of information lay heavy on his shoulders. He had known Ash a lot longer than her, and seemed shocked by what he knew.

'He could lose his job over this – his pension, everything.'

'You don't need to tell me about dodgy acquaintances,' Ruby said. 'I do my best to keep out of trouble but sometimes water and oil mix.'

'Hmm,' Downes said, 'they do.'

'You don't think Ash knows anything about the murders, do you?' Ruby said, finally spitting out the words bouncing around in her brain.

'No, that's not him.'

Ruby folded her arms as she spun around in her chair to face him. 'That's exactly what I've been saying about Nathan. Funny, isn't it? How you can change your perspective when it comes to someone you know.' But their camaraderie was short-lived as both Ruby's desk phone and Downes's mobile rang in tandem. She grabbed the handset, keeping one eye on Downes. Her heart sank as she received the information from control. There was another murder – and it was the last person she expected.

CHAPTER FORTY-NINE

'I know this place, I brought the missus here once,' DC Ash Baker said, manoeuvring the unmarked police car through the streets of London. 'The manager looks like Boycie out of *Only Fools and Horses*.'

Ruby mumbled a reply, wishing it was Downes at her side instead of Ash. A major incident had come in: a double stabbing at the council offices, which warranted his attendance. But it had nothing to do with Ruby's investigation, and he had instructed Ash to attend with her instead. It made sense. Given the killer's theatrics, he appeared to be enjoying the attention, and two sets of eyes on the scene were better than one in case he returned to watch.

'This isn't right,' Ruby said, as Ash killed the engine of the car. 'Sharon was meant to be next on the list, Sharon Connors then Mandy Prentice. Who's this Nikki? And why don't we know about her?'

Nikki Ellis was the name given by the witness, who stated they knew the victim from school. At the mention of being found in fancy dress, the call taker had placed a tag on the incident and alerted her. Ruby turned to Ash as he wrapped his fingers around the door handle. She was better off asking him this now, in the privacy of the car.

'Did you know a Nikki? Was she a working girl?'

The cheerful expression Ash had been wearing slowly slid away. Ruby knew that the incessant chatter and jokey banter was a cover-up for the turmoil inside. 'No, I didn't know of any Nikki.' He released the door handle, looking her earnestly in the face. 'The DI knows, doesn't he? I could tell by the look on his face.'

Ruby nodded. 'We've got a witness statement which provides a list of Ellie and April's regulars when they worked for the Crosbys' escort agency. Your name is one of them. Your phone number matches the one on the personnel system.'

Ash's mouth dropped open as all colour left his face. 'Does Worrow. . .?' A thin sheen of sweat coated his forehead, and he swallowed hard. 'Does she know?'

'Take a deep breath, mate, we'll get this sorted,' Ruby said. But when Ash didn't respond, she leaned forward, touching him on the arm. 'You don't look too good. Do you want me to call a doctor?'

Loosening his tie, Ash looked like a heart-attack candidate as he tried to catch his breath. 'No, I'm OK,' he said. 'It was just a shock. I thought I'd have a bit more time. . .'

Time for what? Ruby wondered. Surely he knew this would come out in the investigation? 'It's on the system as restricted. The only people who know are me and Downes; DCI Worrow will too, at some point. I'm sorry. The DI said he'd back you, but he's pissed off because you didn't confide in him first.'

'I was embarrassed,' Ash said. 'And I thought it would be sorted by now.'

'What do you mean, "sorted"?' Ruby said, her attention drawn to her airwave radio as control demanded an update. Using her call sign, she updated their presence on the scene. She needed to bottom this out with Ash, but he was already slamming the door behind him as he got out of the car. Ruby shook her head. She had a bad feeling about this, and her sense of foreboding was growing by the minute.

The Robin Hood was a gastro pub, which served traditional British food. Popular with the recent influx of Shoreditch hipsters, it was located on Paul Street, just off the main drag. The split-level setting was arranged so that the downstairs area accommodated drinkers, while a climb up a spiral staircase brought them to the restaurant. Such information was conveyed to Ruby by Ash in the car park at the rear of the building. He was back in chatty mode, apparently willing to talk about anything as long as it was not about him.

'I've always meant to try this place,' Ruby said, as Ash paused for breath. 'Doubt I will be now, though. There's nothing more off-putting than going to a crime scene on a night out.'

As she ducked beneath the police tape she was approached by a grumpy-looking man from the pavement, tall, thin and sporting a moustache, just like the character Ash had described.

He glared down his nose at them, the ends of his dark eyebrows raised in two sharp points. 'They told me you're the person in charge. When am I going to be allowed back into *my* business?' He emphasised *my*, as if the police were an inconvenience, daring to waste his precious time.

Ruby gave him a stern stare, chalking up another reason why she would not be dining in his establishment. 'It's a murder investigation, you'll be notified in due course.'

Turning on her heel, she accepted the overshoes and suit as doled out by the bored-looking officer on the scene. While the front of the building belied a tasteful modern design, the same could not be said for the rear. Disused freezers lay in the back yard, which was cluttered with torn-up boxes, overstuffed bins, and a smoking area littered with overflowing ashtrays. The private quarters of the Robin Hood were hidden away from the public, and left a lot to be desired. She picked her way through until she reached the back door, which led to the kitchen.

'No DI Downes today?' Katie, the crime scene officer, said as Ruby stepped in.

''Fraid not,' Ruby said. 'He's been called away.' She consoled herself that at least she would not have to listen to Katie dropping hints about what pubs she frequented in the hope of being asked out for a drink. With a twenty-year age gap between them, Ruby wondered why a girl as pretty as the fair-haired Katie didn't date men nearer her own age.

Katie's voice trailed behind her as she directed Ruby and Ash to the walk-in freezer at the back. 'We've not started yet,' she said. 'Uniform attended in the first instance. The caller thought it was someone who'd broken into the pub and got themselves locked in. Point of entry was through a downstairs window, using a crowbar to force it open. There was no alarm.'

The pub had not invested in double-glazed windows, and the old wooden frames would have held little resistance. Ruby paused at the open fridge door, chilled by the drop in temperature. But just like Jack Downes, Ash was impatient, pushing past her to inspect the body in situ.

'He's around the corner, behind those shelves. He was only a young lad,' Katie said. 'Such a shame.'

'*He?*' Ruby asked. 'I thought it was a girl. . .? Nikki.'

'Nicky, as in Nick,' Katie corrected.

The controller must have got it wrong. Ruby touched the freezer door with a gloved hand, inspecting the other side. The scratch marks ran deep; his desperate attempts to escape engraved in blood. Slowly, she inspected the scene, tracing the footsteps of the person who discovered him in the frosted floor. It was unusual for crime scene investigators to turn up first, but senior officers were thin on the ground. Ruby turned a corner to see Ash standing over the figure of a young man huddled on the cold tiles. She paused to take a breath, gather her strength. Downes's words still rang in her ears, but no matter how hard she tried, she struggled to view this scene dispassionately. The best she could do was to allow her police training to kick in, and wait for the nightmares to come later. It was grim viewing to see a man so young die in such horrific circumstances. She'd had her fill of such scenes, and the sinking feeling never went away. The finger of blame made itself known, feeling as real as if it had physically poked her in the chest. She was meant to be a defender from the evil that roamed her streets, but lately, no matter what she did, it never seemed good enough.

She knelt beside the body, her eyes roaming over him in search of clues. The green tights and feathered cap would have given him little protection from the sub-zero temperatures that claimed his life. Like a waxwork dummy, his face was absent of colour and buried in between his knees. His arms wrapped tightly around his legs, clinging to his own body for a comfort that would not come. A scene played out before her: the young man begging, pleading, scratching at the door for release when, finally, exposure had taken a hold, along with the realisation he was going to die in this place all alone. Had he been unconscious when he came here? Someone had dressed him, surely. The tunic he was wearing seemed cheap compared to the other outfits, and the delivery hurried. A rush of anger rose up inside her as she caught sight of his bloodstained fingers and torn nails. Ruby knew from the previous post-mortems that Ellie and April had been drugged. Had the killer left Nick here? Drugging him just enough to ensure he awoke after he had gone? She shivered as the cold bit through the thin layer of her blazer.

'What do you think he was doing with those?' Ruby said, rising as she peered at a split bag of chips on the floor.

'Trying to keep warm maybe?' Ash shrugged, checking his phone.

'With frozen spuds? They wouldn't provide much comfort.' She sighed, her breath casting a frosted cloud. 'But I get why he's here. He's Peter Pan, the boy who never grew up.'

'Frozen in time, I get it,' Ash said, the words bringing a chilling reminder of a previous case.

Ruby shuddered. 'C'mon, let's leave them to it. The sooner we're through, the sooner they can get that poor kid out of here.' She knew it sounded silly talking as if he was still alive, but she had always held a quiet respect for the deceased.

As they walked to the car, Ruby updated DI Downes, relaying her belief that Nick's death was connected with the case. But the update worked both ways, and she was shocked to discover what her team had unearthed so far. As she ended her call, she kicked the car tyre, expelling her frustration. Nicky Ellis, their Peter Pan victim, had been identified as a rent boy who worked the local area. Just like the others, he was an ex-employee of the Crosby escort service. It was information that had come too late. Muttering as she paced, Ruby gave the tyre another kick, attracting glances from passers-by.

'Are you alright, Sarge?' It was Ash's turn to ask her.

'No, I'm *not* alright,' she said, unable to suppress the anger consuming her. 'I should have asked Frances Crosby if they had any men on their books, but I didn't.'

'You weren't to know. We can only go on the information we're given, isn't that what you always tell me?'

But the words were of little comfort to Ruby, who could feel a lump rising in her throat. 'It's not just that, we've got his address. The kid lived in the same tower block as me. I probably passed him on the stairs.' She inhaled a shuddering breath as she fought back the tears that threatened to engulf her.

Ash fell into silence, his inability to handle her emotions a testament to his inadequacy when dealing with the fairer sex. Wrenching open the door of the car, he got in without saying another word. Ruby took the passenger seat, imagining Ash ignoring his wife when she was emotional and upset. People reacted to stress in different ways. Failing to acknowledge it seemed to be Ash's. But she couldn't worry about him now, she had more important thoughts on her mind. The killer's efforts were becoming harried. He was flying through the motions, hurtling towards the endgame with speed.

'He's nearing the end,' Ruby said. 'It's why he's rushing. He knows we're onto him.'

'My thoughts exactly,' Ash said, his gaze firmly on the road ahead. 'It's why I'd like to take a detour. There's an address I need to check out. You game?'

Ruby glanced at Ash. His fists were curled over the steering wheel; his face filled with determination. The feeling of unease returned, and her sixth sense told her there was more going on here than he had been willing to let on. Whatever it was, now seemed the time to face it.

'Lead the way,' she said, buckling her seat belt into place.

CHAPTER FIFTY

'Shazza, babe, are you going out or what?' Billy Hodges craned his neck from the programme he was watching on TV. He had been sitting there for six hours straight, rising only to use the toilet and boil the kettle to make a Pot Noodle. His hand nestled on his groin underneath the tracksuit bottoms given to him during his last stay in custody.

'You knob,' Sharon said, checking her hair for split ends. 'How can you ask me that when my mates are dead?'

'What? You wasn't that friendly with them.'

Sharon's hair fell from her fingers, and she stretched from her chair to kick his outstretched feet. 'That's hardly the point. You heard that copper, I'm next.'

'Please, babe, I'm climbing the walls here.' A burst of laughter emanated from the television in the corner, maniacal in its deliverance.

Sharon sank back into the chair. 'Well, why don't you get off your lazy arse and earn some money instead of sponging off me all the time?'

'It's not that easy for me. Who's going to give me a job? Please, babe. Just one more job – to take the edge off.'

His voice had taken on a whiny tone, like fingernails scraping on a blackboard. Raising her knees up to her chest, Sharon hugged them in an attempt to get warm. But the chill was not coming from her flat. It was from within: a warning of what was to come. She licked her lips, now dry and cracked from standing on street corners in the bitter chill. She glared at her boyfriend – a constant source of annoyance.

'You said you'd sort something out today – ask that Danny Harris for work. But all you've done is sit on your arse. I told you what that copper said to me. You're the one that should be locked up, trying to send me out there when I'm next on the list.'

'Yeah, well, she was taking a liberty, bringing you back to her flat. You should have reported her for that.'

'God! I wish I didn't tell you now,' Sharon pulled her baggy sweatshirt sleeves between finger and thumb. 'She was only trying to help. I saw their faces. . . those girls he killed. They looked like. . .'

Billy clicked his fingers. 'I know, why don't you hit that copper up for some more money? Tell her you'll report her for harassment if she doesn't pay up?'

Sharon pulled the cushion from behind her back and launched it in her boyfriend's direction. 'I'm not scrounging from the only person that's ever given a damn. Besides, she ain't got none. You should see the state of her place, it's worse than ours.' Looking around the bare flat, Sharon knew it wasn't far off the truth. She tried to keep it clean with the little money they had – it wasn't as if there was much to polish. Billy had sold off anything of value, even the Wade Betty Boop ornaments her mother gave her before she died.

Billy writhed in his chair, wrapping his arms around his stomach to ward off the pain. 'Please, babe, I'm dying here. Just one more go.' He glanced over, watching Sharon gnaw on what was left of her fingernails. 'You're clucking yourself. We'll sort ourselves out tonight and go to the clinic in the morning, I swear down.'

Sharon stared at the television as another burst of laughter ensued. There was something morose about their happiness. But Billy was right: she felt like she was festering inside. It was nothing compared to how she would feel later on if she didn't get another fix. 'Maybe you're right, just a bit of brown to take the edge off so we can get some sleep.'

Billy leant forward, his face hopeful. 'Yeah. I'm not asking you to go off with some psycho, just one of your regulars.'

Sharon rolled her eyes. 'If I still had regulars, I wouldn't be walking the streets, now, would I?'

But Billy wasn't willing to give up yet. 'C'mon, you must know of someone. Offer him a discount, or give him a bit extra. A gorgeous girl like you – they won't be able to say no.'

As Sharon smoothed her limp hair, she knew her days of being gorgeous were behind her. She sighed. A restful night was what was needed, and tomorrow they could start with a fresh slate. 'There might be someone,' she said, bringing up the contacts list on her phone. 'But this is the last time.' Tomorrow she would go to the clinic and get help, with or without her boyfriend.

CHAPTER FIFTY-ONE

'The Queen Elizabeth?' Ruby said, staring up at the looming derelict building. Like many properties in Hackney, it had been earmarked for redevelopment and was currently stalled at the planning application stage. Surrounded by panels of high wire fencing, it was clearly marked with 'no trespassing' signs. The hospital was one of the first properties Ruby had recommended for a visit by uniformed patrol. 'This area's already been checked,' she said. She'd read the report herself. Having tracked down the caretaker, uniformed officers had gained entry, declaring the building devoid of life.

'I'd like to have another look around,' DC Ash Baker said, pulling up the handbrake as the car came to a halt on Hackney Road 'It won't take me a minute. If you want to wait in the car. . .'

The words had barely left his lips before Ruby interrupted him. 'Ash, I know you, and most of the time it's an effort to get you to get out of your chair to briefing, so I'm not buying that you've suddenly decided to walk around a derelict building on your own.'

'Like I said, I. . .' he sighed, wilting under the pressure of Ruby's stare. 'I might have had a tip-off.'

'As in a tip-off to the killer's whereabouts? Why didn't you say?'

'It's going to sound daft. That's why I didn't call it in.'

'I'll be the judge of that. Where did you get your information?'

'From a dead man,' Ash said, giving her a furtive glance. 'Nicky Ellis, to be exact, with the help of a bag of frozen chips.'

'You've lost me,' Ruby said, wondering if Ash had finally lost the plot.

'He left a message written out on the floor. He must have done it when he realised he wasn't going to make it. I guess it was his way of telling us where he'd been.'

Ruby arched both eyebrows. 'With the help of a bag of chips?' A black cab rumbled past – ordinary people going about their business, on this, the strangest of days.

Ash gave a hollow laugh. 'As unlikely as it seems. I found the words "Queen Liz" spelt out on the floor.'

'This is all very Sherlock Holmes,' Ruby said. 'Are you sure?'

Ash nodded. 'I messed them up when I leant over to look at the body, sorry. I didn't mean to, but I figured I was in enough trouble, and I'd check it out myself.'

'"Queen Liz" might not refer to the hospital, it could mean anything.' Ruby tried to contain her annoyance. He was right. It *was* too far-fetched, and she wasn't buying his explanation. Besides, if he had stumbled across the doctor's lair, then why did he want to keep it to himself? Regardless of her reservations, she wasn't leaving without checking it out. 'Right. Well, we can't take any chances. Wait here until I call it in. You're not to go in there without backup. Look at you,' she said, casting an eye over his expansive belly. 'You haven't even got a stab vest on.'

'I won't need it,' Ash said quietly. But there was something about his demeanour that gave Ruby cause for concern. 'Are you alri—' Her words were interrupted as Ash slammed on the brakes.

'Oops, sorry,' he said, pulling up at the pedestrian traffic lights as a woman with a pram walked across. Ruby watched him as he leant towards the car window, his eyes darting from left to right as he stared at the windows of the upper floors overhead.

Ruby followed his gaze to the hospital building looming over them. The tree-lined street that harboured it was bustling with activity. Was it possible that such abhorrent acts were taking place right under people's noses? Ruby stiffened as she caught his gaze, her heart picking up a beat. 'Seen something?'

'What? No, nothing. There's probably nobody there,' he said, releasing his foot from the clutch as the lights turned green.

Ruby took note of the name of the road as Ash turned into Coate Street. They parked down the quiet road, which gave access to the rear of the hospital building. Her attention to street names was a valuable lesson ingrained early in her career. You never knew when backup was urgently needed, and in those days they were not afforded the luxury of GPS.

'Tell you what,' Ash said, pulling up the handbrake. 'Why don't you call it in, and I'll have a look around. . . make sure nobody comes out the back doors?'

Ruby threw him a mistrusting look, wishing she could read his mind. 'Only if you promise not to go inside. If you see anyone just make a note of their direction of travel. I mean it, Ash. I don't want you taking stupid risks.'

'Of course not,' Ash said, delivering another forced chuckle. 'Look at me, I couldn't squeeze through that fence if I tried. I'm just gonna check the perimeter, that's all.' Giving her one last smile, he got out of the car, hands deep in pockets as he walked briskly past the panelled fencing.

But Ruby had barely called for backup when she realised Ash was out of sight. She peered into the distance, cursing herself for leaving her glasses at work. Had he deliberately disobeyed her orders and gone inside? Stretching over, she pulled the keys from the ignition before getting out and locking the car behind her.

'Ash,' she called in a raspy whisper, following his direction of travel. She bit her bottom lip as a crash of glass shattered the silence. Surely not? To go in unarmed to confront such a dangerous killer would be suicide. Unless. . . Raising her radio, she pressed his number to reach him directly on a point-to-point call. No answer.

She prodded the mainstream channel and spoke to control. 'Can I request those units on the hurry up? I'm unable to locate DC Ash Baker by point-to-point. He may have entered the building against my wishes. I'm going in to locate him, over.'

There was no time to waste. Patting her shoulder harness beneath her jacket, she checked her gas, handcuffs and baton were in place. She would have offered to loan it to Ash, but such a thing would have been an invitation to investigate. That was the last thing she'd wanted him to do. Ash was overweight, unfit, and suffering from depression. What the hell was he thinking going in there alone?

'Shit!' she exclaimed, when she came to a gap in the fencing big enough for Ash to squeeze through. She listened for guard dogs, which were sometimes posted in potential building sites, but all that was returned was an icy breeze and a strong sense of dread. Stepping through the fencing, she made her way through the uneven path. Ash was nowhere to be seen. 'Ash,' Ruby whispered, 'where are you?'

Grasping her police issue ASP, she gave it a firm flick, extending it to full length. It always came down to a choice: her baton or her CS incapacitant spray. But the weight of her baton felt comforting in her grip. Raising it over her shoulder, she peered through the broken glass of the back window. There was no time to waste; she had to go inside.

CHAPTER FIFTY-TWO

Holding her breath, Ruby entered the long, dank corridor. Having stood empty since its closure twenty years before, the building carried an eerie sense of desolation. She masked her face with the back of her left hand as the smell of rat urine clawed, thick and heavy, on her senses. In the distance, a scratching noise ensued. Darkness closed in as she entered the bowels of the building. Was Ash creeping down the corridors too? Was the doctor, more to the point? Ruby thought about the post-mortem, and the rat droppings attached to the victim's hair. To end up in a place like this with only the rats for company. . . But it had been searched; she had read the report with her own eyes. She gathered her thoughts as she tried to formulate a plan. Calling out to Ash would only serve to bring attention to her whereabouts, but the building was a literal rat run, a maze of decaying rooms, rotting stairwells and floor upon floor of hollowed spaces. She would never find him in here but she could not sit in the car and wait for backup: she was Ash's sergeant, and wholly responsible for his welfare.

She strained to listen for signs of life and was rewarded with the patter of tiny claws from the floor above. There was more than a nest of rats in this building; there was a commune. And that was exactly where she needed to go. Then she heard it, the echoing tap, tap of leather shoes as they took the stairs. It was Ash; it had to be. Turning right, she followed the sound until she came to a stairwell. Her breath caught in her throat as she heard a voice in the distance.

'No, please, let me go! Please, no, no, no. . .' Hairs stood sentry on Ruby's neck as the young woman's cries for mercy went unanswered.

'Ash,' Ruby said, trying the radio once more. She dialled his number directly. He was much more likely to answer a private point-to-point than talk on the busy main channel.

His voice was sharp and to the point. 'Sarge, I'm fine. Just wait outside for backup, over.'

The woman's cries were silenced, briefly, until continuing for the second time. 'No, please, let me go! Please, no, no, no. . .'

Ruby frowned. There was something off-kilter about this. Her instincts screamed at her to stay put. 'I'm coming up the first set of stairs. We need to regroup. Don't go rushing in there, over.'

'I know what I'm doing,' Ash said. 'Back off, over and out.'

The woman's cries paused for seconds before beginning again. Ruby's heart thundered in her chest as she realised what was going on. 'Ash—,' she said before he cut her off. 'It's a trap. The screaming, it's on a loop.'

'I'm sorry, I've got to do this,' he said, before disconnecting the call.

Swearing under her breath, Ruby fiddled with her radio as she tried again. But Ash had switched his off. She clipped it to her belt before resuming the defence stance and galloping up the stairs. Her muscles tensed, she peered through the gloom as shadows danced on the walls. If someone tried jumping out on her now, it would be a decision they would come to regret. She followed the cries, pausing as she passed the array of open doors. A black rat scuttled past, followed by one more, then another, and another, skimming her shoes as they squeaked in annoyance at the disruption. Was this why the previous officers had denoted the building all-clear? Because they had been put off by the army of rats? Ruby's fingers tightened around her baton. She was used to rodents in the alleyways where she grew up, but she was no fan. She felt the cold release of adrenalin preparing her for what lay ahead. In the distance, a scuffling noise ensued. Footsteps? Had Ash caught up with the doctor?

A choking, gurgling sound echoed in the corridors. That was no recording; that was real. Sprinting towards it, Ruby tried to ignore the possibility that she was heading straight into a trap. Where the hell was backup? Rats streamed from every direction, plump and slick as they scuttled past. The stench was overpowering, but she powered forward through the decay and the desolation, aware of the distant sounds of sirens. Nothing could stop her now because her eyes were set on the open doorway where, cloaked by a layer of rats, a body lay motionless on the floor.

CHAPTER FIFTY-THREE

The polished wooden stairwell in her new Dalston flat was a complete contrast to the sticky metal railing in her old tower block. Inhaling the light scent of cinnamon and vanilla diffusers, Ruby enjoyed the calming silence. Used to loud music and people arguing, the only sound here was the quiet whirr of the lift. She had come to her sanctuary because she could not bear to go back to her flat. After what she had been through, the grey, depressing tower block was the last place on earth she needed to be. More than anything she needed Nathan, but if she could not have him, she would find comfort in the rooms he had furnished, soak in the bath he had chosen, and change into the pyjamas he had bought for her. As her feet tapped up each step of the stairwell, her memory crept back to the horrors of the derelict building where Ash had died, just hours before.

Ruby had insisted on returning to the police station to complete her statement, her fingers shaking as she typed. A shower and change of clothes in the police station locker room had provided her with enough strength to continue with the hunt for the man who had murdered her colleague. The devastation of his loss hung like a dense cloud, not just over their department but the whole station. Ruby felt it like a physical weight on her shoulders, and the pale, shocked faces of her colleagues were more than she could bear. Unanswered questions hung on their lips as small groups gathered in the canteen, smoking area and locker room, trying to make sense of something which could very easily have happened to them. Blame, regret and anger dangled before her, making her sick to the stomach.

It was a relief to be told by the staff at Ash's wife's mental health unit that they would be the ones to break the news when she was strong enough to deal with it. The Kent force would deliver what was termed the 'agony' to his daughters in Canterbury. It was just as well. Ruby doubted she would have been able to keep it together had she attended herself. And why would they want to hear it from the person responsible for their father's death?

Ruby paused on the stairwell, her legs feeling like lead as her mind bombarded her with statements laced with blame. She was in charge; she should have seen through his story sooner, stopped him before he went inside. A message written in chips indeed, what a sorry excuse that was. What had really brought him there? And why hadn't she kept a closer eye on him? She should have been one step behind him, ready to strike out at the killer who was lying in wait. She chewed her lip. Procedure, that's why. She had thought on this occasion that they would be safer if they played it by the book. Two people were not enough to hunt down a psychopathic killer in a building built like a maze. Tweedy had warned her what Doctor Tanner was like: a slippery customer who liked to hide in wait. His level of violence disgusted even Nathan Crosby, someone for whom physical force was a way of life. Armed with a wealth of background information, she *knew* it was not safe for them to go in. But still, the guilt tore through her, accusatory whispers clawing at the back of her mind. She had broken the rules on every other occasion, why did she choose this one time to play it by the book? It wasn't fear that stalled her; she had never backed down when it came to saving the life of another. But after speaking with Tweedy Steve, she was not willing to risk it, preferring to wait for armed officers to flood the building and both follow on behind. And now that had backfired. Yes, her superior officers had told her she did the right thing. She had updated control every step of the way and made it clear DC Baker was acting against her commands. Why? Because deep down she knew he had another agenda? Ruby had risked her life giving chase, but she had not been quick enough. And there, amongst the rats, she had found his body laid out in a pool of blood. Tanner had been waiting for him. He had not used a scalpel to murder him. Her stomach had churned as she caught sight of the length of cheese wire embedded into Ash's neck. It was a horrific death, but one that he had run straight into – giving up his life without a fight. Such thoughts rolled over like rumbling thunderclouds. She came to the landing, taking a deep breath as she pushed her key into the lock. Tonight she would try to get some rest and assess things in the morning.

As she entered the living room, the soft glow of a television told her that she was not alone. The figure on the sofa turned, his smile fading as he took in her expression. It was Nathan, and Ruby was swept up in relief, clinging to the doorway for fear her legs would give.

She kicked off her shoes, dropping her bag and coat onto the floor.

'Babe,' Nathan said, his voice husky as he rose to greet her. 'You OK?'

A small shake of the head was all she could manage as she felt her defences crumble within. She hated crying in front of Nathan, although he never shied away from her tears. Immediately he was by her side, the palms of his hands warm against her cheeks.

'What's wrong?' he said, his tone hardening. 'Has someone hurt you?'

'No,' she said, as the first of her tears trickled onto his hands. 'I lost one of my officers tonight. It was Tanner. We almost caught up with him and. . .' She choked on a sob, blinking the tears from her field of vision, but it was like trying to hold back an insistent tide.

There was only one person who could make her feel better. Her left arm curled around Nathan's waist, while the fingers of her right hand ran through his hair. Drawing him forward, she kissed him softly on the lips.

Nathan reciprocated, his face clouded in confusion as they parted. 'What happened?'

She shook her head. 'I don't want to talk about it, I just want to stay here with you. Please. Sleep with me tonight.'

His eyes reflected the depth of his love, and it was just what Ruby needed to exorcise the horrors of the day. He understood because he had lost people close to him too. Ruby had taken the pain away, now it was his turn to reciprocate. Her senses tingled as his mouth found hers, his tongue carrying the delicate lacing of coffee. Stripping away their layers of clothes, Nathan pressed her against the wall, familiarising himself with her body once more. As she wrapped her legs around him, he effortlessly carried her to the bed, his body pressed firmly against hers. The recriminations that had plagued her all evaporated into thin air.

CHAPTER FIFTY-FOUR

The light that filtered in through the bedroom windows seemed softer today. Everything about her tower block flat seemed harsh in comparison. Ruby rested her head on Nathan's chest, closing her eyes as she savoured the warmth of his naked body. He stirred beneath her, his muscular form wrapping itself around her in a bear hug that made all the pain ebb away.

'I don't want to get up,' she said, her voice muffled as she spoke into the curve of his chest. 'Not yet.'

'You don't have to, babe. Stay in bed. I'll look after you.'

It was a tempting offer. How she had gone back to work after Ash's murder was beyond her. She could not remember DI Downes bringing her back to the station, let alone typing up her statement of what had taken place. It was only when she had broken down in his office that she had agreed to his offer of a cab to bring her home. In her distress, she had found herself reciting the address of the flat Nathan had bought her just months before. Pride had stopped her moving in, but with the stain of Ash's blood still visible under her fingernails, she was in desperate need of solace; somewhere that spoke of home. Finding Nathan here had been more therapeutic than any counselling session, and their night together had been the release she needed.

'I could do with some more sleep,' she smiled.

Here in bed, with their limbs intertwined, there were no barriers to set them apart. Nathan shifted beneath the down-filled duvet, planting tender kisses on the curve of her neck. He nuzzled her skin, murmuring softly to her to stay.

* * *

Her skin pink from the warmth of the shower, she walked across the deep pile carpet, which felt like velvet beneath her toes. She tied the belt of the soft white towelling gown. For the third time that morning she checked her nails, satisfied that all traces of blood had been scrubbed away. But it was still there, lingering in her thoughts. She fought hard to quell the flashbacks scraping her brain, focusing her attention on the breakfast that Nathan had prepared.

He pushed the plate towards her as she took a seat at the polished glass-topped table. Soft fluffy scrambled eggs were loaded onto her plate along with a buttered toasted muffin. She couldn't remember the last time she'd eaten and, despite the thoughts whirling around her head, she began to tuck in. With them both sitting at the table, Ruby in her dressing gown and Nathan in a T-shirt and chinos, they could be any other couple in the world. Finishing her eggs, Ruby downed the last of her tea.

'That's the best cup of tea I've had all week. Thanks, love,' she said, rising to bring her plate to the dishwasher.

Nathan touched her arm, signalling for her to sit back down. Ruby knew he had been curious to know what had happened with the doctor. He had sensed her reluctance, waiting until she had recovered enough to relay the story without breaking down.

She sighed as the real world took over her day. 'We found his lair. It was in a derelict hospital. The place was full of rats, creepy as hell. But you know what? We also found the victims' clothes.'

'Including Lisa Caldwell's?' Nathan said.

'Yes.' She was impressed that he remembered her name. 'They match the description given by her mother. We've got enough forensics to put him away for good.'

Nathan briefly closed his eyes, his face at peace as he took a calming breath. 'Thank you.' He reached across and touched her hand. 'At least now he won't harm anyone else.'

But Ruby could not take any pleasure from such a horrific incident. 'It's not me that found him, it was Ash.' Her gaze fell, shame rising as a warm flush brought heat to her cheeks.

'You shouldn't blame yourself. It's not your fault.' Nathan had pieced together what had happened from her brief explanation the night before.

'I just don't understand. I want to ask him why he acted so strangely, but now he's dead.'

But Nathan was not one to offer platitudes. 'You look beat. Why don't you go back to bed, get some kip?'

'I'm going back to work. I'll need you to come in so we can do a taped interview under caution. Just to tie up any loose ends.'

'Me, go to the nick? You're having a laugh,' Nathan said. 'And besides, today's your day off.'

'You don't get days off when there's a murderer on the loose. Not when he's killed one of your own. Why don't you come with me? It won't take long to—'

'No,' Nathan said firmly, rising from his chair. 'Write up a statement, and I'll sign it. I'm not being interviewed on tape.'

'Fine,' Ruby rolled her eyes. 'Do me a favour, though, tell Cathy to stay in. At least until we find Tanner. If he's tried to frame you, then she could be in danger.'

Nathan smirked. 'She's been under curfew since this all began. It's driving her nuts.'

'Yeah, well, a few more days won't hurt.' Ruby gave him a rueful smile. What would their daughter think if she could see them together now? She glanced around the spotlessly clean kitchen. With glossy designer cupboards, it held every appliance you could possibly need. Streamlined and sophisticated, the Dalston flat was her dream home.

'And you?' Nathan asked, breaking into her thoughts. 'Are you coming back here when you're done?'

Ruby smiled. 'Yeah, I will. I can't live in that tower block anymore. Especially now someone's puked in my bed.'

Nathan threw her a comical look. 'Did you just say. . .?'

Ruby's smile widened. 'Just a girl I was trying to keep off the streets. It's a story for another time. I imagine you'll be keen to get home, get things back to normal.'

'I am, tomorrow. I'll keep your side of the bed warm tonight.'

It was a statement, not a question. Ruby was not going to complain. Nathan was in no hurry to get back to the real world any more than she was. Lenny would most likely have a plethora of things for him to sort out and, from the moment he returned home, his mother would be on his back, trying to bridge the gap between him and his ex-girlfriend, Leona.

But Ruby could not worry about Frances or Lenny now. She took a seat at the dressing table, refreshing her red lipstick and patting her lips against a tissue. Today she would be a force of strength as her team hunted down the man responsible for the loss of one of their own.

CHAPTER FIFTY-FIVE

Shock waves were still spreading as news of Ash Baker's death filtered through the station. Adept at covering up his problems, Ash was known for his practical jokes and smutty one-liners. Even the officers that had not known him felt the loss just the same. Ruby knew she needed to maintain a brave face if she was to carry on with the investigation. Her colleagues were offered a TRIM session, but the police rarely took help on board, the mentality being that they were coppers and should expect such things from their job. They had all become adept at compartmentalising their feelings, and trauma-related incident management would be replaced by a round of drinks in the pub. But it felt like gravity was taking an extra pull in the office today. People answered the phones slower, the receiver heavy on their hands. Footsteps dragged, and heads lowered towards the ground. As Ruby entered the room, apprehensive faces rose, waiting for direction. They needed her to be strong so they could carry on. Her stomach muscles clenched at the thought of their expectations.

DI Downes's platitudes had obviously not been enough as detectives froze in their tracks, waiting for her to speak. Ruby wished she had taken the time to rehearse some words fitting for Ash's memory. A thought-provoking speech on his heroism. . . serving his last days with an unblemished record. But she had a lingering feeling of doubt, and his record was untarnished only because he had died before his acquaintance with the hookers had been brought fully to light. The more she thought about his actions, the louder the question became. Was it really an accident?

Had he a death wish all along? She recalled their meeting when he mentioned ending it all in an off-the-cuff remark. Had he wanted to do so? Was that what this was all about? She shook the thought away. It was incomprehensible that he would leave his family in such a way. Yet. . . The insurance pay-off would be substantial.

Sending his daughters to his sister's, putting his wife in care… had he been putting his affairs in order? Ruby swallowed back her grief. She was wrong; she had to be. Such thoughts rose because she could not bear the alternative: that it was her fault. She had let him down. Wearily, she leaned against Ash's desk, still cluttered with paperwork and files just as he had left it. A framed photo of his family sat in the corner next to a chewed-up pen. His cup still carried a brown ring from the remains of his coffee, and his jokey posters were still stuck to the wall.

She took a deep breath, vowing to keep her voice strong and steady, yet not unfeeling in the way that DCI Worrow's clichés would portray.

'I know we're all feeling Ash's loss today. Most of you are probably still in a state of shock. Given I was with him when it happened. . .' she paused, a wave of guilt rising and stealing her words, 'I can't help but feel somehow responsible.' She raised her hand as Luddy began to speak, most likely to reassure her that it wasn't her fault. 'It's OK,' she said, 'I just need to work through it. Ash's loss is going to be immense, and I don't just mean workwise. He had such a huge personality, and it's tragic that it had to end this way.' A thought entered Ruby's head as she remembered a group discussion about retirement. The way Ash spoke it was like he knew he would never see it. Ruby sighed. If only such theories would stop infiltrating her mind.

'You've all been offered TRIM, and yet here you are, all at work today. God knows these cases need a hundred per cent. If anyone here isn't feeling up to it, there's no problem in getting you signed off. Go home, or go for a drink. I know which Ash would have preferred.' She gazed around the room, but nobody was forthcoming. 'I'll be going to The Eagle pub after work to raise a glass to our friend for anyone that wants to join me. If anyone else has a few words that you'd like to put together, just email your comments to me for the memorial service. I'm sure you all have a story that you'd like to share. Nothing too embarrassing, mind.' She thought about Ash's wife and his daughters, who had already had to cope with so much. Thoughts of their young lives made tears well up inside her, and rather than cry in front of her colleagues, she swiftly turned away. 'I'll be in my office if anyone needs me.'

The shrill ring of her desk phone infiltrated Ruby's thoughts, and she jabbed at the volume button to turn it down. Insistently the red dot of light flashed, alerting her that the caller was not going away. Straightening in her chair, she picked up the receiver.

She was greeted by the gravelly voice of front counter staff. It was June, and Ruby immediately recognise her smoker's drawl. 'Sorry to trouble you, Sarge, but I've got a young man down here that's very keen to speak to you.'

Ruby sighed as her computer dinged to alert her of ten new emails. 'Can you take his details, and I'll call him back? I'm a bit busy right now.'

'I can do, but he's saying it's urgent. He said he's Sharon's boyfriend, and she hasn't come home. He'll only talk to you.'

'I'll be right there,' Ruby said, before placing the receiver back on the cradle. Clenching her fists, she banged them on the table, venting her growing frustration. Just like Ash, Sharon had ignored her advice to stay put.

As she made her way to the front office, Ruby hoped that was where the similarity stopped.

CHAPTER FIFTY-SIX

'Sit down,' Ruby said, as Billy paced the room. His hair was greasy, his eyes intense. This was a man who was experiencing pain. Sweat rolled off his body, dampening his clothes, each movement drawing out the sweet tang of body odour. Not that he would have noticed; he was too busy trying to focus on his missing girlfriend.

'I can't believe that after everything I told her she went out on the job. What was she thinking?' Ruby said, standing over Billy as he rocked in the hard plastic chair.

It was of great relief that the interview room was free. The last thing she wanted was to bring him inside the realms of the police station, where he would see his own face staring back at him from the prolific offender posters on the walls. With a history of petty offences a mile long, he was no stranger to the custody suite.

'She listened to you, she really did, said she was gonna get help,' Billy said. Eyes wide, he was barely blinking as he relayed Sharon's last movements. 'But she was clucking bad, we both was, so she went for one more job with someone she knew.'

Someone she knew? She had warned Sharon about Doctor Tanner. So who was the mystery client? 'Go on,' she said.

'She called him, set it all up. But she's not come home. She knew how worried I was. Something's happened to her, I know it.' Billy clenched handfuls of his short stubby hair as he bent over in agony. His eyes were wild as he rose up, pain and concern stabbing him in equal measures. 'Please. You've got to find her.' His words were laced with spittle, landing on the small desk between them. He was going cold turkey and it was hitting him hard.

But Ruby had little sympathy for the man who sent his girlfriend into danger so that he could score. 'Pity you weren't so concerned when she was with you. It doesn't look like you've done a lot to stop her, does it?' She placed her hands on her hips as if talking to an errant child. 'How could you let her out there? What sort of boyfriend are you?'

Billy wiped his nose with the back of his hand, smearing his fingers in slime. 'You don't know what she's like. Once she gets somefink into her head there's no stopping her. She just needed one last fix so that we could sleep through the night. And it wasn't as if she didn't know him.'

'Who?' Ruby said, sick of hearing his excuses. Her hands itched with the need to grab him by the scruff of the neck and squeeze the information from his scrawny throat. 'Who was her punter?'

'I don't know,' Billy said. 'They don't give their real names most of the time. She said she'd be an hour, tops. Promised she'd ring the minute she came out. But that was yesterday. I've been searching the streets all night. I thought maybe she went to the dealers, but they've not seen her either.'

'And you've tried calling her phone?' Ruby said, a familiar knot in her shoulders making itself known as her body tensed.

Billy looked at her miserably, tears welling in his red-rimmed eyes. 'Yeah,' he sniffed. 'It's turned off, and her punter's number is off the hook.'

Ruby froze, wondering if she had heard him correctly. 'Hang on a minute. You've got the number of the client that booked her?'

'Yeah, I thought I said. She's got two phones. Her private one that I call her on, and the other one that she takes bookings with. She left the booking phone in the flat. I've got the number here.'

Ruby stared in disbelief. 'The whole time we've been talking, and you've had the number all along?'

'Yeah, but I don't have the address or nothing. Here, see for yourself.' He handed over the phone: a small white diamanté-studded Nokia. Ruby peered through the cracked screen, pressing the buttons as she brought up the list of calls. She clicked on the call timed at one o'clock in the morning. 'This is a landline,' she said.

Billy nodded. 'She leaves it with me when she doesn't want to take no more calls. I should have come sooner, but I didn't want to get her into trouble.'

Ruby's brain was whirring as she worked out the next course of action. 'When you say Sharon's phone is turned off. . .'

'Well, not switched off. It rings out and goes to answer machine. She keeps it on silent, so I thought maybe she didn't hear it at first.'

'Good, that's good,' Ruby said. 'We can triangulate her phone and trace the address of the landline – see if they match. I need you to stay here. I'll get an officer to take a quick statement and book this evidence.'

'But I. . .'

'You want to find her, don't you?' Ruby said, in no mood for excuses. She raised the phone. 'This is good. As soon as I hear anything, I'll let you know. Do you understand?'

Billy nodded dumbly, tears gathering in the corners of his eyes.

Ruby sighed, a small pang of sympathy making itself known. 'Go to the medical centre when you're done here, get a prescription. You'll need to keep a clear head. If you hear from Sharon, let us know straightaway, alright? No waiting around.' She shuffled in a back pocket for a weathered card, along with some loose change.

Nathan had pressed some cash into the palm of her hand before she left for work, telling her to get a round of drinks in for her shift. She guessed he had checked her wallet, seeing nothing but a twenty-pence piece and an Oyster card inside. It was the same Oyster card that was magically topped up every month online. Such actions were typical of Nathan and, although she hated taking his money, she had appreciated his help today.

'Here,' she said, handing the business card and change over. Billy may have had a phone but, like most of the drug users she knew, his credit was probably low. 'Call me if anything happens.'

As Ruby sped up the stairs to her office, her heart skipped a beat. It was an alien emotion when it came to this case: hope. If this was a landline then there was a small chance they had the killer's address. Did the doctor have an accomplice? And could they reach Sharon in time?

CHAPTER FIFTY-SEVEN

Armed officers bundled out of the van as they prepared for the raid on the ramshackle East London semi. There was no way Ruby was going to miss this. Piles of work were overflowing on her desk, overtime needed to be sorted out, as well as tackling the spreadsheets that DCI Worrow had provided her, but at this moment in time nothing was more important than finding Sharon alive. The case had got under her skin, and there was nothing she could do to stop it.

Ruby shifted the ugly stab vest poking into her ribs. She had forgotten how heavy these things were. Each time she wore it, she was transported back to when she was in uniform, weighed down with heavy boots, a utility belt that carried everything except the kitchen sink and bulked up with layers of clothing and protective wear. She remembered tucking her hands into the armholes of her stab vest to keep her fingers warm in the winter, and loosening the Velcro belts at the side when sweat trickled down her back. Things were much more straightforward then. Not easier, but straightforward. Work had always been a constant stream, no matter what department she frequented, and she had witnessed many people leave because they could not hack the pace. And now, crouched behind the hedge of the alleged perpetrator's home, this seemed the most important day in her career to date. So near but so far... All she wanted to do was to see the killer behind bars; to make him pay.

Officers positioned themselves around the back of the building, updating their counterparts by radio. They had all areas covered – what was keeping them? Ruby's breath frosted as her impatience grew. She stood, just as the command was given to go. There was no soft knock, or the ringing of a doorbell for this high-profile case. Officers drew back the heavy metal battering ram, aptly named the 'big red key', and sent the door hinges clattering to the floor. As the door slammed to one side, they announced their presence, their boots stamping in unison against the grimy tiled floor. Ruby remained vigilant close behind, the memory of Ash's death lingering in her thoughts.

Shouts of 'clear' echoed in the building as each room was checked in turn. She wished she could rush ahead of the wall of officers, but they were firm in their instruction that she should stay one step behind. Footsteps thundered up the stairs, and Ruby followed them, her heart sinking as she realised that downstairs was all clear. Unlike their last big operation, there was no basement to be found.

'We've got a body in here,' a gruff voice shouted in a voice that suggested it was too late for an ambulance. But was it too late for Sharon?

Dozens of questions flooded Ruby's mind as she caught sight of the blood-saturated duvet. But the matted black hair did not belong to Sharon, and she did not recognise the face of the portly man on the bed. So who was he, and how did he die? Naked, and drenched in blood, he lay splayed across the mattress, the sheets tightly gripped in his chubby fingers. Was this Sharon's client? More to the point, where was Sharon?

She raised the radio to her mouth, pressed the side button and updated control. As with all such operations, they had their own channel tagged under the operation name devoted solely to the raid. The words had barely left her lips when she became aware of a voice requesting an ambulance to the scene. Gripping her radio tightly, she rushed across the foot-worn flooring to the bedroom across the way.

'Let me see,' Ruby said, aware she was contaminating the scene by traipsing from one room to another.

She paused at the doorway, craning her neck as wide-shouldered officers moved to one side. The image of a woman on a single bed came into view. Feeling like she was stepping into a nightmare, Ruby gazed at the pink satin costume. Long satin gloves reached her elbows, and a delicate tiara adorned her newly dyed blonde hair. 'Sleeping Beauty,' she breathed, the words touching her lips in a whisper as she recognised the costume from one of the images on their briefing room wall. Bent over Sharon's body, the attending officer swivelled his head, giving Ruby a nod.

'She's alive.'

Eyelids flickering, a sudden breathy rattle emanated from Sharon's throat. Swearing under her breath, Ruby tugged at the ropes binding her flesh to the metal bedposts. The long white satin gloves were spotless, except for a single pinprick of blood that seeped through from the index finger of her right hand. It was heartbreaking to see Sharon trussed up in this way. With her pale skin and impossibly pink lips, the doctor had perfected her to the last detail. They had found her just in time – or had they?

As the paramedics poured in, Ruby stepped aside. Plucking her mobile phone from her pocket, she dialled her office number. After three rings, DC Eve Tanner's voice spoke on the other end of the line. She and the doctor may have shared the same surname, but that was where the similarity ended. Eve was one of the most caring and conscientious workers in her team, and it took her just seconds to find the original version of 'The Sleeping Beauty' fairy tale in her notes.

Eve's voice was steady as she read from the text. This was not a story she would be reading to her baby when it was born. 'As the prince tried to wake her, the princess seemed so incredibly lovely that he began to grow hot with lust…'

Ruby listened as Eve filled her in. The modern day fairy-tale, based on a later version of the story, saw the princess put to sleep after she pricked her finger on a spindle, only to be awoken by her true love's kiss. But the original version relayed a harsher reality. Taken by the king for his pleasure, the princess was continuously raped, bearing two children while still asleep.

Ruby ended the call, clearing her throat as she spoke. 'Guys, when you seize the bedding, can you bear it in mind that we may be dealing with a rape scene here too.'

CHAPTER FIFTY-EIGHT

Dr Tanner's fingers gripped the edges of the brick wall as he watched from a safe distance. Disbelieving of the scene before him, his shopping bags had fallen to the ground as officers raided the building. How was this possible? And so quickly? He had only broken in there in the early hours of the morning. Since his encounter with the police in the derelict building, he knew time was in short supply. That's why he had to be clever, using one of Sharon's clients as a way of getting her all to himself. He was familiar with her old haunts; such places were listed in the records he had kept after he left the Crosbys' employment. And he had been watching her home for some time, knowing her addiction would eventually force her outside. He did not miss the freezing cold hospital building, the unforgiving cement floors or the way the wind howled through the corridors in the dead of night. More and more rats were flooding the rooms, nipping him as he slept, insistent in their demands for food.

He had treated his last victim differently and gained little satisfaction from his presence. But then again, he did not have the same affinity for men: there were no long, flowing locks to caress, no silky body to feel the tip of his barber's brush. After his initial hysterics, Nicky had calmed down enough to plead for his life. With the Peter Pan costume draped over his arm, the doctor stood, unspeaking, as the young man recounted his abusive childhood. His sobs echoed through the building, punctuating his words. 'Please don't hurt me. Please, I'll do whatever you want. Please, just let me go. . .' Nicky had misjudged the doctor, presuming he was abducted due to his choice of profession, but that meant very little to him: it was the beauty of the transformation that made his artwork complete.

He had disposed of him quickly, but not before he had infiltrated the contents of the young man's phone. He had heard of DC Ash Baker but his liaison with Nicky brought an interesting twist to the tale. The intimate texts left him in no doubt that Baker swung both ways. But the hypocrisy infuriated him. According to the papers, DC Baker was one of the officers working on his case. The gall of it! He had used Nicky to gratify his needs, just as the doctor had done. The temptation to teach him a lesson was strong.

Texting from Nicky's phone could have backfired. By the time Ash responded to it, Nicky was dead. So why did he come thundering in with no regard for his safety? He was a big man, twice the width of him, yet he'd dropped his hands to his sides, refusing to put up a fight. Death had come quickly and without fanfare. Only then, with his blood staining his coat, did he realise that Ash Baker was not alone. He had made his escape with haste, the rats diverting attention as his colleague came racing up the stairs.

But the death of one of their own had made the police all the more determined to find him. Doctor Tanner had been warned. His beneficiary had instructed him from the start: have your fun but frame Nathan Crosby. Don't leave evidence, stick to the plan and don't get caught. But with each murder he had grown more self-indulgent, enjoyed it a little too much. The keepsakes... why had he held on to their clothing? He would receive no protection now.

The best he could hope for was to finish what he had set out to do. It was why the doctor had wasted no time in locating the last person on the list: 'Randy Mandy', as she was known. The one working girl who had refused to sleep with him. He couldn't think of a more suitable candidate for his plans. She called herself

Amanda now. She was fleshed out – a far cry from the skinny waif with protruding cheekbones that he had known. Mandy wasn't like the others, not anymore, but that didn't necessarily make her clean. And he was looking forward to reminding her that she could never truly shake off her roots.

He would deal with her just like the others. He had watched Sharon in the darkness as she earned her keep. On her hands and knees, eyes tightly closed, she groaned as the pot-bellied man rutted her from behind. Too engrossed in the moment, he had not noticed him standing in the darkness; his head craned to one side. Death had come quickly as he'd slit his throat, enjoying the sound of blood slapping against Sharon's naked flesh. It wasn't until the dead man slumped to one side that she became aware of the doctor's presence. It was a constant source of fascination to watch how people reacted in extreme situations. Fight or flight, it was called, and he had observed it many times during his employment with the Crosby family business.

Sharon was a fighter. Her teeth flashing, she had kicked and lashed out at him as he cornered her in the dimly lit bedroom. Holding his scalpel in his right hand, he showed her what was waiting if she didn't comply. The last thing he wanted was to kill her – nowhere in the story did Sleeping Beauty have her throat slit. She had dug her nails into the woodchip wallpaper, leaving bloodied hand trails in her wake. As if that would save her. In the end, he laid the scalpel to one side, calmly telling her that she had nothing to fear. He was her protector – killing the man to save her, because the police had got it all wrong. It had all been a misunderstanding, he said, and his efforts at helping the girls had set him up as a suspect in their murders. As he approached, her eyes flicked to the door, planning her escape. Tearing into the chloroform bag, he whipped it from his coat pocket and without hesitation slammed it on her face.

Such a shame he had been unable to finish his work. He had known that one of his plans might fail. It was the nature of the game, he would accept it and move on. Like a metronome his thoughts flicked back and forth, finally halting on Mandy: it was time. He would enjoy getting reacquainted with her again.

CHAPTER FIFTY-NINE

It was a rare and wondrous occasion to have time for a lunch break, but Ruby found herself with minutes to kill. The matron at the hospital where Sharon Connors was currently admitted had advised her to call back in half an hour. Having cleared it with DI Downes, Ruby decided to eat a sandwich on the go, while conducting a long overdue visit to her mother in Oakwood Care Home. She tried to squeeze in a visit every day, pushing back the guilt when the time would not allow. She liked Oakwood. It had been worth selling their family home to keep up the fees, subsidised by a monthly payment out of Ruby's wage. Even so, the fees seemed remarkably low. Was Nathan assisting towards the payments without her knowledge? Did she need to know? The fact her mother was living in comfort was all that mattered. As she entered the bright, airy building, she took in the clear vases of freshly cut flowers from the beautiful landscape at the back of the home. Expansive French doors afforded a wonderful view, and patients were encouraged to step outside and enjoy the garden when they could. As she took a seat beside her mother, Ruby knew that she would not be judged. Due to her dementia, Joy had lost all sense of time. Giving her a hug, she inhaled the scent of lily of the valley, taking comfort in the perfume lacing her mother's skin.

Ruby was pleased when she noted the red hairclip in her bun. Joy always wore something red. It was a throwback to the days when her father joked she was his little robin redbreast, always sporting a flash of red – a spark of her individuality. For Ruby, the dash of red lipstick she wore was in tribute to happier days: Mac Ruby Woo. It seemed kismet when she found the brand name, and she had worn it ever since.

'How are you today, Mum?' she asked, as her mother stared into space.

'Killing the minutes and watching them die.'

It was her mother's usual response, followed by a soft sigh. Ruby tried to ignore the fact that Joy had got a little thinner and paler since her last visit, her attention always that bit further from her reach. She knew it was inevitable that her mother would age and deteriorate, but she wasn't ready to face it, not today.

Their small talk exhausted, they sat in silence, listening to the finches chirping as they bobbed from branch to branch in the garden outside. Ruby liked that the care home kept the windows open – forfeiting savings on heating bills to allow the residents the wistful pleasure of enjoying the birdsong.

'Hey, girl, where you been? You look bushed,' Harmony said, pushing a silver trolley laden with pots of tea, coffee and white china cups. Ruby had a particular fondness for the Jamaican woman whose personality was as broad as her waistline.

'Oh, hi,' Ruby said, so deep in her thoughts it took seconds to resurface. 'Heavy workload. Is that tea you're making?'

'You know it,' Harmony said, emitting a soft chuckle as she passed her a cup. 'I've given these teabags an extra squeeze for you.' She turned to Joy, handing her a cup of tea. 'Here you go, precious.'

As Harmony walked away, filling the corridors with a song, Ruby felt a pang of envy for the woman who appeared happy with her lot. Ruby's job as a sergeant made her feel fulfilled, but when was the last time she was truly happy at work? She thought of her last moments of pleasure, her snatched hours with Nathan as they curled up in bed.

'You know what?' she said. 'I've been working really hard this week. It's not easy being a woman in the police, but I lead a good team.'

'Are you in the police?' Joy said, her eyes offering recognition. 'When did you do that?'

'Years ago,' Ruby said, happy that, at least today, her mother appeared to know who she was.

Joy frowned. 'Why didn't you tell me you've joined the police?'

Ruby shrugged. She had, many times. Even now she couldn't help but bring it up in the hope her mother would say she was proud of her. She'd received a lukewarm reception when she first broke the news all those years ago. Ruby had grown up in a world where the police were best avoided, and liked as much as the debt collectors that called to her neighbours' doors. Joy had her reasons. Back then it wasn't the nicest establishment to be a part of, and people had their own perspectives on things. Joy wanted Ruby to work in retail, not part of a vocation where you put people in prison. But Ruby had told herself she was destined for greater things.

'Ooh no, the police isn't for you.' Joy wrinkled her nose. 'Why don't you get a job on the shop floor? I hear that Debenhams is taking on. Mrs Delaney's daughter works there, and she's just been promoted.'

'You know, Mum, I might just do that.' Ruby stifled a smile. Some things would never change. She checked her watch: a visit to the hospital was due. The heavy weight she had walked in with seemed to have lightened, and being in her mother's company had made her breathe easy again. She parked any concerns to the furthest recesses of her mind. Kissing Joy lightly on the forehead, she promised to visit again soon. Ruby was so close to finding the doctor she could almost taste it. Their enquiries had been intense, making her wonder how he had managed to elude them so far.

She stopped halfway across the car park as her mobile phone buzzed insistently from the back pocket of her trousers. It was Downes, and Ruby frowned as she answered the call. 'I'm just on my way to the hospital now,' she said, wishing he would not keep such close tabs on her.

'I know,' he said. 'There's something you need to be asking young Sharon when you see her.'

'Go on,' Ruby said, pulling the car keys from her bag.

'We've had a look at Ash's phone, which was seized at the murder scene. You were right to doubt his explanation of what took him to the Queen Elizabeth hospital.'

Ruby had explained it all in her police statement – how Ash had said he found the name of the hospital on a message spelt out with frozen chips on the freezer floor. She sighed with relief, glad that she had been truthful and explained her reservations of such an implausible excuse. 'I had a feeling he was lying,' she said, opening her car door and taking shelter from the biting winds.

'Ash received a text from Nicky's phone asking to meet him at the hospital,' Downes said. 'But it was sent while you were in the Robin Hood pub, where Nicky was found dead. Ash must have suspected his killer sent the request to meet.'

'But why?' Ruby said, answers already forming in her mind. 'And why was his number on Nicky's phone?'

'That's what I was about to tell you. It wasn't just the girls Ash was seeing. Judging by the texts that passed between them, he was visiting Nicky too.'

'Bloody hell!' Ruby exhaled, almost dropping the phone from her grasp.

'Exactly. Who knows what was going on there? He could have been blackmailing him,' Downes said with a shrug. 'We'll never know for sure.'

'All the more reason to end it all,' Ruby said. 'Ash would have been mortified at the thought of you finding this out.'

'Hmm, well, we don't want to be spreading that around. I was talking to his sister. He's taken out some serious life insurance policies. Those daughters of his deserve the payout after everything they've lost.'

CHAPTER SIXTY

'You tried to warn me,' Sharon said, speaking through lips stained pink from whatever concoction the doctor had used to dye them. Her low mood was in contrast to the eyebrows he had drawn: arched in an expression of permanent surprise. Everything about her 'makeover' appeared rushed; it told Ruby that Tanner knew the police were closing in. It ignited a glimmer of hope. People who hurried made mistakes.

Sharon squirmed in her hospital bed, pulling the blankets tighter to her chest. Her abnormally white skin could not hide the dark circles under her eyes. There were no 'Get Well Soon' cards on her bedside locker. No flowers or chocolates from family or friends.

'I had to go out, didn't I? After everything you did to warn me.'

'It's over,' Ruby said, her voice low and comforting. 'You're safe now.'

Tears trickled down Sharon's cheeks as the enormity of the situation hit home. 'If you hadn't found me. . . If. . .' she gulped as a sob hit the back of her throat.

Ruby leant forward, her hand resting on Sharon's wrist. It was cold to the touch and painfully thin. 'I know this is difficult, but I need to know. Who did this to you?' Unable to lead the witness, Ruby waited for answers. She caught the flicker of fear in Sharon's eyes and squeezed her wrist. 'We've got a police officer on the door and nobody will get in without your say so.' Taking a small recorder from her jacket, she laid it on top of the blue waffle blanket and pressed 'record'. She went through the usual introductions, citing the time, date and people in the room. A full account would be taken when Sharon was up to it but, for now, she needed something to go on.

'I don't want to talk about it,' Sharon said, as Ruby posed the question for a second time. 'And besides, you know who. . .' her sobs showed no sign of abating. She raised her hand to her face to block out the memory, but Ruby did not have the luxury of time; she could not let it go.

'Please, I need you to be strong. There's one more girl on the list: Mandy,' Ruby said, her words firm. 'Who was it, Sharon? Who did this?'

'Doctor Tanner,' Sharon said, choking on the memory. Accepting the tissue that Ruby drew from the box on the bedside cabinet, she loudly blew her nose. 'It was Billy's fault. He kept nagging me to go out. "Just one more score," he said, then we'd knock it on the head and go to the clinic in the morning. So I rang one of my old customers, Larry Driscoll, and he invited me around.'

Ruby nodded. It was the same person they had traced through her phone. A single middle-aged man, he rented the run-down property where Sharon had been found.

'The doctor. . . he must have followed me to the punter's house. Larry was doing me from behind when I felt something warm on my back. At first I. . . I didn't know what it was. Then he fell to the side. There was blood everywhere, in my hair, up the walls. The doctor. . . he was standing there with a blade in his hand. All I could hear was screaming. It wouldn't stop. Then I realised it was coming from me.' Twisting the tissue between her fingers, Sharon took a deep breath. 'I remembered those photos you showed me, and I told myself that I wasn't going down without a fight. So I ran for the door as soon as he dropped the blade. But he put something over my mouth, and the smell. . . I gagged. I must have passed out.'

'And you woke in hospital?' Ruby said, hoping this was the case. More than anything, she prayed that the old version of the fairy tale had not come true.

Sharon's chin trembled. She stared at the tissue, now broken into pieces on the bed. 'No. When I came to my skin felt too tight for my body and stung like hell. I tried to move but my hands and legs were tied. I was wearing this long pink dress, and he… he kept saying how beautiful I looked.'

'Oh, Sharon,' Ruby said, knowing what was coming next.

'Please, let me finish,' Sharon said, holding up a shaking hand. 'He raped me. And I know I won't get much sympathy because people will say that's what I do. But this was different – I said no.' Tears filled her eyes, her face contorting with the rush of emotion. 'I said no.'

'Come here,' Ruby said, taking Sharon in a hug. It was stretching the boundaries, and her superiors would not approve, but she could not just stand there and observe such raw pain.

Sharon sobbed, staining Ruby's jacket as her tears flowed, unchecked.

'Nobody has the right to do this to you,' Ruby said, slowly releasing Sharon and delivering an intense stare. 'Don't ever forget that.'

'I swear down, I'm never going back to that way of life again,' Sharon said.

'You're alive. That's all that matters right now,' Ruby said. 'But I need your help. Did the doctor give you any clue as to where he's staying or what he's doing next?'

'We never left the punter's flat. It made me sick, knowing that Larry's body was in the bedroom across the way.' She exhaled a heavy, painful sigh. 'I cried, I screamed, I even had a go at him for killing Nicky and the girls. But he just looked at me like I was a creature in the zoo. He had no trouble speaking when he was on the phone though.'

Ruby stiffened. 'On the phone? To who? What did he say?'

In the doorway a nurse entered – pausing as Ruby raised her hand, mouthing the words, 'five minutes?' her eyes pleading for a little more precious time. With a nod of the head, the woman retreated.

Lost in her recollection, Sharon barely noticed the intrusion. 'The doctor thought I was out of it, but I could hear him arguing.'

'Did you hear the phone ring? Who made the call?'

'They called him. I couldn't hear what they were saying but it was heated, something about not sticking to the plan. The doctor hung up then switched the phone off, muttering under his breath. That was when he shook me hard, said it was time to complete the fairy tale. That was when he. . . he. . .' Sharon said, gathering her words. 'He forced himself on me. Then he said he was getting some supplies. He put a needle in my arm. Then the next thing I remember was waking up in the ambulance.'

'Please, try to remember. What was said?' Her senses were on high alert now, the thoughts of an accomplice raising her pulse rate.

Sharon shook her head. 'I can't remember their exact words.' Her eyes flicked up to the left as she forced herself to recall the memory. 'They were arguing about Nicky. At least, that's what it sounded like, because he was saying he *hadn't* gone too far.' She paused for thought. 'That's right, he said he was going to finish what he started and that was that. There's one thing I can tell you though,' she said, her eyes haunted with the memory of the past. 'Whoever it was, they knew Nicky and the girls.'

CHAPTER SIXTY-ONE

The doorbell delivered a distorted 'Yankee Doodle Dandy', enough to rouse the dogs on the other side of the door into life. The Victorian property was one of many which had been renovated by the council to make room for the larger families in the area. The intelligence system had brought back a plethora of results on the family. There wasn't one child out of their brood of ten that was not in trouble at some stage or another. From shoplifting to handling stolen goods, social services had been involved on more than one occasion. Much of their benefits had gone on alcohol and cigarettes rather than the food and clothing the children desperately needed. Judging by the racket coming from within, it seemed that things had not improved. It was little wonder that Nicky had ended up on the streets. After updating the investigation, Ruby was keen to speak to Nicky's family. Sharon's words played on her mind. Given that the overheard phone call had focused on his murder she had thought it best to start close to home.

As the door opened, Ruby held her warrant card aloft, introducing herself to the pimply teenager on the other side. Sandal-footed, he wore blue tracksuit bottoms and an Eminem T-shirt that was two sizes too big, his short bleached blond hair suggesting he was a fan.

'Yeah?' he said, grabbing the larger of the three mongrels by the collar and pushing him back from the door.

'Can I come in?' Ruby said. 'I need to speak to your mum and dad. It's just some enquiries, nobody's in any trouble.' Calling on a grieving family was not ideal, and Ruby knew her visit would be unwelcome, but she had no choice. After the slip-up with officers checking the derelict building, she would not be satisfied until she spoke to the family in person. The boy shrugged, pulling back the door to allow her inside.

A waft of something foul rose up to greet her, and Ruby cast her gaze to the floor. 'Your dog's had an accident,' she said, pointing to the ice-cream shaped turd.

Sloping further down the corridor, the boy picked up a piece of newspaper, slowly layering it on top before stamping it down. 'Come in,' he said, closing the door behind her.

Ruby arched an eyebrow. Someone needed to have a word with this kid about the fundamentals of house-training his pets. All the same, she would be following up with children's social services upon her return to the station. Previous reports spoke of children who had grown up in their pushchairs, stewing in their nappies in front of the TV. Such children became lethargic and disinterested in life when released from the confines of their straps. Ruby guessed that the young man leading her into the living room was once one of the children involved.

She followed him down the dim corridor, passing several green-tinged tanks, and peeping into each one. A languid iguana flicked his tail in annoyance as she tapped the glass to check for signs of life. She peered into the next tank, temporarily forgetting the urgency of her call. Ruby had always wanted a pet. The only thing holding her back was her inability to commit herself to caring for another living creature – a problem which apparently did not bother Nicky's family, given the state of the tanks on show. She recoiled as a tarantula scuttled under a piece of wood. As she peered into the tank containing scorpions, Ruby wondered what purpose such creatures served in a family home. She smiled as a mixed-race toddler came running up to greet her, tugging her trouser pockets in search of sweets. Nick was the oldest in the family, and his parents seemed to have had a child every year since his birth. Judging by their different skin colours, not all of them shared the same father, but the couple had been living together for over twenty years, just the same.

Standing by the fireplace with arms folded stood Michelle Ellis, Nick's mother, her gaze weary as she observed Ruby enter the room. The flowers on her dress evaporated into a washed-out grey hue. Ruby blinked under the dim light, realising, as she stepped closer, that it was not a dress at all, it was a nightie. Michelle's hair hung limply around her face, black; the same colour as Nicky's, except for a few strands of grey. Everything about her appeared disinterested, and Ruby wondered if it was because she was suffering a loss or if that was her permanent expression.

Ruby picked her way through the broken and chewed plastic toys littering the grubby carpeted floor. A small curly-haired boy sat in the corner of the room, amusing himself by hammering nails into a piece of wood. Nick's father, Phil Ellis, sat in a leather armchair, staring obliviously at the one pristine piece of furniture in the home – a forty-eight inch television.

It was another familiar sight. Amongst the chaos of neglected children, unruly dogs, and faeces minefield was a top-of-the-range TV, and, judging by the Sky box, with access to hundreds of channels.

'Sorry to disturb you,' Ruby said, trying to find a clean space on the floor to stand. 'Is there anywhere we can speak in private?'

Phil Ellis jabbed his thumb towards the door, his gaze on his wife. 'Sod off to the kitchen, I'm trying to watch the telly here.'

The *X Factor* rerun was on subtitles due to the constant stream of noise echoing within the four walls.

'It's about your son. It would be better if you both came through,' Ruby said, raising her voice to be heard over the din.

'You talking about the queer? 'Cos we had your lot here yesterday,' Nicky's father said, raising his gut from the chair.

Ruby felt her temper flare: if there was one thing she could not abide it was homophobia but she also accepted that her outrage would not change a thing, apart from getting herself thrown out of the house. She clamped her lips tightly together, swallowing back her response. They were still his parents, and it was a tragedy. The fact that she found Phil Ellis wholly offensive was something she would have to keep to herself.

After finally getting them to sit down at the kitchen table, Ruby endured Phil's mumblings as she took out her pocket notebook and pen.

'We have to pay for the funeral now,' he said, his little finger buried in his ear. 'More money.'

Ruby's lips parted as she exhaled her disgust. She turned to look at Nicky's mother, whose eyes were swimming with tears. At least one of them cared.

'I'm sorry for your loss,' Ruby said. 'I don't wish to intrude on your grief, but it's crucial that we find the person who killed your son before they strike again. Have you ever spoken to or visited a Doctor Tanner?' she said. 'We believe he may be connected to the case.'

'Nah,' Mr Ellis sneered. 'We see that Indian bloke down the precinct.'

Ruby nodded, grateful that at least she had been spared a racial slur. 'Do either of you recall an acquaintance by the name of Mandy? Ever seen her around?' Ruby forced herself to return her gaze to Phil after Nick's mother delivered a blank stare.

'Acquaintance, my arse! I know what he's been up to,' Nicky's father sneered. 'And 'im getting killed, it's all he deserved. Made me a laughing stock down the Horse and Hounds, he did, selling blow jobs down the alley for a tenner. I can't show my face round there again, thanks to 'im.'

'You didn't mind taking his money,' Nick's mother said, finally opening her mouth to speak. Her tone was cold and brittle, and she clasped her fingers tightly together as she leant over the kitchen table, her knuckles turning white. 'You didn't ask about where the money came from when he was handing it over so you could go boozing. How are we going to manage now? The benefits barely cover the food. How are we going to survive without his money?'

Ruby could feel the atmosphere thicken between them, and knew an argument was about to erupt. She felt sorry for the children who would witness what was to follow, but they were most likely immune to it now. She remembered something a social worker had said to her once: it was not the youngsters who screamed and cried after a domestic that you had to worry about, it was the ones who accepted it as everyday life. Such children grew up to be perpetrators and victims themselves. Water found its own level, she had said, and there were enough damaged souls in the world to find each other and begin the cycle all over again. The little girl that had tugged on her trousers now stood in the doorway, her eyes devoid of emotion. In a fleeting moment, Ruby could see her life all mapped out for her. It made for depressing viewing.

'Here's my card,' Ruby interrupted, returning her attention to the arguing couple. But as they exchanged expletives, it was as if she wasn't there at all. 'If either of you recalls anything about Mandy, I'd appreciate it if you'd let me know. I'll show myself out.'

Walking to her car, Ruby took a few breaths of air to expel all remnants of the Ellis household. She knew what social services would say because they had heard it all before: their hands were tied. As long as the children had a roof over their heads, a warm bed and food in their bellies, then the best they could do was to work with the family if they were willing to engage. She did not blame the partner agency because they were doing the best they could. Like the police, they were over-stretched and under-resourced, and the first in the line of fire when the media highlighted their failings in the worst possible way. Everyone was a critic. She thought about the headlines that the fairy-tale killer wanted to create, and how hard she had worked to ensure details of Nick's case had not come to light. No family wanted to see their son portrayed in such a way, not even the Ellises. She glanced at her watch, well aware of the seconds ticking past. There was still so much to do, and time was running out for Mandy Prentice.

CHAPTER SIXTY-TWO

As Ruby approached her office, she felt as if she was walking in a nightmare. Everything seemed off-kilter. She glanced at Ash Baker's desk, still littered with his belongings. It seemed his colleagues were content to allow his presence to linger another day. She could not believe he was gone. In a box marked 'do not open', she had stored the details of his murder into the recesses of her mind. It would live there along with countless other monstrosities, creeping out in the dead of night when her defences were down. But she could not stop the niggle at the back of her brain. Ash's final words replayed on a loop: 'I'm sorry, I've got to do this.' What was he sorry about? Deep inside, she knew. But the fact Ash may have sacrificed himself to provide for his family was not one she was ready to deal with just yet.

'Any results on Mandy yet? Someone must have something?' Ruby leaned across Luddy's desk. A quick cup of tea and a fresh coat of lipstick had helped her face her team again. It seemed likely that Danny Smedley would not be convicted at court, leaving the team under increasing pressure to find the real killer and bring him in. At last, DCI Worrow had agreed to link Lisa Caldwell's murder with the other victims. It was something the press was quick to point out. Her eyes roamed across the newspaper laid open on the desk. The so-called fairy-tale killer was gaining momentum in the press, reaching front pages far and wide. While sympathy lay with university student, Lisa, the other victims were known by their profession rather than their names.

'We've heard from social security,' Luddy piped up, 'nothing new since the Northolt address.' Every avenue had been explored, but the trail had gone cold after Mandy's last-known address in Northolt.

'Any luck with the hospitals?' It was a long shot. Mandy had been AWOL over a year, but there was still a possibility that the doctor had already disposed of her.

DC Ludgrove shook his head. 'Every time we get a lead, it turns into a dead end. No family, no friends, nothing.'

Mandy had been a loner, and the second of the girls brought up in care. 'Keep trying, mate. We barely got to Sharon in time, I don't want to leave it that late for Mandy.'

Luddy ran his fingers through his hair, his frustration evident. 'But surely if we can't find her…?'

'How's he going to?' Ruby finished his question. 'Because he has personal knowledge.' She turned to the rest of her team. 'Think about it, doctors are like barmaids, people confide in them. It wouldn't surprise me if he were keeping notes on all of the girls. He would have asked about their family history too. We're going in blind, he's not.'

Luddy shook his head. 'Then what hope do we have? You've seen the papers; the press is baying for our blood. Don't they realise that we're doing everything we can?'

'Don't take it personally – the journalists are doing their job the same as us. If nothing else, at least it's raising awareness.' She forced a smile. 'I've spoken to the drug crisis centre. Their referrals have doubled, and there are fewer girls on the street.'

Both their glances fell on Ash's empty desk. 'The office is quiet without him, isn't it?' Ruby said, noticing that someone had finally cleared his things away. The only sign that he had been there was the swear chart still pinned to the wall. A pin was missing from one of the corners. Ruby guessed whoever had started to take it down had lost the will to continue.

'We should do something to remember him,' Luddy said. 'Maybe have his picture on the wall.'

'We'll not forget him,' Ruby said, 'but he wouldn't want us being maudlin. Have you had a refs break today?' Refreshment breaks were few and far between.

'Now seems a good a time,' Luddy said. 'Want me to make you a cuppa?'

'You know me too well. Can you stick it on my desk? I've got a call to make.'

✳ ✳ ✳

Ruby was reluctant to begin stirring things up with Sharon again but she was the only connection with Mandy she had left. The phone rang three times. Ruby prayed Sharon had saved her number to her mobile, otherwise she wouldn't be picking up.

'Yes?' the response was cold, cautious.

'It's Ruby. . . Sergeant Preston from Shoreditch serious crime. Are you alright to talk?'

'Sure. Is everything OK?' Sharon's voice thawed.

'Nothing to worry about. I've got a couple of questions to ask about Mandy Prentice. Are you on your own?'

'Yeah. Billy came in to visit me but I binned him off.'

Ruby wanted to say 'good' but she held back the words. 'Are you OK?' she said, hesitant.

'I'm going to a women's refuge when I'm discharged from here,' Sharon said, keeping her voice low. 'Sold them a story about Billy forcing me to work. They've got a room for me. I've sorted myself out with methadone and everything.'

Ruby smiled. It was good that Sharon trusted her enough to tell her the truth. The refuge was very select about who they took on – given the lack of funding, they had to be. But the fact Sharon had almost become a murder victim would have put her ahead in the queue. They would provide a support network for what was to come, and Sharon knew the system well enough to turn it to her advantage.

'Good,' she said. 'Sounds like you'll be in the right place to get the support you need.'

'Plus there ain't no crazy coppers trying to keep me in their flat.' But her voice contained a smile, and Ruby knew she harboured no ill feelings towards her actions that day.

'God,' Ruby said, feeling like their experience was a world away, 'the less said about that, the better. Listen, Sharon, I don't mean to go raking things up, but I'm desperately trying to find Mandy. Is there anything you can remember about her that you haven't mentioned already? Any clue about where she might be?'

Silence fell, and just when Ruby thought she was not going to respond, Sharon drew an intake of breath. 'She was strong, stubborn. If she said she was gonna do something, she'd do it. Out of all of us, she was the one most likely to get off the gear and start again.'

'No mention of family, friends?'

'She ain't got none. Her foster parents emigrated, poor cow.'

Ruby nodded. The information was nothing new. They had already been traced and spoken to; they shared the same apathy that Sharon had hinted at with no knowledge of Mandy's whereabouts. She decided to try a different tact. 'You must have chatted for her to tell you all that. Had she any aspirations? Tell you what she wanted to be?'

'I wanted to be Victoria Beckham – didn't mean it was ever gonna happen.'

Ruby snorted a laugh. 'True, but you'd be surprised where clues sometimes hide. Did she ever talk about any clients in particular? Anyone she might develop a relationship with?' she said, knowing such questions had been asked before.

But Sharon was stuck on the previous question, an answer forming on her lips. 'She did say she loved kids. She couldn't have none, thanks to the doctor.'

Ruby stiffened. This was news to her. 'The doctor, as in Doctor Tanner?'

'Yeah, a botched abortion left her infertile. She was in bits. I ain't told no one that before – I figured it was her business. If she were working anywhere, it would be with kids. She loved them too much to let them go.'

'In what capacity?' Ruby said. Sharon's silence relayed that she didn't understand the question. 'Sorry, I mean, there's lots of jobs with kids. In schools, hospitals, girl scouts... I don't know where to start.'

'I dunno. She liked toddlers, she hated hospitals, though – couldn't stand the smell. That's all I can tell you. Sorry.'

'It's something. If you think of anything else, will you send me a text? I'll ring you straight back, save your credit.'

'Sure. And Ruby?'

'Yes?'

'I hope you find her.'

Ruby was already online, printing up lists of local pre-schools, and anywhere toddlers visited during the day. She paused, her words thick with emotion: 'I'll find her. I just hope it's in time.'

CHAPTER SIXTY-THREE

'I've got an address for you.'

Resting her hand on her suitcase, it took Ruby a moment to discern the voice on the other end of the line. 'Nathan?' she said, having answered the phone without getting a proper look at the screen. Impatient to see the back of her flat, she had packed quickly.

'It's Lenny. Do you want Mandy's address or will I go round there myself?'

'Call it out,' she said, shoving her hand down the side of the sofa for a pen. It didn't matter where she kept them they always seemed to end up there. The pen rose between her fingers, along with a ball of dust. Clicking it on, she wrote on the back of her hand as Lenny recited a street name and number. 'Are you sure this is Mandy's address?' she said, clenching her fist for the ink to flow smoothly. It was in Dalston, not far from her new flat. All this time they had been looking for her, and Mandy was only half an hour away. How on earth could she afford to live there?

'I'll give you tonight to sort this out,' Lenny said, ignoring her question. 'After that, we do it my way.'

'I need more time,' Ruby said, knowing how slowly the cogs of police investigation turned.

'Just get your evidence and get him nicked. This is the last night my brother's a wanted man.'

The phone went dead in her hand. Ruby hadn't told him that Nathan was already in the clear. Finding Doctor Tanner was her priority now. She stared unblinkingly into space, working out a plan. She had two choices: she could go through the proper channels and wait for procedures to be put in place, or she could go it alone. Police attendance could frighten off the doctor from attending Mandy's address, leaving him free to kill again. As soon as she called it in, a police unit would visit and put safeguarding in place. If they took it seriously enough, they might set up a sting. But such operations took time to approve. Lenny had given Ruby one night before he took the law into his own hands. And the alternative? She could go round there, speak to Mandy and lie in wait. Given what had happened to Ash it was risky but this time she would be prepared.

Within five minutes she had washed her face and removed the mascara shadows from underneath her eyes. She dragged a brush through her hair, quickly winding her long dark locks into a bun: she had to look professional if she had any hope of winning Mandy over. She shrugged on her suit jacket. It felt empty without the reassurance of her police harness beneath it, but it did not mean she was vulnerable. She reached for the tin box she had excavated from beneath the floorboards of her home. Popping off the lid, she wrapped her fingers around the handgun Nathan had gifted her some years before. Nestling it in the waistband of her trousers, she covered it with her jacket before walking out the door.

CHAPTER SIXTY-FOUR

'Mandy, can I speak to you?' Ruby jogged up the steps to the flat as she followed the girl to her front door. Mandy turned around, a glint of distrust in her dark brown eyes as she took in Ruby's warrant card.

'The name's Amanda,' she said, her keys jangling as she pulled them from her handbag. 'You'd better come in.' Her dark wavy hair was thicker than Ruby's, trailing halfway down her back. Dressed modestly in a tracksuit and padded jacket, she looked nothing like the young woman Ruby expected to meet but the presence of the small love heart tattoo on her forefinger told her she had the right person.

Ruby peered down the lamp-lit streets, a gust of icy wind playing with loose strands of her hair. Was Tanner out there, watching them? As Mandy opened the door wide, she wasted no time in getting them both inside.

'It's about the murders, isn't it?' Mandy said, pushing a living-room door open. 'Have a seat, I'll be with you in a second.' Her shopping bags rustling, she set them down in the kitchen.

Her calmness seemed odd given the situation, but, for once, Ruby did as she was told. A police officer or not, the only power that allowed her to be there was the goodwill of her host. The sitting room carried a Laura Ashley theme; neatly decorated with floral wallpaper, soft furnishings, and a beautiful ivory antique fireplace that took centre stage. For the second time, she wondered how Mandy could afford to live in such a nice area. Her pistol dug into the waistband of her trousers as she reclined on the sofa. It made her heart skip a beat, reminding her of the urgency of the situation; she could not afford to make any more mistakes.

'Lovely place you've got here,' she said, keeping her tone light as Mandy joined her.

'It was my mum's,' Mandy replied. 'She left it to me in her will.'

'Oh, I thought your parents had emigrated?' Ruby said.

Mandy raised an eyebrow. 'My biological mum. I knew nothing about it until her solicitors tracked me down.' She pushed back a floral cushion before taking a seat. 'Am I in some sort of trouble?'

Ruby shook her head. 'I take it you've heard about the murders in the news?'

'Yes, but I've been trying not to watch TV,' Mandy said. 'It's very depressing. And we all have our lives to lead. If I paid any attention to that, I'd never go out at all.'

But Ruby knew there was more to it than that. 'You knew some of those girls, didn't you? It's all right. I know you've worked hard to leave that part of your life behind.'

'And that's where I want it to stay,' Mandy said. 'I'm not being rude, but why are you here? I'm sorry to hear about those girls dying and all, but I know nothing about it.'

'I'm not here to question you, I'm here to warn you. We've good reason to believe that you're next on his list.' Ruby hesitated. Despite her reservations, she had to offer safeguarding but limited funding meant the best she could do was to take her to stay elsewhere while officers put a safety plan in place. An alarm and some practical advice would be provided, but there was no way a police officer could stand guard at her door. Even if she stayed elsewhere, she would have to return at some point.

Mandy's face fell as Ruby brought her up to speed. 'I'm not moving out,' she said. 'That bastard has taken everything from me. It stops here.'

'I appreciate the sentiment,' Ruby said, 'but I warned Sharon, and she's come to regret not listening. Is there anyone staying with you this weekend?'

'My boyfriend's at a music festival. I was meant to go but I've just got a job, and it's too early to be asking for time off.'

'Where are you working?' Ruby asked, wondering how close she'd come to finding her.

'Little Ducks Nursery, just up the road from here,' Mandy said. 'So you see, I'm not moving out, and I'm not going to any safe house.'

A local children's nursery, of course; it was one of the places on Ruby's list to check. But Lenny had found her first, most likely by offering a reward. Ruby took a breath to speak, but as Mandy stood up, she cut her off.

'No police – I mean it, I don't want my new friends knowing about my old life.'

Ruby rose with her. 'Surely if they're that fond of you they'll accept you for who you are?'

Rolling her eyes, Mandy looked at her as if she was mad. 'It doesn't work like that. Every time they looked at me I'd see judgement in their eyes – whether it was there or not. I can't take that risk. It's taken me a while to get here but I like who I am now.'

'Come on, Mandy, surely it's not worth risking your life for? This man is dangerous. He's capable of anything.'

'You don't know me, so where do you get off, telling me what to do? I would never have fucking let you in if I'd known what you wanted. Bloody coppers, I hate the police!'

Ruby raised an eyebrow. 'Steady on, girl, I came around here to help, not to be verbally abused.'

Mandy muttered under her breath. 'You've been here five minutes and I can feel the old Mandy seeping back in. The new me would never act like this,' she said. Her face reddened as her voice grew louder. 'Do you see what you're bringing me back to? I never want to go there again.'

Ruby couldn't believe her ears. 'I'm not here to wreck your life, I just want to catch this killer before he strikes again.'

But Mandy was not listening as she shooed her towards the door. 'I want you to leave now. Your work is not my concern. As long as he stays away from my door then he can do what he wants.'

'That's where you're wrong. It's your door he'll be knocking on next.' Ruby stood her ground. She had to find a way of making her listen.

Mandy frowned. 'He'll never find me here.'

'I did.'

'You're the police.'

'And he's ingenious. Please, at least promise me you'll call the police if you see or hear anything suspicious.'

Mandy shook her head. 'I told you, no cops.'

'Then what about me?' Ruby said. 'There may be something else I can do.'

CHAPTER SIXTY-FIVE

Some children had imaginary friends growing up, but not the doctor. His friends came in all shapes and sizes and were very, very quiet. He did not have to wait until the weekend for a sleepover either. In a bed lined with satin, they stayed in the small Chapel of Rest attached to his home. As a child, he was too young to understand the concept of death. He would talk to their sleeping visitors, fascinated by the coldness of their skin as Mummy layered their face with make-up and carefully blow-dried their hair. Not until he witnessed his father piece back a car crash casualty did he fully comprehend his parents' work.

Doctor Tanner peered from the undergrowth outside Mandy's home. A warm pulse beat inside him at the thought of claiming her flesh. But it was much more than having the joy of toying with the human form. It was about revenge for every misfortune that had plagued his life, and the teasing promise of fame that would follow his name for years to come. He watched in the distance as a dark-haired woman trotted down the steps of the dull grey building that was Mandy Prentice's home. Her head dipped, she had briefly turned, saying something about seeing Mandy tomorrow, before walking to her car. His heart skipped a beat as he recalled where he had seen her before: she was the police detective who was present as paramedics took his Sleeping Beauty away.

He looped his scarf around his face until it was almost touching the woollen hat. The gloves were awkward when it came to his work, but he would not give the police the satisfaction of leaving his fingerprints at the scene. He was stretching his luck coming here so soon; he could almost feel the police snapping at his heels. The death of one of their colleagues had been a glorious moment. Propelling him into the limelight, it had no doubt brought the police renewed conviction. He would not go unpunished, it was said. If only they knew he had received his punishment tenfold.

With a soft breath, he dragged his feet through the undergrowth, approaching the back entrance of Mandy's home. The garden was long and thin, easily accessed by climbing the wall at the rear. He landed on the other side with a thud, jarring his knees on the frostbitten ground below. Narrowing his eyes, he peered through the half-open window blind. Pop music was playing in the kitchen, and he watched as the back door was opened to allow a tabby cat inside.

Switching off the kitchen light, Mandy retreated from the room, allowing the doctor to advance under the cover of darkness. He would have to make his entrance quickly, before she returned to lock the door.

Dipping his hand into his coat pocket, he felt the comforting rustle of the plastic bag containing the chloroformed cloth. It wouldn't do to contaminate himself before he'd even begun. The element of surprise always won him a few precious seconds. He would be quick in his reprisal – dressing her in the red hood and placing her on the bed. It was a slip of material, but enough to send the message home. How he missed his surgeon's chair and the symphony of music that raised colours in the air.

Slowly, he placed his hand on the kitchen door, scalpel in his right pocket, cloth in the left. Dew had gathered on the bridge of his scarf, and he lowered it from his face, licking his lips as his excitement grew. In the living room, a news channel blared, and the doctor held his breath as he snuck into the downstairs hall, his feet slowly pressing on each stair as he made his ascent.

He stepped inside the open bedroom door on the right. It carried the scent of jasmine, and his eyes fell on the remnants of a candle now melted into a puddle on her dressing table. In the dim light he squinted at the photographs Blu-Tacked to the wall; snapshots of people he did not recognise. She did not acquaint herself with the street girls any longer, having moved on and made a valiant effort to start her life again.

He opened her wardrobe, a huge thing, packed with coats and unattractive baggy clothes. Nothing like the skimpy outfits she had worn in the past. He pushed the clothes aside, the metal hangers jangling as he assessed the space: he could easily fit inside if he made room. Touching the cotton material of a blue flowery dress, he brought the cloth to his face, inhaling the scent of fabric conditioner. A ghost of the past loaded into his memory – the old Mandy smelt of sex and cheap perfume.

His knees ached as he shuffled into position behind the wardrobe door. Today, he was feeling his age. A fleeting thought entered his mind: he was getting too old for all of this. Perhaps it was time to give it up while the going was good. After all, he had inflicted his revenge on Nathan Crosby, sending him scampering into the shadows like the rats he had left behind. But there was a lot more to it than that. Like him, the reasoning behind his behaviour was multi-layered and complicated. The satisfaction he received working on the street girls far excelled enjoyment gained from his revenge. And now there was just one more left. All he could think about was reacquainting himself with Mandy, the one woman who turned him down. He had repaid her for her belligerence by botching the abortion, which left her infertile. But it had never been enough. The thought of her carrying on with a normal life had always played on his mind. A smile graced his lips: he had just the fairy tale in store for her. Not many people knew the true message behind 'Little Red Riding Hood'. It was a message to young women about giving up their virginity to the Big Bad Wolf. He bared his teeth in a sharp grin. Mandy may have refused him once; she would not refuse him again.

CHAPTER SIXTY-SIX

The doctor's eyes snapped open as the television silenced below. Downstairs, Mandy's chatter filled the air. He stiffened as he realised she was not alone. But she had to be. He had been standing in her room for a good twenty minutes, and she had not opened the door to anybody. Creeping to the window, he peered outside. Cars lined the street; empty shells devoid of life on this frost-stricken night. Nothing resembling the police presence he expected to see. He pressed his ear to the bedroom door, listening to the voice downstairs. Like a game of Jenga, any deviation from the plan could bring it tumbling down around him. His annoyance subsided as he realised that only one set of footsteps was climbing the stairs. It was only then that he understood that she was on the phone. Forsaking the cramped wardrobe, the doctor concealed his presence behind the bedroom door.

'I'll be fine,' she said, hovering outside on the landing. 'You have a good time.' Soft laughter filled the air. 'What's there to feel guilty about? Those tickets cost a fortune. Don't go spoiling it now.' She giggled. 'Well, OK, if you want to make it up to me I won't try to stop you. Oh, and Aidan? I might not be here when you get back, I've got to pop down to the police station tomorrow.' She breathed a sigh. 'No, nothing to worry about. I'll fill you in when you get back.'

The doctor's heart was galloping now, a thin layer of sweat coating his brow.

Humming, she entered the bedroom, lightly pushing open the door. The room remained in darkness, lit only by the glow of the street lights outside.

The doctor's nose pressed against the other side of the door. Muscles tensed, he prepared to pounce. He would have to act quickly. The amount of chloroform he had soaked into the cloth would ensure her silence for some time to come.

He could take her now, wash her in the bath and tie her to the bed, just as he had with Sharon. He would work through the night to make her realise her full potential. A smile touched his lips as he imagined what was to come.

Mandy stood at her dressing table, failing to notice the doctor's form in the mirror behind her. He held his breath as he slid his hand over the chloroform cloth in his pocket. It was time to tear it from its bag and put her to sleep. A rush of excitement flooded his senses but creeping forward, he realised something was wrong.

As the woman spun around, he realised it was not Mandy at all. Cold liquid slapped against his skin and, for one horrific moment, he relived the acid attack all over again. He blinked furiously, staggering back as the unwelcome substance stung his eyes. But as he caught sight of the bottle in her hand he could see it was not acid, but nail varnish remover. Yes, it would sting, but there was no long-lasting damage to be had. Setting his jaw tight, he launched himself at her, only to receive a sharp punch to the face.

'Hands on your head, you're under arrest!' the woman bellowed, her voice hard and commanding.

'You're not Mandy,' the doctor said, swallowing the blood leaking from his nose. Steadying himself, he reached for the scalpel in his pocket.

'I'm the sergeant of the police officer that you killed. Drop the knife. NOW!'

The words had barely left her mouth before he lunged at her with the blade.

CHAPTER SIXTY-SEVEN

Clasping Doctor Tanner's arm, Ruby's fingers bit into his tendons as she tried to force him to release the scalpel. But he was stronger than he looked. Wearing thick-soled boots, he had an advantage over her as she slipped on the wet laminate floor. The clothes she had swapped with Mandy offered little protection, and the pumps on her feet were a half size too big. Ruby knew what Tanner wanted to do, and he voiced the fears taking centre stage in her mind.

'If Mandy's not here,' he said through gritted teeth as he grabbed her by the hair, 'then you'll do instead.' Kicking her legs from beneath her, he flung her to the corner of the room.

With a sickening thud, her head smacked against the corner of the wardrobe on the way down. Searing pain spiked her temple as stars flashed in her vision. Feeling the grasp of the doctor's hand on her hair, she winced as he took a handful and shook. But as he threw the scalpel to the floor, she knew he was in no hurry to impose a quick death, unlike the one he administered to Ash. He would do to her as he did to Sharon; use her body for his pleasure before disposing of her in some undignified way.

With one hand, he pulled the scarf over his nose before delving into his coat pocket and ripping the bag within. His breath heavy and rasping, he bent over her form.

'Back off,' Ruby coughed, the smell of sweat and urine infiltrating her senses. Then she saw it; the steely glint of madness in the doctor's eyes which made her blood turn cold. The wisest thing would have been for him to turn on his heel and run but this was not a man who backed down. He smiled, his sharp yellow teeth glinting in the moonlight pouring in through the bedroom window.

Ruby groaned as she clawed at the wardrobe, a trickle of blood making a path down the side of her face. Her head injury brought double vision, and as she pulled her body upwards, the wardrobe handle broke off in her hand. The doctor was upon her now, the cloth in his hand filling her vision as it clamped tightly over her mouth and nose.

'Shh now, don't fight it,' he said, swaying from side to side as she tried to fight him off. 'Go to sleep. Soon it will all be over.'

Don't inhale, she thought, the sweet smell of chloroform watering her eyes and burning her throat. It would be all too easy to submit, to shut her eyelids and let go. Easy for others who had nothing to live for and no way out. Ruby jerked back her head as Tanner's fingernails pinched the sides of her face. She thought of Ash, whose life he had extinguished without an ounce of remorse. It stopped here… with her.

Grappling in the darkness, the doctor backed her up against the wall. She needed to put some distance between them to draw her gun. The thoughts of introducing such a lethal weapon made her blood run cold. She was concussed and dizzy. What if he turned it upon her? Unable to hold her breath any longer, she drove her stiffened fingers into the doctor's eyes.

His howls filled the air, buying her enough time to roll to the side as his grip on the cloth weakened. Anger coursed through her as she thought of the innocent lives taken, and for what? A headline in the newspaper or some warped sense of revenge?

As the doctor clambered onto his hands and knees, he picked up the scalpel he had discarded.

'Turn around. Put your hands against the wall,' Ruby commanded. 'You're under arrest.' Heaving for breath, she found her feet.

'I'm not going anywhere,' the doctor said, his knuckles tightening over the glinting blade. He nodded in the direction of the bed. 'Why don't you lie down? I've got a bedtime story to tell you.'

She was cornered, and the only way out was through the door he was blocking. That's if she wanted a way out; what she wanted was to finish this for good. She pulled her pistol from the belt looped under the waist of her tracksuit bottoms. Gripping the handle, she clicked off the safety switch, her face determined as she held it in both hands. 'I said, turn around, put your hands against the wall.'

Wide-eyed, the doctor inhaled a sharp breath. 'You wouldn't.'

Ruby's lips thinned into a smile. 'Don't tempt me. Drop your weapon. NOW! Turn around, hands against the wall.'

Blood seeped from her forehead into her left eye, coating her vision in a red hue. Squeezing her eye shut, Ruby raised her gun as the doctor advanced upon her.

'Drop your weapon or I'll shoot,' she said, swiping the blood from her forehead.

But picking up the cloth from the ground, the doctor took one step, then two. 'You're not going to hu—'

'Thank God, you're here,' Ruby said, her relief evident as she stared at the door.

But as the doctor swivelled to see who had come in, she drew back her right hand. The doorway was empty, but the bluff afforded her enough time to distract her attacker. Metal hit jawbone as a sudden cracking noise filled the air. In quick succession Ruby hit him a second time with the barrel of the gun. As he spiralled backwards onto the floor, she drew back her foot and kicked him hard between the legs.

'That's for Ash,' she said, drawing back her foot a second time. 'And that's for the others.'

Wheezing and groaning, the doctor curled up into a ball.

Pushing the gun back into the band of her tracksuit, she panted as she stood over him, feeling the satisfaction of a job well done. 'You weren't worth the price of a bullet,' she said, pulling the belt from a dressing gown, which lay on the bed. Tying his hands behind his back, she glanced around the room. Her eyes focused on the trinkets and ornaments taking up shelf space on the dresser. 'That'll do,' she said, taking the thick glass ashtray and pressing it down on his bloodied face. She examined the surface, satisfied contact had been made, and dropped the ashtray to the floor.

Plucking her phone from inside her bra, she dialled 999 and waited for backup to arrive.

CHAPTER SIXTY-EIGHT

'Funny about old Tanner, wasn't it?' DI Downes said as he stood with Ruby at the back of the police station.

'Everything about that old fucker is funny,' Ruby said, sliding a cigarette from the pack. 'Want one?'

Downes shook the offer away. 'Let's head out for a wee dander…' Guiding her by the elbow, he turned her away from the eyes and ears of Shoreditch police station.

'Sure,' Ruby shrugged.

Dawn seeped through the sky; the sounds of the birds drowned out by the traffic gaining momentum as early-morning commuters travelled to work.

'So, are you gonna tell me what really happened?' Downes said.

'It's all in my statement,' Ruby replied, her words peppered with smoke.

He snorted. 'Do you think I came down the Lagan in a bubble? That statement's a work of fiction. C'mon, tell me the truth.'

Ruby resisted a smile. 'I told you. I was given an address by my sources. I didn't expect anything of it, so I was surprised when Mandy opened the door. I offered safeguarding, but she declined. I persuaded her to spend the night in a hotel. We agreed that she'd come to the station in the morning.'

'And you just happened to swap clothes before she left? She's around the same height as you, same colour hair. You could easily mistake who's who on a dark night.'

Ruby took another drag of her cigarette, buying some extra seconds as she figured out what to say. Mandy was open to the idea of trading places, and Ruby had been thrilled when Doctor Tanner took the bait. Coming in through the unlocked kitchen door was a risk he had been foolish enough to take, and she had listened from the living room as he crept upstairs. She even went as far as chatting in an imaginary phone call to cement his belief that it was Mandy, not her. But if it hadn't been for her gun, things could have turned out very differently.

'Mandy and I share the same taste in clothes,' Ruby lied. 'I was at home when I got the address from an informant. I didn't bother changing out of my casual gear for a quick call to her door. After she left, I heard someone prowling around the back of her house. It turned out she'd left the door insecure.' She threw Downes a sideways glance. Brows knitted, he was staring at the pavement as they walked along. 'I crept up to her bedroom and found Doctor Tanner there. We struggled, he assaulted me, and I whacked him across the face with an ashtray. End of.'

'That's not what he's saying.'

'I'm surprised he can say anything with a broken jaw,' Ruby grinned.

'He's not, but I caught the words "gun" a couple of times. And his injuries appear more consistent with being pistol-whipped than being battered with an ashtray.'

'Oh that,' Ruby said, stubbing out her cigarette before flicking it into a bin. 'It was dark in the room. I said I was armed. It was worth a shot, pardon the pun. But when he came for me I grabbed the ashtray and hit him with it.'

'Sent him into next week more like. Remind me never to piss you off.'

Ruby laughed. 'Then stop asking questions. It's all good. He's in custody, and Mandy's gonna be OK.'

'How's the head?'

Ruby touched the egg-shaped bruise which was rising on her temple. 'Sore, but no lasting damage.'

'I was hoping it would knock some sense into you, but given that pile of tripe you've just fed me, I can see it hasn't.'

Shoving her hands in her pockets, Ruby turned back to the station. 'I think this is the point where you praise me for a job well done.'

DI Downes fished out a set of car keys from his pocket. 'No, this is the point where you dispose of whatever heat you're packing, go home and get changed into your own clothes. Take the job car. You might fancy taking a spin past the canal – I hear the water's very deep over there.'

'But. . .' Ruby said. She had yet to tell him she was in the process of moving home.

'No buts. You've done all you can today. Go home, get some sleep and report to work as normal tomorrow.'

As Ruby nodded, she knew that rest would not come until she had tied up the last loose end. It was not enough that Doctor Tanner was in police custody, because he had not been working alone: it was time to speak to his accomplice.

CHAPTER SIXTY-NINE

A twinge of regret made itself known. Ruby had progressed the investigation without fully exploring who had implicated Nathan in the crimes. Her team had covered the basics, checking out alibis and speaking to all involved. But she should have done more. She had hoped that by capturing the doctor a connection could be made.

It was only now that answers were forthcoming, and Ruby did not like what she'd found. Tweedy's comment about not wanting her death on his conscience replayed in her mind. His explanation that he had visited her out of concern had only muted the alarm bells ringing. There was nothing to disprove his statement, which said he was at home that night. Cross-checked with the account given by Fingers, the police believed that Nathan was responsible for hiding the evidence beneath his bed. That was until the investigation took a turn and Doctor Tanner was caught for the crimes. Given his ingenuity, it seemed acceptable that Tanner had gained entry into the Crosby home. As if he would return to the very people responsible for his injuries. It was all too convenient and that morning, as Ruby visited the working men's club, she knew what she had to do.

In the tiny back office she was left alone to view the CCTV. Sitting amongst cardboard boxes full of junk and out-of-date newspapers, she prayed her suspicions were wrong. She could not bear for her old school friend to be lying to her. How would she break it to Nathan? The level of trust he carried in his heart would shrink even smaller. Ruby drew in a sharp intake of breath. There, in black and white was a figure she recognised. Propping up the bar was Nathan's employee, Fingers, and the time and date matched when he was supposed to be covering for Tweedy Steve. She pressed the pause button, leaning in for a better look.

'*No*,' she whispered.

It changed everything. If Fingers wasn't working, Tweedy had been lying about his whereabouts that night. Ruby felt like she had been punched in the gut. Tweedy could get time in prison for perverting the course of justice. Then there was Lenny Crosby to think about – what would he do to Tweedy if he found out? This wasn't just a murder investigation, this was a serial killing, a high-profile one at that. It came down to one thing: could her old school friend have been working with the doctor to set Nathan up? Had he got in over his head and was unable to escape? This was something she would have to deal with herself.

Ruby gathered up all her strength as she knocked on Tweedy's door. He did not appear surprised to see her as he allowed her inside.

'I know why you're here,' he said flatly, as her stern expression relayed that this was not a social call.

'Best I come in then,' she said, wiping her boots on the doormat in the hall.

'You know about my alibi, don't you?' Tweedy said. 'I knew I was taking a risk coming to the nick to warn you, but I couldn't let you walk into danger knowing that I had a part to play in it.'

Ruby shook her head, unable to comprehend what she was hearing. 'How could you? After all Nathan's done. Were you jealous of his success, was that it? Or were you being blackmailed? What sort of trouble have you got yourself into, Steve?' She dropped the nickname; such things were reserved for friends, and their friendship had been broken in two.

Steve crossed his arms, tucking his hands under the armpits of his sweater. 'It's not what you think. I knew that you'd get Nathan out of it eventually, and it did him some good getting away from his family. We never really talk much when he's at home. When he stayed here, he really opened up.'

'Your bromance is very touching. How about you tell that to the victims' families?' Ruby inhaled a deep breath as she calmed her rising temper. 'You directed Tanner to the girls so he could get his revenge. Then you told him you'd protect him in exchange for Ellie's organs, and I'm guessing you stole Nathan's watch. It makes me sick to the stomach. Yet here you are pretending to be his friend when all along, you planted the evidence under his bed.'

'You've got it all wrong,' Steve's face paled. 'I never intended for any of this.'

'It seems pretty clear to me,' Ruby said, her gaze imparting little sympathy.

'I couldn't tell you the truth – Lenny would have killed me. Besides, the damage had been done. I just had to place my faith in you, that you'd find the killer and bring him in.'

'You sat back and allowed him to slaughter those poor young people, all the while knowing who it was. You know I just can't leave it at that, don't you?' Ruby unfurled her handcuffs from their pouch. 'I'm bringing you in for this.'

'Wait.' Steve raised his palms open in a gesture of surrender. 'Please, sit down. It's time you knew the truth.'

CHAPTER SEVENTY

'Fresh air has never felt so good,' Nathan said, placing the shopping on the counter of Ruby's new flat. A smile broadened his lips. 'Thanks, you risked a lot to clear my name.'

'Well, I'm honoured. It's not every day I get thanks from you.' But the pleasure of Nathan being in the clear was marred by the news on her tongue. As he shoved the empty shopping bag into the overhead cupboard, Ruby took a step towards him and hugged him from behind. 'Thank *you*. . .' she whispered, wrapping her arms around his waist, '. . .for the flat.'

Turning around, Nathan silenced her words with a kiss. He had told her before he did not want her gratitude. According to the legal documents, the flat had been left to her in her deceased aunt's will. But Ruby knew the truth and, much as it pained her to accept such an extravagant gift, she could not face another day in her rodent-infested tower block. As they parted for air, she leant into his taut chest, taking in the sound of his heartbeat from beneath his crisp white shirt. Dressed in his suit, he had come straight from work. He had spent little time at his own house since Ruby moved in, and their time together made her feel the happiest she had been in years. Unlike many couples, they did not speak about work – they lived in their own little bubble, just as they did in their youth. But now Ruby was about to put a pin to that perfection, and the words weighed heavy on her tongue.

'There's something I need to tell you,' she said, staring deep into his blue-grey eyes. 'But I don't want you to lose your head – enough people have been hurt. You have to learn from this and let it go.'

'Let *what* go?' Nathan said, his face clouding over.

'I know who tried to frame you for the murders.'

It took less than a second for the atmosphere to change, and the quiet anger Nathan had suppressed came bubbling to the surface in an instant. 'Who?' he said, his voice low and rumbling.

Feeling his muscles tense, Ruby took a step back, preparing to impart the identity of the person who almost sent him to prison. 'It wasn't the doctor who planted the evidence, it was someone much closer to you. It had to be to get inside your house unchallenged.' She sighed, waiting for their happy world to come tumbling down. 'But what worries me now is where to go next with this information. The doctor's the one who committed the murders, so I'm tempted to let sleeping dogs lie. On the other hand, I'm conscious of the fact that they tried to frame you, and I really don't want that to happen again.'

'Who. Is. It?' Nathan said, each word sounding pained.

Ruby checked her watch as the air chilled between them. 'They're due here any minute. But you've got to promise me one thing, you can't lose your rag.'

'You're kidding me, aren't you?' Nathan said, his face incredulous.

'You told me when I moved in that this is my flat. If you raise one finger, I'm walking. I still have the lease on my old place for another month.'

'Fuck's sake!' Nathan ran his hands through his hair. 'If you think I'm letting him get away with this. . .'

But Ruby stood firm. 'I mean it, Nathan. Raise one finger and I'm gone. This is going to be dealt with by talking. If you lose your temper, you'll be waging war. You listening to me?'

The sound of the doorbell had never sounded so menacing as it delivered a light chime. Nathan's biceps tensed as he folded his arms across his chest. 'I'm listening,' he grumbled. 'But I don't know what the hell you're on about.'

'You will soon enough.' There was a light tremble in her hand as she activated the buzzer and allowed them access to the flat. She prayed she would not have to act as referee between them. And if it came to blows? Her relationship with Nathan would be over before it even got going.

'Come in,' Ruby said, allowing their guest inside.

Ruby did not need to introduce herself to Leona – the young woman knew exactly who she was. She stood tight-lipped, wearing a red dress that clung to every inch of her figure beneath her expensive fur coat.

Nathan's eyes narrowed. 'Leona,' he said. 'What are you doing here?'

'You texted me,' she said, her face pinched as she looked Ruby up and down. Sliding the phone from her pocket, she recited the words. '"I've had time to think. Miss you, meet me at this address so we can talk." I presumed this was one of your hideouts.' She cast her eyes around the room. 'Now I'm not so sure.'

'I sent the text,' Ruby said, her face firm. 'I knew you wouldn't come any other way.'

Leona looked from Nathan to Ruby. 'I don't know what sort of messed-up game you're playing, but I'm not having any part of it. If I'm not invited by Nathan, then I'm going home.'

'You're not going anywhere until I have an explanation,' Nathan said, his tone commanding. He turned to Ruby. 'What's she doing here, babe?'

The term of endearment made Leona visibly flinch. There was love there, Ruby could see that, but it was all one-sided, and the sort of love that could turn to hate at a flick of a switch.

'Leona set you up.' Ruby took little pleasure from the words.

'She's lying,' Leona said, reaching for her phone.

But Ruby was ready and slid it from her grasp. The last thing she wanted was Leona calling her father, and him sending his heavies around. This is what she meant by Nathan waging war. Leona's dad Ray Delaney was well known in the criminal underworld and had been good friends with Nathan's father, Jimmy, when he was alive. But he was a violent man who thought the world of his daughter and if Nathan harmed a hair on her head, he would unleash his fury. Such a war would have far-reaching consequences, and enough blood had already been shed. Leona may look sugary sweet on the outside, but she got her spirit from her father, having chosen the worst possible way to wreak revenge on the man who had so callously dumped her.

Ruby examined Nathan's face for clues: a flicker of compassion, a glance of appreciation for the woman he had once shared a bed with. But there was nothing but hatred delivered by an icy stare. It sent a chill down her spine, and she hoped it was never a situation she would find herself in. She took a breath, wanting to get this sorted. The sooner Leona could leave, the better.

'This is off the record because I don't want to get mixed up in your mess,' Ruby said. 'We've got our man, and he's remanded at Her Majesty's pleasure, but I couldn't understand why he wanted revenge so long after the crime. And as for planting the evidence, it seemed oddly convenient it happened when the CCTV was out.'

The three of them stood facing each other. Ruby knew there was little point in asking Leona to sit down. The young woman was looking less self-assured now, her gaze on the floor.

'So I began compiling a list of all the people who held a grudge. But it just didn't fit. Then I remembered where Nathan was on the night it happened – in your father's house, playing poker. He kept up his weekly routine, despite the fact you had split up. You were there too, weren't you?'

Leona nodded, a flush rising to her face.

'Only, you weren't there very long. While Nathan thought you had parted amicably, you slipped off, pretending you were in your room. In reality, you were delivering a present to Nathan's house, and it was Tweedy who let you inside.'

Nathan shook his head. 'Fingers was working that shift, not Tweedy.'

Ruby sighed. 'Fingers didn't turn up for his shift until later – he was too busy boozing down the working men's club. Tweedy covered for him because he didn't want to get him into trouble. By the time the police arrived, Fingers had taken over. He lied, saying he'd been there all evening. He wasn't to know that it would turn into a murder investigation.'

'Then why didn't Tweedy just tell me what happened?' Nathan said, frowning as he tried to comprehend her words.

'Because Miss Leona here made sure he had plenty to stay quiet about.'

Leona emitted a small gasp, her hand rising to her face as Ruby spilt her shameful secrets.

'She fucked him,' Nathan said, the harshness of his words slicing through the air.

Ruby nodded. 'It bought his silence because he didn't want you to know. He didn't find out about the package until later, and by then he'd guessed her involvement. But Leona here told him to keep his nose out unless he wanted to start a war between her family and yours. That's when he came to see me to find out how the investigation was progressing.'

Ruby turned to face Leona, counting her misdemeanours with her fingers. 'You went looking for revenge, and you found the doctor. You gave him the list of working girls along with enough money and food so he could stay underground. Then you gave him free rein with no compassion for his victims, offering him your father's protection. Doctor Tanner was still carrying enough anger to undertake your wishes, even if he did decide to use his own turn of hand. After you planted the evidence, you tipped off the police as an anonymous source.'

Leona fell silent but she did not need to speak. Guilt was etched all over her face.

'It was you who took Nathan's watch, wasn't it? Jealous, because you saw our names engraved on the back. Then you gave it to the doctor so he could plant it at the leisure centre – another damming clue.'

Nathan shook his head in disbelief. He would never hit a woman, but he had a right to be angry and owned a temper that could not always be controlled. 'You fucking bitch!' he spat the words. 'You fucking psycho bitch! I should have you killed for this.'

'Not on my watch,' Ruby said, coming between them. 'This ends today.'

'I didn't mean for him to kill *all* those people,' Leona said, her voice trembling. 'Doctor Tanner came to my dad for help after he strangled that girl in the park. Dad owed him a favour and promised he'd make it all go away.'

'And that's when an idea hatched in your head,' Ruby said, as things became clear. So Danny Smedley had been telling the truth – Ray Delaney had got to him and persuaded him to confess to Lisa's murder. Her attention returned to Leona, her discomfort evident as she confessed.

'After he left, I followed him home.' Leona's eyes flicked to Nathan and back to the floor. It was doubtful she would have been so truthful, had Ruby not been there to protect her. 'I gave him the list of women so he could pick just one. Later, I planted the evidence under Nathan's bed when he was visiting our house. I wasn't to know the doctor would kill them all. And Nicky. . . he was just a kid. I told him he went too far.'

'And what about Ash Baker?' Ruby said, fighting the urge to smack Leona in the face herself.

'That wasn't my fault,' Leona's chin jutted in defiance. But she could not hide the pain. She still cared for Nathan, and it hurt her to be spoken to with such harshness by the man she once wanted to marry. As Nathan's hand slid around Ruby's waist, Leona's eyes burned with a look of jealousy and hatred – a cocktail inflamed by desire. But Ruby was more than ready to take her on, and she had the law on her side.

'Does your father know?' Ruby said, her words cold.

'No, and he's not going to. I'm not admitting to anything.' Leona stared at them with contempt. 'All that time I thought you loved me, and you were just stringing me along. I don't ever want to see either of you again.'

'That suits me fine,' Nathan said, anger simmering beneath his words. He pointed to Ruby. '*This* is the woman I love. You're just a stupid kid playing at being a grown-up. If I ever see you around Ruby or me again—'

'You won't,' Leona said, tears filling her eyes as she made for the door. Emotional manipulation was a tool Nathan would use to his advantage when physical violence was off the agenda.

Guilt speared through Ruby. She gained no satisfaction from seeing another woman humiliated in this way. She squared her shoulders. She had to get the final word in to ensure that it ended here.

'I've got enough evidence to send you down for conspiracy to commit murder,' she said. 'If anything comes from this – and I mean *anything*, I won't hesitate to arrest you. Do I make myself clear?'

'More than clear,' Leona said, her voice breaking as she opened the door. She paused as she twisted the handle, tears falling down her face. 'I went too far… I'm sorry.'

CHAPTER SEVENTY-ONE

One Week Later

'Did you think it was that easy?' Lenny said. 'You thought you were going to ride off into the sunset, just like that?'

'What do you want, Lenny?' Ruby said, stepping back as she allowed him inside. She did not want to spend any more time in her old flat than she had to and, gathering up the last of her things, she was just about ready to leave.

'I heard you're moving in with my brother. Setting up home, are we?'

'You heard wrong. Now, if you'll get out of my way, I've got things to do.'

Lenny blew out his cheeks and shoved his hands deep into his coat pockets. He was suited up today, somewhat overdressed for a visit to her old address. 'You can't leave until you settle your debts.'

'I'm paid up until the end of the month.'

Lenny smirked. 'I'm not talking about the rent. Did you think I was giving you Mandy's address out of the kindness of my heart?' he tutted. 'You should know by now that my favours don't come for free.'

Ruby frowned, her voice rising an octave. 'I helped you; I put my neck on the line to put Nathan in the clear.'

'Not true. He was already in the clear before I gave you Mandy's address. Not that you had the courtesy to update me. Oh come on, did you really think I didn't know about that?'

Ruby frowned, her heart plummeting in her chest. To be indebted to Lenny Crosby was not a good situation to be in. 'You never said. . .'

'I didn't need to. You know the code of practice. Did you think you were exempt?'

'I was clearing up your mess. You started all this by advising him to throw acid in Tanner's face.'

'Such slander. I don't think Nathan would like to hear you talk about the family like that, do you?'

'Whatever. Tanner's on remand in prison. It's over.'

'He's in the morgue,' Lenny said, a hint of satisfaction in his voice.

Ruby picked up her coat from the back of her chair and shrugged it on. Every second in this flat was tainted. She wanted to move on, but Lenny would not let her go. 'What are you talking about?'

'Haven't you heard? He hung himself in his cell about. . .' He pulled back his shirt-sleeve and checked his designer watch. 'Oh, about ten minutes ago... nasty business, that. Still, as you say, it's over now. He won't be troubling us again, and you don't have to worry about any awkward questions in court.' Silence fell between them as the implication of his words became clear. He leant against the chair, blocking her movement. 'Do you still have it?'

'Have what?' Ruby said, her blood running cold.

'The shooter.'

She shook her head – she had taken Downes's advice and disposed of the gun the next day.

Lenny gave a slow nod, making it clear he was enjoying every second of this game of cat and mouse. 'So, about this debt... I'm just kidding. You did a good job.' His face broke into a vicious smile. 'Don't want to spoil the housewarming, now, do I? How's your mum, by the way?'

'She's fine.' Ruby swallowed.

'Ah, good. Sorry I haven't been in to visit. I don't like those places. Care homes, prisons, they're pretty much the same to me. Know what I mean?'

Ruby nodded. She knew exactly what he meant. If he could get to Doctor Tanner in prison, then he could get to her mother just as easily. He was putting on the squeeze so he could use her in the future. He could try all he wanted. Helping Nathan was a one-off, she wasn't for sale.

'Great! Well, enjoy the move.' The words trailed behind him as he walked away.

Ruby closed the door behind him, her hands shaking as she fumbled with the lock. She did not need to check with the prison to see what fate had befallen the doctor. Tanner was the last person she was worried about. Her thoughts were focused on the veiled threats made against her mother. She should have known that Lenny would try to gain control now that her relationship with Nathan was restored. They had a future together. She would make it work. As she gathered up the last of her belongings, she decided on one thing: she would not allow Lenny's interference to blight her relationship with Nathan. Whatever came her way, she would sort it out on her own.

LETTER FROM CAROLINE

As mentioned in my acknowledgments, I'm so very grateful for the support of my readers. Every social media share, every review and every word of mouth recommendation means so very much.

On a further note I would like to mention my use of the derelict building which is featured in this book. I decided to use the recently demolished Queen Elizabeth Hospital as a tribute to the building, which was a landmark of deep significance for generations of East Enders for many years. Sadly, many iconic buildings are now being demolished to make way for new developments. It is only through our writing that we can keep such places alive.

I hope you enjoy reading about Ruby's latest adventures. You may also be interested in checking out my other books, which are available now: *Don't Turn Around, Time to Die, The Silent Twin* and *Love You to Death*. If you'd like to keep up-to-date with all my latest releases, just sign up at www.bookouture.com/caroline-mitchell. Your email address will never be shared and you can unsubscribe at any time.

Best wishes,
Caroline

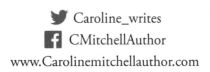

Caroline_writes
CMitchellAuthor
www.Carolinemitchellauthor.com

ACKNOWLEDGMENTS

I always find it difficult to write the acknowledgments section of a book. Firstly, because I'm in a daze as I cannot quite believe I've written another novel. Secondly, because a few lines in a book never seems like enough to express how I feel. I am incredibly grateful to everyone who has helped me to progress my writing career, and blessed that I am in a profession where I get rewarded for doing what I love.

To Madeleine Milburn, thank you for everything. I still can't quite believe I'm signed with such a wonderful agent. To my publishers Bookouture and the talented team of people behind it, thank you as always for bringing my book to fruition. To my editor Keshini Naidoo, I know I'm on the right track when I get a side note on my edits saying "It's disgusting...I LOVE it!" Dark minds think alike and yours is always a joy to behold. Speaking of dark minds, I could not write this without mentioning the wonderful Angie Marsons, Julie Forrest and Mel Sherratt. It's true, crime authors really are the nicest people you could meet. I've been very fortunate to befriend many more fantastic people this year. Facebook has a lot to answer for! To my family and extended family, thanks for putting up with me as I throw myself into producing yet another book.

To the book clubs and all the lovely people who have read and reviewed my books. Thanks so much to you all. I love hearing from my readers and you truly brighten my day.

As a former member of the emergency services, I was thrilled to spend my first Christmas at home with my family. I will never lose sight of how lucky I am. Thank you to everyone who has supported me along the way.

22626581R00175

Printed in Great Britain
by Amazon